T0208684

The Path of Evil

Leo J. Rogers

iUniverse, Inc.
New York   Bloomington

iUniverse books may be ordered through booksellers or by contacting:

iUniverse
1663 Liberty Drive
Bloomington, IN 47403
www.iuniverse.com
1-800-Authors (1-800-288-4677)

Because of the dynamic nature of the Internet, any Web addresses or links contained in this book may have changed since publication and may no longer be valid. The views expressed in this work are solely those of the author and do not necessarily reflect the views of the publisher, and the publisher hereby disclaims any responsibility for them.

ISBN: 978-1-4401-9361-3 (sc)
ISBN: 978-1-4401-9362-0 (ebook)

Printed in the United States of America

iUniverse rev. date: 12/02/2009

1

Jeff moved softly through the leaf strewn forest floor. He had been quietly working his way toward this spot for the past hour. This was the same area where he'd had a shot at that big buck last fall and he was hoping that he could find the same spot again. But this afternoon, if his luck held and the big deer stepped out in front of him, he didn't intend to shoot him, but simply take his picture!

The actual hunting season didn't open for several weeks yet and this was just a scouting expedition to refamiliarize him with the terrain he hadn't experienced since last year. He'd left his Blazer parked off the side of the fire trail a half mile or so behind him and he'd been enjoying this quiet stalk through the early fall afternoon. He had seen a number of small wild life creatures during his careful movement, but no deer.

He was about to move off the direction he'd chosen, when he saw the ragged remains of a fallen oak just ahead. And there at the left end of the rotting trunk of the old tree, was the stump that he had sat against a year ago. He quickly moved toward it, hoping for a glimpse of that big deer before heading back to the Blazer.

He sat with his back against the stump, camera at the ready, but there was no movement other than the rustling of the leaves as a gentle breeze played through the trees.

After an hour, he decided to start back, thinking maybe he'd be luckier on his walk out of the woods. As he got stiffly to his feet, he suddenly glimpsed movement off to his right and froze in an awkward half standing crouch while searching the trees for the movement that caught his attention.

And there he was, about a hundred feet off the end of the fallen oak. The big buck stood looking at Jeff, ears tilted forward, head held high, a large majestic rack on his head.

Jeff felt a surge of excitement at seeing this magnificent animal, standing as though posing for a wild life magazine. Jeff slowly started to bring his camera into position, but the buck, sensing this movement, turned and quickly bounded deeper into the forest and out of sight.

Jeff stood upright, heart pounding, experiencing an adrenalin rush from the close encounter with the big deer. He took a few steps down the length of the old oak tree in the direction the deer had disappeared into the thick forest.

But stopping, he realized that trying to see the deer again was going to be impossible today. Turning to return to the Blazer, he suddenly saw, what appeared to be bones, strewn along the ground beside the old tree trunk.

Thinking it must be the remains of a dead animal, he stepped nearer to take a closer look and was suddenly horrified to see what appeared to be the skeletal bones of a human being!

Jeff felt the hair on his head move and was sure it must be standing on end! He had seen dead bodies before, but this was not a body, but the rotted remains of a body, the sight of which was so unexpected and so gross that he was nearly nauseated. Obviously, these remains had been strewn about by prowling animals and the very thought made Jeff gag.

Stepping back and away without conscious thought, he raised his camera and began snapping picture after picture of the scene. There were still bits and pieces of flesh and body parts clinging to the bones, as well as putrefied remains of skin and hair on the skull. Jeff instinctively decided that this was what remained of what had once been a woman ... but from these remains, he had no idea what her age might have been.

Controlling his nausea, he stepped several feet away and reached for a cell phone clipped to his belt. It was habit more than anything, that he had the phone with him at all. Normally, when he went tramping or just walking through his hometown neighborhoods, he would leave the cell phone behind, just so he would have the freedom of being away from business for a while. Now he was grateful that he had not left the phone in the Blazer, or worse yet, at home in his cabin.

Dialing 911, he was suddenly concerned that he might not be able to send or receive in this remote area. His fears were quickly relieved however, when the surprisingly clear voice of the 911 operator answered his call. After several cursory questions, she transferred his call to the Sheriff's office and he found himself explaining the situation to a Deputy Carstairs.

Jeff had some difficulty trying to explain exactly where he was, but solved the situation by directing the deputy to the fire trail where his Blazer was parked, saying that he would go back and wait for him there.

By the time Jeff had worked his way back to the fire trail, he could hear the sound of automobile engines coming from the county road a mile away. As he stepped out into the open, he glanced down the trail at his Blazer parked a short distance away and saw a sheriff's car already there. A deputy was standing behind Jeff's Blazer and talking on his radio. Jeff realized that the deputy must have been running a check on his vehicle and probably him too.

As he started walking the short distance to the Blazer the sounds of engines he'd heard were suddenly close behind him. Turning, he saw two more sheriff's cars and what appeared to be an oversized van. Jeff wondered how in the world they could have arranged all these vehicles this quickly.

"Mr. Lawson?" The deputy by the Blazer said as Jeff walked up.

"Yes sir, that's me," Jeff said. "You must have flown to get here this fast."

"Yeah, well I got the call and I was only a couple of miles from here checking on a dog complaint," the tall deputy said. "My name is Tuttle and I understand you've found something interesting out here," sweeping his arm in the general direction from which Jeff had emerged on the trail.

Jeff said, "Well, I'm not sure I'd call it interesting, I'm still trying to keep my lunch down!"

At that moment, an older man came walking up, although as Jeff watched, he felt that the term 'bustling' would have been a more appropriate description of the way this fellow approached him. He was somewhat overweight and carried what could only be described as a 'beer belly' over a tightly drawn belt.

He too, was in the uniform of the county sheriff and as he drew closer, he in fact introduced himself as, "Sheriff Tommy Beck." Which struck Jeff as a peculiarity for a man of his years being called 'Tommy'!

Taking immediate control of the situation, Sheriff Beck said, "Bill, you better get on the horn to Irma and have her get ahold of Jerry over at the state post. We're going to need some lights out here and get some heavy equipment out here too. We're going to have to break a trail for some of this equipment to get to the scene. Mr. Lawson, how far back in there did you find those bones?"

"I'm guessing it to be about a half mile, more or less," Jeff said. "But, Sheriff, it was pretty easy walking, it isn't too thick in there."

"Well thank the lord for that," the sheriff said, then, "Okay, now then, can you tell us what you've found back there and what you were doing there in the first place?" As he was asking this he had fished out a small hand held tape recorder and held it out in front of Jeff's face.

"We'll get this transcribed when we're done here and we'll have you walk us back in there in just a few minutes," the sheriff explained.

A short time later, Jeff led the sheriff and a number of his deputies back through the trees toward the fallen oak. As they approached, the sheriff held up his hand and gestured to the following deputies to stop and hold their position.

Sheriff Beck asked, "Is that the tree right there? The one you were telling me about?"

Beck had stopped and held his hand across Jeff's chest. Jeff nodded, pointing in the general area he had seen the remains.

"Okay." Speaking now to Tuttle, "Start right here and start stringing tape around this area out at least a hundred yards in all directions."

And louder now for the group following, "Don't any of you guys come any closer than this, I want to keep this area as clean as I can, for the time being at least."

Turning to Jeff, "Okay, show me." They started walking slowly toward the stump where Jeff had sat earlier in the afternoon. When they reached the stump, Jeff pointed down the trunk of the old oak tree toward the area where he had seen the scattered remains.

Stepping carefully around the stump where he had been sitting earlier, the Sheriff followed as Jeff carefully worked his way the few feet to the area where the bones were scattered about.

Sheriff Beck was seemingly, not in the least affected by the site as Jeff had been earlier. He did not approach the remains but rather stopped a few feet away and carefully scanned all about the immediate area of the bones.

"Sure looks like she's been here for a while doesn't it?" the sheriff commented. Jeff noted that the sheriff must also believe he was seeing the remains of a woman.

"I'll bet if you hadn't happened on this spot when you did, we probably never would have found this much of her."

Seeing the look on Jeff's face, the sheriff explained, "See how those bones are scattered. All kinds of critters have been working on this body. There's wild pigs, raccoons, buzzards and every kind of flesh eating animal you can think of in these woods. They would have kept working on this poor soul until her remains would literally disappear."

Hearing this, Jeff felt the bile rising in his throat again and was afraid he was going to be sick. The sheriff sensing this told him to move on back to the growing group of deputies. He said he'd be along in a minute.

When Jeff reached the deputies, they were busily stringing a yellow tape through the trees. A glance at the ribbon showed the words 'Crime Scene' printed on it every several inches. He reached out to lift the tape so he could slip under and just at that moment one of the deputies off some distance to his right, started shouting for the sheriff.

The sheriff was just walking up and was talking into a hand held radio. "What in Hell are you yelling about Johnson? Use your radio for crying out loud ... why do you think we've got them?"

Seconds later, Deputy Johnson's voice could be heard. "Sheriff, you'd better get over here ... I just found another bunch of bones! They look like they've been here quite a while."

Sheriff Beck looked aghast ... "What kind of bones, animal or ..."

Before Beck could go on, Johnson replied, "They're HUMAN bones ... at least the skull is!"

Beck said, "Well don't touch anything, I'll be there in a minute, and don't move ... I don't want anything disturbed!"

Beck turned to Deputy Tuttle … "Bill, did you get in touch with the state boys yet?"

Tuttle replied, "Yes sir, they were going to send someone over."

Beck said, "Well, get them back on the horn and tell them they better send a team over here right now! This is turning into a situation!"

With that, he turned and started up the tape towards deputy Johnson.

As Jeff reached his Blazer, a nearby deputy was listening on his radio to the sheriff and his deputies back in the woods. He looked up as Jeff approached and said,

"Man, you've really opened up a hornets nest out there. From the sounds of things, they're finding bones and remains all over the place back in there!"

'Well, if that's the case, I'm sorry I even came out here today. Wasn't what I had in mind at all!'

'Yeah, I'll bet,' the deputy replied. 'Sounds like you stumbled onto somebody's private killing ground!'

2

After leaving his address and phone number, along with his office address and phone numbers, Jeff headed back to his cabin near Lakeview. Jeff loved this small northern Minnesota town of 3,500 or so population, most of whom Jeff had come to know on a first name basis. He had been living here since taking a position with a small manufacturing company with the somewhat pretentious name of Wildwood Dynamics.

Jeff had come to this community eight years earlier at the invitation of his closest friend, Dwight Sutherland. He and Jeff had gotten acquainted and become fast friends while both were in the Army and about to be sent to Saudi Arabia as part of the Desert Shield, later Desert Storm operations.

Dwight had been wounded and Jeff, at considerable risk to himself, had carried his friend out of harms way. Although neither will talk about their experiences, Jeff had been decorated for his actions.

While visiting with Dwight, he learned of an opening for an assistant plant manager at George Gunderson's factory. Jeff had been employed with a paper mill in southern Wisconsin before coming to visit Dwight. Although he felt secure in his job there and was making a decent income, he really hated his job.

Dwight had inherited a large dairy farm just outside of town and from all appearances was doing quite well with it. The farm had 6 acres of unproductive heavily wooded acreage, which backed up to a small ten or twelve acre lake. At the time there was an old log hunting cabin on the property that appealed to Jeff.

After he was hired at Wildwood Dynamics, Dwight sold the property to Jeff on a ten-year land contract. While restoring the cabin, which took the better part of four months, Jeff lived in Dwight's 25-foot motor home. When Dwight married his childhood sweet heart a few months after Jeff was settled, Dwight had asked him to be his best man.

When Jeff had joined Wildwood Dynamics, it had been privately owned by George Gunderson, an outgoing friendly Swede who took an immediate liking to Jeff. There were only 55 or 60 employees in the company, most of whom had spent most of their adult lives working there for George.

The company made a variety of wooden table lamps. Wood for the lamps was supplied by a local saw mill with kilns for curing and drying the hardwood used in the lamps produced by George's company. The finished products were then shipped to a number of national retail chain stores where demand seemed to be ever increasing for lamps from the little company with the impressive name.

It had been an ideal situation for Jeff. He loved to fish

the bountiful lakes in the area and was likewise enthralled with the surrounding heavily forested countryside, where he spent much of his free time just tramping or hiking the fire trails, or during the season, hunting for deer, which could be found in abundance in the area, but were wily and elusive during the hunting season.

Jeff had several poker pals, most of whom he'd met after George introduced him to the local Rotary Club. They got together every two weeks and rotated from one home to another.

Jeff was the only bachelor and his friend's wives always seemed to have someone they wanted him to meet. As a result, he had met and dated a number of different young women over the years, but nothing serious had ever developed with any of them.

It seemed that the wives had finally run out of available friends, because it had been some time since he had been introduced to anyone new. Even Donna Sutherland, Dwight's wife, had told him she was 'throwing in the towel' and giving up on him.

He began his career with Wildwood Dynamics as the Assistant Plant Manager and five years ago, the Plant Manager decided to retire and George had moved Jeff up into that position. Since then, he had progressed rapidly in the small company and had recently been offered the opportunity to buy the company from George Gunderson.

George had long since passed retirement age, but no one had ever been able to pin him down just how old he actually was. George had lost his wife to cancer last year and it seemed that with the death of his wife, he had lost much of his enthusiasm and interest in the company. And now, he was talking about going to Florida for the winter and just lying in the sun and playing a little golf ..... A game that Jeff himself had introduced George to. So he had offered Jeff the opportunity to buy the business.

Jeff had at first, been reluctant to take George up on his offer. First of all, he had limited personal capital to invest in the enterprise. But Gunderson had quickly convinced him that wouldn't be a problem because, he himself would carry the debt on a personal contract.

No down payment would be necessary and the interest rate on the total debt would be kept at a bare minimum. George had said that he had no particular need for a lot of money, most of which the IRS would probably get anyway!

But, there was another consideration, which gave Jeff pause. George had a daughter. Brenda was about Jeff's age and she had lost her husband in a plane crash a year or so after Jeff came with the company. Her husband had been a light plane pilot with the National Guard at the time. During a routine training flight, something had gone wrong and the small plane had crashed, killing everyone on board.

It took Brenda several months to accept that Bill was gone. These past years she had been teaching in the local Middle School and staying pretty much to herself. Jeff had no idea what the relationship between father and daughter might be.

When Jeff brought up the subject, Gunderson had suggested that the three of them have a meeting to discuss the situation and find out Brenda's feelings on the matter. As he spoke, Jeff sensed a great deal of pain and love that George felt for his daughter. He spoke of how lonely she had become after her husband's death and how she had gone through extended periods of depression as a result.

George had tried to get her to come and work with him at the company and learn the business. But she had told him that she had no interest in the business and she preferred to continue teaching.

The meeting was going to be this evening at George's home.

Jeff quickly showered and changed before stopping for something to eat at the small cafe where he ate most of his meals. To his surprise, several patrons spoke to him about the remains that he had found that afternoon.

One old gentleman in particular, who always seemed to have the 'inside' information on most of the gossip in town, was sitting at the counter and telling those around him, about the 'killing field' that young Jeff Lawson had found that afternoon! Jeff was soon inundated with questions concerning the event.

When it became obvious that Jeff didn't have any more information than they already knew, they lost interest in further discussion on the matter. Jeff was grateful for the seemingly lack of interest of the cafe patrons, but he sensed that as soon as he would leave, the conversations would pick up where they left off.

He quickly finished his meal and as he left the cafe, became aware of Quint Mason following him out the door. Quint was the local town marshal and took his position a good deal more seriously than the townspeople did. Jeff stopped at his car as Quint approached.

"Hello Jeff, I didn't want to talk with you in there," nodding toward the café. "But I did want to ask you why you didn't call me this afternoon instead of the Sheriff's office? Seems like I should be involved in this thing too, don't you think?"

Jeff replied," You know what Quint, I never even gave it a thought. I just called 911 and the call went right through to the Sheriff's office. Sorry if you think I did something wrong"

"Oh no, nothing like that," Quint said quickly. "I just couldn't get any information at all from that fat Sheriff, or his deputies, when I called them this afternoon. And I guess they ticked me off. I never have understood how he keeps getting re-elected every four years!"

Jeff said, "I wonder why he wouldn't tell you anything about what's going on out there. Seems like you, of all people should be involved in something like that."

Then ... "You don't know of anyone that's come up missing around here in the past few months do you?"

"No I don't," Quint replied. "And that's just it Seems like that would be one of the first things he would have asked me! I just don't get it."

After a few more minutes of discussion, Jeff got in his Blazer and left for Gunderson's home located on the outskirts of town.

3

Driving up the long winding driveway to George Gunderson's home, Jeff kept running the conversation he just had with Mason through his mind. Why hadn't the sheriff called the local Marshal and brought him up to date on the situation? It seemed logical to Jeff, that the Sheriff would get in touch with the local town Marshal right away, to verify if there was information of any missing persons within the local law man's jurisdiction. Particularly with the close proximity of Lakeview to the discovery of the remains.

As he approached the old house, he saw George standing out on the front porch waving to him.

There was another car parked just ahead of where Jeff stopped his Blazer and he assumed it belonged to George's daughter Brenda. It was an older model Honda Accord two door. It was dull beige in color, but Jeff noticed that in spite of its unattractive color, it was spotless in appearance and appeared well cared for.

As Jeff got out of the Blazer, George came down the steps smiling to meet him. No matter what the occasion,

George always had a ready smile for any situation, which immediately put people around him at ease.

Shaking his hand, as if it had been weeks since he had seen him, instead of just that morning, he reached with his left hand to Jeff's shoulder saying, "We have heard of the terrible thing that you came across today. Are you alright?" he asked with concern.

"Oh sure, I'm okay now. I was a little queasy earlier though," Jeff replied sheepishly. "I don't know why it affected me the way it did. I've seen things like that before."

George said, "I'm sure you did. With your Desert Storm experiences and all, you've probably seen a lot worse."

They were climbing the steps to the porch, George still had his hand on Jeff's shoulder. "I didn't think I'd have to see anything like that again," Jeff said. "But in any event, the Sheriff seems to be taking charge out there now, so maybe they'll have it cleared up in a day or so."

"Huh," George snorted. "That fat belly Sheriff couldn't find his own shoes if he didn't have help! I don't know how he keeps getting re-elected every four years."

Jeff was taken aback by the disgust in his friend's voice, particularly since it hadn't been more than twenty minutes since he had heard virtually the same words from Marshall Mason.

Before Jeff could respond, George said, "Well come on in the house, Brenda's already here. We had a light dinner together and I talked to her a little bit about what I had in mind with the business. She doesn't seem to take much interest in it, one way or the other. But then, she never has had much interest in the company."

As they walked in the kitchen, Brenda was standing at the sink rinsing off dishes from their dinner earlier. She placed the last few items in the dishwasher and turned and smiled at Jeff.

Jeff was struck by the nearly radiant appearance of this young woman. She was dressed casually in walking shorts, golf shirt type top and sandals on bare feet. She had beautiful blonde hair that fell straight to her shoulders, which framed a lovely Scandinavian face. And the way she was dressed, accentuated her lush figure.

Jeff had often admired Brenda, but had always been very careful about developing a relationship with her, mostly because of his association with her father. Nonetheless, he thought of her often.

"Hi Jeff," she said. "I guess I'm looking at the new owner of Wildwood Dynamics."

"Whoa, whoa, hold on there just a minute!" Jeff exclaimed. "I thought that was why I'm over here tonight. To talk about that."

"Well Dad told me pretty much what he had in mind and I think it's a fine idea," she said.

"I don't know what to say," Jeff said. "I was sure that you should be involved in the business. It certainly seems like you would be his beneficiary or partner ... or something," Jeff stumbled on.

"Oh, I think Dad and I have worked out that problem. You see," Brenda continued. "Dad doesn't feel he needs any further income from the business, he's got quite a retirement built up over the years, so he wants the proceeds of the sale to come to me!"

"Whaat?" Jeff exclaimed. He glanced at George seeing

him sitting back in a kitchen chair with a smug grin on his face.

"That's right Jeff," George said. "I'm afraid I mislead you some. You see, I've discussed this with Brenda several times before tonight and although she was against the idea to begin with, she now feels it would really work out the best for both of us. After all, we all know that I'm not going to live forever and whatever money I would get from the sale would end up in my will anyway."

"And there's a plus side to this whole thing too," George continued. "If we waited for my demise," he commented wryly, "Brenda would end up paying a lot of inheritance taxes. This way, she'll get the whole thing and only have to pay taxes on this as annual income."

Jeff, shaking his head said, "How long have you two been discussing this anyway?"

Brenda laughing said, "Well, I admit we've been talking about this for the past several months."

Then not smiling she said, "Really, since a month or so after mom died. Dad wanted to give up the business and try and enjoy a few years of retirement. Right from our first talk, he made it plain that he wanted you to have the business."

"But, but, how can you be the recipient of the proceeds of the sale, when your dad is the actual owner of the business?"

"That won't be a problem Jeff," George replied. "You see, Brenda's name has been on the business since the day she was born. As a matter of fact, her name is on this house and everything else I own ... including my bank accounts, IRAs, CDs and safety deposit boxes. So when we go talk with Larry in the morning, it will be Brenda that will be signing the Bill of Sale and all other necessary papers."

"Larry?" Jeff said. "Larry Dunson the attorney?" Then after a few seconds, "You've had this appointment set up already? You were that sure of all this before now?"

"Oh sure," George said with a grin. "Like Brenda said, we've been talking about this for quite a while! I made the appointment with Larry a week ago!"

Brenda came over and took Jeff's hand. "Jeff, when Dad and I first started to talk about this, I wasn't sure he was really serious about giving up all that money, but, he assured me he didn't need it, or, want it. And after he shared all his financial holdings with me, I became convinced that this would be okay."

"You know," she added, "I think Dad has always been afraid someone else would end up with his company and wouldn't care for it the same way you will."

Jeff was overcome with the moment. With Brenda standing next to him, still holding his hand and George beaming at them, it suddenly occurred him, that George may have more in mind here, then just selling his company. At that moment, Jeff wasn't sure how he felt about that.

His feelings for Brenda, although carefully hidden, ran disturbingly deep. When she had taken his hand just now, his heart had jumped as he experienced her closeness, the sweet smell of a subtle perfume and the soft touch of her breast as it brushed his sleeve briefly.

"Well, how about it Jeff," George said. "Do we have a deal? You're not going to make me call Dunson and cancel our appointment are you?"

"You've been practically running the company for the past couple of years anyway," George continued. "So I know you've got the stuff to carry on without me looking over your shoulder every day!"

It took Jeff a moment to accept the idea. Until this very minute, he had not been able to believe that this was actually happening. He had often considered leaving to start a business of his own, however, his loyalty and affection for George had always stopped him from pursuing that idea.

When he'd been in the Army, he had taken a number of advanced educational courses and continued taking night courses at a nearby Business College after coming to Lakeview. He had earned a number of college level credits, more than required for a degree, but not enough of the 'right subjects' to qualify for one.

And now, here was the greatest opportunity of his life, presented from a man he greatly admired and yet he hesitated.

After several moments, with George beginning to appear uneasy, Jeff finally said, "George, thank you for this opportunity. This has to be the most exciting thing that's ever happened to me!"

"But," he hesitated, "I won't take it without the understanding that I can call on you anytime when I need help making some of those tough decisions."

George was smiling and nodding his agreement as Jeff continued, "So I guess you won't have to make that call to Larry, except to tell him we'll be there in the morning."

George reached out to shake Jeff's hand but was forced to step back as Brenda put her arms around Jeff and held him for several seconds. Jeff was suddenly aware of her firm breasts pushing against his chest as she said something in Jeff's ear and for the life of him, he later couldn't remember what she had said. All he would remember was the closeness of her body against his.

A short time later, they were standing on the front porch saying good bye when George suddenly said, "Say Jeff, I wonder if you'd mind dropping Brenda off at her house. I've got a couple of things to take care of here."

"I thought that was Brenda's car out in front," Jeff replied.

Before George could answer, a young man walked around the corner of the house and seeing George on the porch, stepped closer.

"You're all set Mr. Gunderson," the young man said. "It's running like a top now. Just needed the fuel lines cleaned out."

"Thanks Red." George replied, turning to Jeff saying, "This is Red Waters Jeff. He's been working on that riding lawn mower of mine. It quit running yesterday and I had Red come out to have a look. That's his car out front and one of the best small engine mechanics in the county."

"Sure," Jeff said, "I know Red." Smiling he nodded at the young man saying, "How are you Red and how's that new baby coming along?"

"Just fine Mr. Lawson. He's growing like a weed and keeping us up half the night." Red said with a grin. "That was sure nice of you to send over the flowers and baby blankets after he was born. It sure meant a lot to Birdie and me too." he finished.

"Birdie Waters is your wife?" Brenda exclaimed. "I had no idea. I've had Birdie a couple of times to clean house for me."

"Yes maam, I know. And she really thinks the world of you Mrs. Dexter. You've all been real good to us."

4

"Well, he finally succeeded in getting us together," Brenda said as Jeff turned out of the driveway.

Jeff looked at her in surprise." What do you mean?" he asked.

"Oh he's such a sly old dog. For the last couple of years we haven't had a meal, a visit or anything together, that your name hasn't come up. He talked about having us meet for dinner a couple of different times, and I wouldn't let him do it," she said.

Jeff was at a loss for words. He just didn't know how to respond to this bit of information. "George never once said anything to me," he finally said. "I've always been reluctant to call you because ...." he let his words trail off.

"You didn't want to interfere with the young widow's grief?" She said somewhat bitterly.

"Jeff, it's been nearly seven years since I lost Bill! My days of mourning have long passed. I'll always love and cherish our memories together, but I've come to accept the fact that he's gone and will never be a part of my life again. I want to move on!"

Jeff was somewhat taken aback at this. He said, "Well it wasn't that I didn't want to interfere on your grief alone .... because I didn't come near ..... It was also because ...... well," he stumbled along ... "You know, boss's daughter and all that. I wasn't sure how George would...."

"Oh for crying out loud," Brenda exclaimed. "Dad has been after me for three years to 'get better acquainted with Jeff', as he put it. So I don't think you ever had to worry about that!"

"But in any event, you're the boss now, or at least you will be tomorrow, so," she looked at him with an impish smile, "Can we take the time to get 'better acquainted' from now on?"

"Yes of course," Jeff blurted. "How about if we start by having lunch together tomorrow after we leave Dunson's office?"

"How about if we start right now by you coming in and having a drink with me tonight .... this is where I live, by the way," she pointed as Jeff jammed on the brakes as he suddenly realized he was about to drive past her house.

"Sorry." he apologized. "I knew this was your house but, I was just so

surprised by what you just said."

Brenda lived in a small one-story ranch type house on a quiet side street. Jeff pulled up behind a late model Chevrolet Impala parked in front of a two-car garage.

"Dad picked me up on his way home this afternoon and didn't give me a chance to pull the car in the garage," she explained.

"I wondered why he didn't want me to drive over there

by myself," she said with a smile. "But now I know. The old devil," she finished with affection.

As they walked to the front door, Brenda suddenly turned and said, "Jeff, I'm putting you on the spot. I didn't think. Do you have other plans for the evening? I'll understand if you do," she said looking at him anxiously.

Jeff replied, "Are you kidding, even if I did have plans, which I don't," he grinned, "I'd change them to spend time with you!"

Brenda laughed at this and said, "Okay, well come on in then. I hope you like scotch because that's about all I have to offer, except maybe a bottle of wine or two. That's usually what I drink, I keep the scotch for dad when he comes over."

"Scotch is just fine," Jeff said, thinking, that he really hated scotch and maybe he should have a glass of wine instead.

"This is nice," Jeff commented as he stepped into the living room entry. He saw the room was furnished with a comfortable appearing couch and overstuffed chairs. At one end of the room was a stone fireplace with bookshelves on either side. On the mantle there was, what appeared to be an antique clock and it was striking the hour just as they entered the room.

"Come on out in back," Brenda said. "That's where I spend most of my time."

'Out in back' turned out to be a large open room with beamed ceilings that had obviously been added to the original structure. On one end of the room were more bookcases, heavily laden with books. On the sidewall was a small bar area with three bar stools.

Jeff was looking around the room with admiration

when Brenda stepped behind the bar and came up with a bottle of Famous Grouse scotch in one hand and a bottle of White Zinfandel wine in the other. Placing them on the bar top, she reached below the bar and came up with a wine glass and a 'rocks' glass.

"I like a little ice in mine and I suppose you want a lot of ice in yours. That's the way Dad likes it." As she spoke she reached behind her to a small refrigerator and came out with ice trays.

"That's fine," he replied looking about. "This is a wonderful room. Was this here when you bought the house?" he asked.

"No, we added it on the first year we lived here," she said. "Bill insisted we needed the extra room. It turned out to be a lot more than we really needed, but it's been nice and I'm really glad to have it."

Jeff had sat on one of the stools and was reaching for his drink when Brenda said, "Come on, let's sit on the couch. Would you like to turn on the Television or listen to music?"

"Music would be nice," he said. He saw the stereo equipment on the opposite end of the room, with a large screen television to the right. Again, there were bookshelves loaded with books on each side of the TV set.

Brenda sat down on a tan leather couch with reading lamps at each end. A book was laying on an end table with a ribbon marking her stopping place. He realized that the room was softly lit by an indirect lighting system that made the room appear warm and intimate.

As Jeff sat down beside her, she picked up a remote and pointed it in the general direction of the stereo system and was immediately rewarded with the soft sound of classical music that filled the room.

"This is very nice," Jeff said. "My little cabin looks like a shack compared to this."

He suddenly had an overwhelming desire to reach out and touch her but felt awkward and afraid of what her reaction might be.

She sipped her wine and they made small talk for an hour or so. It was very pleasant sitting there together. Jeff got up and fixed a second drink. He discovered he rather liked scotch after all.

He had placed his drink next to Brenda's on the coffee table in front of the couch, when she suddenly snuggled against him and said something to the affect that she was feeling a little chilly. Jeff placed his arm around her and suddenly they were kissing, without thought, as though it was the most natural thing in the world.

"I can't believe this," he mumbled. "You have no idea how badly I've wanted to do that, ever since I walked into George's kitchen this afternoon and saw you standing there."

He realized he must be babbling. "I'm sorry, I just ....."

"Shut up Jeff," Brenda said. "That was nice. Kiss me again."

And he did .... many times.

5

Sheriff Beck was sitting in his office trying to make some sense out of the scene that Jeff Lawson had come upon earlier today. His deputies had carefully searched the entire vicinity of the forest where the first two remains had been discovered, only to come upon three more victims.

All appeared to be women, but, the coroner would have to make that determination for sure. What baffled the sheriff was the lack of any clothing, jewelry or anything else that could give a clue as to the identity of the victims.

From the condition of the remains, it seemed apparent that the bodies had been unceremoniously dumped in the forest months ago. All seemed to be in relatively the same stages of deteriation, but it was difficult to tell anything for sure, because in all cases the bones had been scattered by wild animals in the area.

He was reviewing Missing Persons reports that had been filed with his office, as well as those that he had examined from the State Police 'on-line' computer information. The description of missing women shown on any of those reports didn't seem to match anything that he could tell from the remains found in the forest.

Until he heard from the coroner for sure, he was assuming that all were young women that had been killed as a result of some sexual predator in the area. As he sat there thinking, the phone on his desk rang.

"I thought I'd still find you there," the gravelly voice of Doctor George Schmidt said. "Thought you might be interested in something I just discovered," he said.

George Schmidt, along with his normal practice, had been the county coroner for the past fifteen years or so.

"Hi Doc," the Sheriff responded. "What's up? You don't have anything this soon do you? You just got the bones a couple of hours ago."

"Yes, that's true and I've only got the remains of the first one so far. But I've seen enough at this point to make a couple of pretty good judgments on a couple of things," the gravely voice continued.

"What have you got?" the sheriff asked. "Anything that will help us determine who these girls might have been or how long they've been dead?"

"Well that's why I'm calling," doc replied. "I don't know about the others yet, but I suspect the one I have here has been dead for eight months to a year."

"Any indication of a cause of death?" the sheriff asked.

"Nope, nothing that I can tell at this point. Lot of damage to the bones, but that appears to be the result of animals working on the body after it was dumped out there."

"Ah Hell," the sheriff replied. "That really makes me

sick. To think of some young girl just dumped out there for the animals to feed on ......"

"You might have to rethink this situation Tommy," the coroner interrupted. "This thing doesn't look like what you're thinking right now."

"Oh, how's that?" the sheriff replied.

"Well, from everything I can tell at this point and this is pretty preliminary you understand, but I'm sure I'm right about this. These bones I've got here are not from any young girl. In my opinion, these are those of a much older female. I'd say at least seventy five years old!"

"What?" the sheriff exclaimed. "Are you sure about that? My God, why would anyone want to kill an old lady like that?"

"Yeah, I'm pretty sure. The first thing I noticed was that little bit of hair that was still attached to the skull. It wasn't dark at all, although it might have been years ago, but now it's a silvery gray! And also," he concluded, "There is a decided indication of arthritis in several of the joints."

The sheriff was silent for such a long moment that the Coroner said, "Are you still there Tommy. Did you hear what I said?"

"Yeah, I heard alright, I just don't know what to make of it. I sure wish you could come up with a cause of death. That might help."

"I might be able to tell you more when I get the other remains in here. Any idea when that'll be?"

The sheriff replied, "I'm guessing you'll get the rest of them tomorrow sometime. As far as I know the state boys are just about done out there and when they are, you'll get them."

As an after thought, he said, "Listen George, I don't

know what this is all about yet, but I'd appreciate it if you kept what you've just told me to yourself for the time being. Keep me advised and when you've found out everything you can, send me a copy of your findings will you?"

"Sure will Tommy. The state boys might be able to come up with something from dental records or even old health records that could help identify these remains. This old girl suffered a broken leg sometime within the last few years. Those are the kind of injuries that there should be a record of somewhere."

"That's good thinking," the sheriff said. "I'll start looking into that idea in the morning."

The sheriff sat back and thoughtfully reached for a diet Coke from a small refrigerator behind him. His thoughts were interrupted by a soft knock at his door. Looking up he recognized Quint Mason, town marshal of Lakeview.

Waving to him, he called, "Come on in Quint, what's got you out this late at night?"

Pointing him to a chair in front of his desk, he said, "I was just opening a can of Coke, do you want one or, maybe something a little stronger?"

"No thanks Tommy, I thought I'd drop by and see if I could be of any help with your investigation. I was surprised you didn't think to give me a call today," Mason replied somewhat petulantly.

"Well, to tell the truth, it must have just slipped my mind," Sheriff Beck replied. "There was so much happening out there, I couldn't keep up with it all."

Sitting back he said, "I just got back to the office a little while ago myself. Those state boys are still out there taking pictures and picking up bones scattered all over the place.

Looks like they'll be there all night and maybe tomorrow too."

Mason, somewhat mollified, said, "How many bodies did you find out there anyway?"

Beck replied, "No bodies, just the putrefied bones of what appear to be five females."

He was careful not to divulge what he had just learned concerning the estimated age given him by the coroner.

"They look like they've been there a long time. Animals have scattered the bones all over the place. When all is said and done, we may find that there were more than five victims involved. It's going to be a tough job getting I.D.s on any of them," he concluded.

"Well, after I heard about all this today, I went back through any files I had, to see if there was anything that would tie into this," the Marshall said. "But Lakeview is a pretty small town. Nothing much has happened there that might be mixed up with anything like this, at least not in the last couple of years."

"That's right, you did have a little excitement up there two or three years ago when that Indian went on a rampage there didn't you?" the sheriff exclaimed. "What was his name again, Waders, Wanders, something like that?"

"Waters," Mason answered, "Yeah, he got a little too much firewater and that got his blood up one night. Seemed like he was going to get the scalp of a couple of old boys that had been making fun of him in the bar that night."

"What happened to him anyway?" the sheriff asked. "Didn't he get locked up for that?"

"Yeah, he got two years for assault with intent to do great bodily harm. Big dummy, if he hadn't pulled that knife on those guys, we could have put him in jail for the night and it would have all blown over in a day or two."

"But, that was the Raeford brothers that he was mixed up with and they're just plain mean and hate anybody that isn't white, and especially Indians! So, they pressed charges and that's all she wrote" Mason finished.

"He should be out by now, is he behaving himself these days?" Beck asked.

"Yeah, he isn't going to bother anybody again, poor devil, he got released after eight or nine months, good behavior I guess, and wouldn't you know, first thing he did was get a bottle and drink himself blind, falling down drunk and walked right into the side of a moving freight train!"

Mason shaking his head said, "Lot of folks over that way figured he committed suicide, but there are also those that think maybe he was thrown into that train by someone who just didn't like Indians!"

"He had a son didn't he?" The sheriff asked.

"Yeah, Red Wing. He's a nice kid. Got his girlfriend pregnant while they were still in high school and she had to drop out, but he stayed long enough to graduate. They got married before he was out of school. Darned shame too. He probably could have gotten a scholarship for almost any sport. And he's a real smart kid too. Just a darned shame." Mason said again shaking his head.

"How are they getting along? Young kids like that, without an education, they don't have much of chance anymore, especially if they're an Indian," Beck said.

"Well, Little Bird, everybody calls her Birdie, she cleans houses around town. She even does my house once a week. Red took over his Pa's small engine repair business. You know, lawnmowers, snow blowers, and things like that. He's a real whiz when it comes to fixing things like that. So they're getting by," Mason finished.

"What about those Raeford boys? What's happened to them?" the Sheriff asked.

"Well, Thad, he's the youngest one, he fell out of his fishing boat a year or so ago and drowned. The other one, Jeremy, he's still around, but he ain't good for nothin anymore. He was working at the sawmill and as usual he was drunk and somehow he fell against one of those big saws and got his right arm cut off at the shoulder. Now all he does is lay around drunk all day, every day. He's just good for nothing," Mason said.

"Quint," the sheriff said, "He couldn't have anything to do with this situation could he? He ever have a record of assaulting women or anything like that?" The sheriff was careful not to specify the age of any potential victims.

"How does he live anyway, even a drunk has to have an income of some kind?"

"Ah naw, only trouble he's ever had was because of too much to drink, which has been pretty much the story of his life," Mason replied. "The sawmill arranged a small annuity for him after his accident, even though they weren't liable for anything. Plus, old Jeremy, he's sixty-three or four, he was the older of the two, and he qualifies for Social Security now. But he just blows it all on booze every month!"

"How about the kid, what'd you say his name is?" the sheriff asked.

"Red Wing, but everybody just calls him Red. He's okay. Never been in a bit of trouble and was doing real well in school. Cracker jack of a baseball player, everybody says he'd of gotten a scholarship for that or football, either one. There'd been a couple of colleges looking at him."

"Other than that and a few kids raising Hell on Saturday night, not much of anything happens in my neck of the woods."

"What do you know abut Jeff Lawson? He's not from around these parts is he?" the sheriff asked.

"Naw, but he's been here a pretty long time. Works over at the lamp factory. George gave him a big job over there."

Then, "That sure was something, him stumbling onto those bones like that. What the heck was he doing out there anyway?"

"He isn't married is he?" the sheriff asked, ignoring the question.

"He got any girl friends over there, or doesn't he like girls?" Beck asked with a smirk.

"Oh naw, I don't think there's anything like that with him. He's dated a few gals from time to time, but nothing ever seemed serious." said Mason.

"Old George would sure like to match him up with that daughter of his, but he says Jeff hasn't taken the bait yet, but he will one of these days."

"Well, I guess I'd better get on back to Lakeview. Let me know if there's anything you need that I can help you with," Mason said as he headed out the door.

Beck said, "You bet Quint, I'll sure do that," with a casual wave to the Marshall as he headed out the door.

Sitting back in his chair, he took a long pull on the can of Coke thinking about the conversation he'd just had with Mason. Without conscious thought, he reached down to a lower drawer of his desk and pulled out a bottle of Jack

6

Jeff, Brenda and George were having lunch together at a local downtown cafe. Jeff was nervous, wondering just how George would react when he learned that the relationship with his daughter had apparently changed since he had last seen them the previous evening.

The meeting with the attorney had gone smoothly and was quickly concluded. Jeff had been a little surprised at the number of documents and agreements that he and Brenda had signed. George too, had signed a few papers giving up his interest in the business to Brenda, and by virtue of a purchase agreement, finally to Jeff.

He was now the sole owner of Wildwood Dynamics and he was a little overwhelmed by the whole idea.

George tried not to take notice of the two, but when he realized Brenda was holding Jeff's hand under the table and they were sitting very close in the booth, he couldn't help but smile at them with a knowing grin.

"All right you old Devil," Brenda said. "We took your advice and we're starting to get 'better acquainted'!" Jeff's face turned scarlet red with embarrassment.

"Turns out that we really do like each other," she said looking at Jeff, "very much." She finished.

"Well," George said with a big smile, "I couldn't be happier. You two are the most important people in my life these days and I'm just sorry it took you so long to 'find each other.'"

"Now dad," Brenda said. "Just slow down a bit. We've just realized we want to see more of each other. That's as far as it's going for the time being. So just take it easy and stop pushing," smiling to soften the rebuke.

George was not put off in the least. "Well, I don't care what you say, I know how this is going to end and all I can say is, hurry up and get it done! I'm not going to be around that many more years and I want to see my grandchildren!"

Now both Jeff and Brenda were red faced. Jeff thinking they had come pretty close last night, but Brenda had finally pushed him away saying, "We better stop this right now."

But she had leaned forward and kissed him again. Then, "Come on. Get going. We've got time now and we don't need to rush things."

She had stood up, reaching for his hands to pull him from the sofa. As he got to his feet, she pulled him close and she became aware of what their passionate kisses had done to him. Nonetheless, she pushed her hips forward to make closer contact.

Then suddenly, realizing what she was doing to Jeff, she quickly stepped back saying breathlessly, " I think we'd better stop this and say good night."

And that had been it. Jeff didn't even remember driving home after that. His head was so full of Brenda and the closeness of her warm body against him that he could think of little else. He had difficulty getting to sleep but he finally drifted off and his dreams were filled with visions of her throughout the night.

And now here they were, with George grinning at their discomfort and making comments about grandchildren. For Jeff's part, he was thinking that he might at last, be at the end of his lonely bachelorhood. There didn't seem to be much doubt in George's mind about that.

Changing the subject, George said, "I think we should call a meeting of everybody over at the plant this afternoon and let them all know what's happening and that you're the new ramrod of this outfit from now on."

"Good idea," Jeff replied, grateful to change the direction of the conversation. "I thought I'd go on over to the office and try and get things in order. What do you think of moving Les up a notch or two, so he can kind of look after things with me?"

'Les' was Lester Noonan, a young accountant who had started working for the company a year or so earlier. He had moved his new wife into the area at that time and they had soon made friends with a number of town's people. He had a friendly outgoing personality and had quickly been accepted by his fellow workers.

Before George could respond, Attorney Dunson stopped at the table and said to Jeff, "I'll have all the papers ready for the county court house in the next hour or so. You had mentioned that you'd like to take them down there yourself. Do you want to come by and pick them up around three or so?"

"Sure," Jeff replied. "But it might be tomorrow before I can get down there. Will that matter? While I'm there,

I want to stop by and see the Sheriff for a few minutes too. I'm not going to have the time today," with a grin. "We've got a big meeting to take care of this afternoon."

"No problem," Dunson said.

But then, "Just don't let it drag on too long and keep all that stuff locked up somewhere until you take it over. If it turns out that you can't get over there in the next couple of days, let me know and I'll send somebody from my office."

"Why don't I just leave it all in your office till I can pick it up on my way?" Jeff said.

More small talk and finally Dunson shook hands with Jeff and wished him good luck in the new venture and walked away.

Discussion continued between George and Jeff concerning the meeting they were going to have that afternoon, but the pressure of Brenda's hip and leg against him in the narrow booth distracted Jeff.

Too soon the lunch was over and Jeff was standing in front of the small cafe saying his goodbyes to Brenda as George waited impatiently at the curb.

Glancing at George, Brenda smiled and stepped forward and kissed Jeff saying, "Call me later today. We'll talk some more," glancing again at George, "without an audience."

She turned and hurried away, leaving Jeff staring after her.

7

The rest of the day for Jeff was filled with exciting and challenging details of owning a new business. The meeting with the plant employees went well and all congratulated Jeff on his new position of ownership.

He met with Lester Noonan after the meeting, asking him to take on the challenges of becoming the Controller for the company. Noonan was surprised and pleased that Jeff considered him capable of handling the new position, especially after Jeff told him how much he was going to rely on his judgment and guidance in the weeks and months ahead.

George spent most of the afternoon with Jeff, covering a number of issues that had to be taken care of. Then, without fanfare, George stood and shook hands with Jeff, saying, "Well it's all yours now Son, take good care of my company."

And as an afterthought, "You've got some really good people out there and you can always count on them." With eyes slightly tearing, shook Jeff's hand again and left the company that he had started so many years before.

As Jeff left his office, glancing at his watch, he realized he hadn't called Brenda and thought back to that last conversation with George. In all the years he had known him, George had never before called him 'Son' and Jeff was moved by the reference.

When he turned into his driveway, he saw a sheriff's car parked there. Directly in front of that, was a blue Chevrolet that he recognized as belonging to Brenda. As he got out of his car, Sheriff Beck and Brenda stepped out the front door and Brenda waved happily.

As he walked up Brenda came forward taking his hand in hers and leading back toward the cabin. Jeff said, "Hello Sheriff. What brings you over this way?"

"Oh, I just had some unfinished business over here and thought I'd stop by and see if I could catch you at home."

"Well come on in the house," Jeff said. "Can I fix you a drink, a beer, or anything?" Jeff asked as they stepped inside.

"No, no thanks," Then, "Wow, this is okay. I'd never guess this old cabin could look like this inside."

The sheriff was looking around at a very comfortable appearing main room with a kitchen off to one side. A small breakfast area could be seen off the kitchen. Another doorway on the far wall presumably led to the bedrooms and bathroom. The walls appeared to be the highly varnished logs that comprised the exterior of the main building itself. Masculine looking curtains were hung at all the windows.

The main room had neat overstuffed furniture scattered around in a random, but carefully arranged pattern. The floor was covered with beige, tight nap carpeting that extended into the kitchen area as well as the hallway extending towards the bedrooms. In one corner was a medium size flat screen television, sitting so it could be viewed from any point in the room.

Jeff was looking at Brenda and marveling again at how this beautiful woman could be having such a profound affect on him.

She was looking at him somewhat anxiously saying, "I hope you don't mind my coming over here without an invitation. I thought maybe you'd be home and the door was unlocked, so I just came in and made myself at home."

"Don't be silly. I'm very glad to see you," Jeff said.

The Sheriff was looking, with interest, at the two of them standing there. He couldn't help but remember the comments Quint Mason had made concerning these two and wondered how long this relationship had been going on. From the way they were looking at each other, something was definitely happening between them.

"Well Sheriff," Jeff said, finally taking his eyes off Brenda, "What can I do for you? Anything new on those bones we found? Come in, come in," motioning towards a chair while he and Brenda moved towards a large couch to one side.

"Actually," the Sheriff began, "I wanted to ask you a few questions and also follow up on something you mentioned in the woods the other day."

"Okay, what do you want to know?" Jeff replied, as he and Brenda sat together on the couch. The Sheriff noted that it was quite a large couch, but Brenda was sitting very close to Jeff.

"I didn't make anything of it at the time, but didn't you

tell me that you had been taking pictures out there that day?"

Jeff replied, "Yes, I was. I had hoped to get a picture of a big buck that's been moving around in that part of the woods. He showed up, but when I tried to bring up my camera, he took off. That's when I found those bones by the log."

The Sheriff said, "Didn't you say you took some pictures of those bones too?"

"That's right, I did. I forgot all about that till you just mentioned it. Do you want the film?"

"Yeah, I think so. The state boys took a lot of pictures too, but I guess a few more won't hurt."

"I'll go get my camera, it's back in my bedroom." He started to get up and the sheriff waved his hand stopping him.

"That's okay Jeff, I'll get it before I leave. By the way, if you haven't taken the film out of the camera I'd like to take the camera and all with me. I'll let someone else take out the film and develop it."

Seeing the questioning look on Jeff's face he continued, "Oh don't worry, I'll give you a receipt for it and get the camera back to you as soon as we're done with it."

Brenda asked, "Have you found out anything about that woman? That's scary to think that sort of thing could happen in this area."

"How do you go about finding out who she was anyway?"

"Well," the Sheriff replied. "Normally we'd check with the local dentists for matching dental records, but that won't work in this case because whoever did this to her, also knocked her teeth out!"

Jeff shook his head, saying, "Good grief, what kind of monster have we got here anyway? I can't think of anybody that could be that sadistic."

Suddenly turning to Brenda, "What's wrong honey? Oh, don't get upset over this thing, the Sheriff will figure it out," glancing at the Sheriff.

Brenda was shaking and had turned quite pale listening to the two men talk. She snuggled closer to Jeff, clutching his arm saying, "I can't help it. Just the thought of what that poor girl must have suffered."

Again the Sheriff didn't offer any information as to the age of the victim. Then he said, "Jeff's right Mrs. Decker. We'll get to the bottom of this pretty soon I think. I talked with Doc Schmidt again this morning and he told me he'd come up with something, but wanted to check it out for himself."

Jeff asked, "Who's Doc Schmidt? I thought I knew all the local doctors".

"Oh, he's the county coroner." the Sheriff replied. "He's been around the block a time or two and he's seen it all. I don't know what he thinks he's found, but I'll bet it'll be something interesting, that's for sure."

Brenda said, "I sure hope so. I don't think any of us will relax until this animal is caught and dealt with. And by the way Mister," she said turning to Jeff. "What's the big idea of leaving your house unlocked like that? All I had to do was open the door and walk in this afternoon!"

"I've never locked my doors since I've lived here. I don't even know if I've got a key for the doors." Jeff replied somewhat sheepishly. "I guess you're right though, I'll look around and see if I can find one."

The Sheriff said, "That's probably a good idea. And

until we get to the bottom of this, it'd be a good idea for you to spread the word for everybody over here to start taking some precautions."

After additional small talk, Jeff retrieved his camera for the Sheriff and as he was leaving, turned and asked Jeff, "You've been here in Lakeview for a long time now haven't you? Where are you from originally anyway?"

"I came here shortly after I got out of the Army," Jeff replied. "Before that I lived in a small town over in southern Wisconsin."

"Oh," the Sheriff said. "Do you still have family over there?"

"No, afraid not," said Jeff. "Actually, I'm not sure if I have any family or not. You see, I was raised in an orphanage and spent most of my life living with a young couple that acted as my guardian until I was eighteen."

"Oh my," Brenda said. "I never knew that about you. Dad never said a word about it to me."

Jeff laughed and said, "I suspect there's a lot George hasn't told you about me."

The Sheriff noted this and saying his good byes left the two of them standing on the small deck in front of the cabin. Driving away, he glanced in his rear view mirror and saw the young woman reach for Jeff and step back into the house.

In the house, Brenda was kissing Jeff with passionate abandon. Drawing back a little, she looked into Jeff's eyes and said, "Finally! I thought he would never leave!"

8

fter turning around and driving down the gravel
entry and onto the county road in front of Jeff's
cabin, the Sheriff picked up his radio mike and
contacted his office. Irma, his fifty five year old dispatcher
answered immediately.

"Sheriff, where've you been? I've been trying to get in
touch with you for almost an hour."

"Well, you've got me now, what's up?" the Sheriff
replied.

"You didn't have your cell phone either," Irma
exclaimed, not to be put off. "When I tried to call you on
that, it was ringing behind me in your office! As long as
the county pays for that thing, you should carry it with
you," she scolded.

"Okay, okay, I'll make a point of picking it up on my
way home. In the meantime, will you please tell me why
you've been trying to get in touch with me?"

"Well, first of all, you remember you sent Deputy
Tuttle back out there to those woods to clean up all that
crime scene ribbon, well he's still out there," Irma said.

"What? I sent him out there three or four hours ago. He should've got back by now. What's going on?"

"Well, unlike some people," Irma replied haughtily, "most people carry their cell phones with them and can stay in touch. He was cleaning up out there when he tripped over another one," she finished.

"Oh no," The Sheriff thought, then asked, "Tripped over another what?" he asked, knowing what the answer was going to be.

"Actually, it was a skull. All covered up in a bunch of grass, he said. He started looking around and found a whole bunch more of bones lying in the area. He said the grass was so tall and thick that that's probably why you missed them the other day."

The Sheriff couldn't believe what he was hearing. There had been a veritable army of deputies and state policemen in those woods. They had covered the whole forest for hundreds of yards in all directions and yet he was now being told that they had missed this one!

"For crying out loud, how could we have missed that?" he asked. "It sounds like it was right where we had strung the ribbon. This is bad, we should have found this one when we found the others. There'll be Hell to pay when this gets out."

"Hang on to your hat Sheriff," Irma was saying. "I've got some more bad news for you."

"What else could happen today that could be worse than this mess?" Beck said.

"Sheriff," Irma said, "If you're driving, I wish you'd pull off to the side cuz this is gonna really upset you."

"What? What are you saying?" Beck said, as he was

slowing and pulling off to the side of the road. "What now, what's happened Irma?"

"Sheriff, I'm sorry I have to tell you this, but your friend Doc Schmidt was found sitting in his car over behind the Walgreen's drug store a couple of hours ago. They figure he had a heart attack, Tommy," Irma said softly. "He was dead."

It felt to Beck, like someone had hit him across the chest with a hammer. Without thinking, Beck brought the cruiser to a stop, flipping on the flashing emergency lights and half blocking the blacktop highway he'd been traveling. His mind was reeling with confusion and emotion as he sat there trying to make sense of what Irma had just told him.

He and George Schmidt had grown up together. Although George had been a couple of years older than Tommy, a strong bond of friendship had grown between the two of them over the years. The two of them had married local girls, coincidentally with George marrying a close cousin of Tommy's.

"Tommy," Irma said. "Are you okay? Do you need anything? Tommy?" she repeated. "Tommy, answer me please." she said pleadingly.

"Yeah, okay, okay," Beck replied as in a stupor, then, "Has anybody called Sharon? Have you called Lynda?"

Lynda was Beck's wife. "She should be over there with Sharon. Where did they take George?"

Beck felt like he was babbling and couldn't stop asking questions. Finally, hearing Irma trying to break in he just sat there listening to Irma's soft voice explaining that, yes Lynda was with Sharon and George had been moved to Decker's Funeral Home and George's son and daughter had been contacted and were already on their way from the Twin Cities.

Gathering his thoughts, he finally said, "Alright, first things first I guess. Have Tuttle retape the area and give the state boys a call. They were out there too,"

Beck said, thinking, we weren't the only ones to miss it. "Tell Tuttle to stay there until the state boys get there," he finished.

Irma said, "We already called the state office, but they weren't sure if they could get back out there yet tonight. Do you want Bill to stay out there all night?"

"Hell yes," Beck yelled into the mike. "Keep him there until next week if need be! Dammit anyway, how'd we ever miss something like that anyway?"

"Tommy," Irma's soft voice came over the radio. "Bill is already on overtime and I don't really think those bones are going anywhere tonight. Do you really want him to stay there all night?"

"No, No, of course not," Beck said. "Have him go on home and send someone out there first thing in the morning to meet the state boys."

Then, "Sorry Irma, I'm upset and didn't mean to shout at you. I'm going to stop by George's office on my way home and see if he left anything for me. He said he was onto something, but wouldn't tell me what it was."

"Okay Tommy," Irma replied. "And I'm real sorry, I know how close you two were. Will you be stopping by to see Sharon tonight too?"

"Just as soon as I can, after stopping at his office."

"Have someone run that damned cell phone over to my house will you. I'm sorry I missed your calls. I should have had it with me," he said.

"Okay Sheriff," Irma said, back to the official dispatcher voice. "We'll see you here in the morning. If you need anything from us, just give a call on the radio, Rhonda will be on the board for the rest of the night."

Beck drove several miles before realizing that he hadn't flipped off the cruiser's flashing lights. His mind was full of conflicting emotions and he was more upset than he'd ever been in his life. He couldn't seem to focus his thoughts. It seemed that he was suddenly dealing with death everywhere he turned.

It was forty minutes later when he pulled up in front of the Coroners office. He went inside and found the night watchman sitting behind the receptionist desk outside George Schmidt's office. The watchman looked up and saw Beck coming through the front door. He got up quickly and went to meet him slowly shaking his head as he came forward.

"Terrible, just terrible Sheriff," the watchman began. "We just couldn't believe it when we got the news a couple of hours ago."

"I know what you mean Ed," the Sheriff said. "I'm not sure I still believe it. Is there anyone out in back?" ' Out in back' was the examination room, a cold sterile facility where Beck had visited his old friend a number of times over the years, for both county business or just to stop by and say hello.

"Yeah, Stony's back there. He was looking over that last bunch of bones that came in yesterday." Stony was a young intern that was studying to be a pathologist and was presently earning credits working with George.

"Give him a jingle will you and ask him to unlock the door. I want to go in and look around."

"Okay Sheriff, just hold on a minute." as the old watchman moved behind the desk, he punched an intercom on his desk and the Sheriff heard Stony respond. A moment later a buzzer sounded at the door in back of the office and the Sheriff passed through into the examination area and was struck again at the sterile stainless steel atmosphere of the room.

Stony was waiting just inside the door and extended his hand to Beck as he came through the door. "Hi Sheriff," he said. "Sorry about Doc. He was a great guy. I sure did learn a lot from just being around him."

He hesitated and then said, "They called me this afternoon when they found him and I had to go over and pronounce him. I'm not sure if I had the authority to do that or not, being just an intern and all, but they needed someone to do it. I didn't sign the death certificate though, as to the cause of death I mean," he finished.

"Yeah, I'm sure it'll be okay," Beck said. "I was told it looked like he had a heart attack."

Stony replied, "Yeah, that's what the druggist over there said too. I'm not real experienced yet at this sort of thing, but Doc looked funny to me, not what I've been led to expect a heart attack victim to look like."

"What do you mean, 'looked funny'?" the Sheriff asked with a frown.

"I don't mean 'funny' as in 'funny ha, ha'. I mean unusual, different from what I expected, that's all," Stony finished.

"What did you expect?" Beck asked.

"Well, for one thing, I was expecting to see a grayish pallor to his complexion, but instead he looked like he always did. If you didn't know better, you'd have thought he was just sitting there asleep."

"Anything else," Beck asked?

"Sheriff, please understand, I'm pretty inexperienced at this sort of thing and haven't seen many actual victims till now. But another thing I expected would be the individual's eyes. I've always thought that a person dying of a heart attack will generally have some considerable pain and normally will have their eyes squeezed tight, you know what I mean? Well, Doc's eyes were open and there was no sign of stress or muscle constriction that you'd expect if someone was experiencing a lot of pain."

Sheriff Beck thought about what he had just been told, but didn't know quite what to make of it. He hadn't been aware that his old friend even had heart problems, but knowing that George wasn't one to burden his problems with anybody, he wasn't surprised he hadn't been told. Nonetheless, what Stony had just told him started nibbling at the back of his mind.

"Okay, well anyway," Beck said, "I need to see Doc's notes, or any report he was working on concerning those bones they found. He was going to send something over to me but hadn't gotten around to it yet."

"Sure," Stony replied. "I've been going through what he had so far, but can't seem to make heads nor tails out of most of it. Here's his lab notebook right over here," he said walking over to an examination table, where the skeletal bones of one of the victims were laid out.

Beck picked up the notebook and quickly glanced through the first few pages. He asked Stony, "Do you mind if I take this with me. I'd like to look through it and see if anything I find makes any sense. I'll get it back to you in a few days."

"No problem," Stony replied. "But you might also try and get that little notebook he carried in his shirt pocket. He was always making notes in it. Said it helped him think and he'd look it over when he got home."

"Alright, well thanks Stony," holding up the notebook. "I'll get this back to you in a couple of days."

As he was driving to his friend's house, Beck was dreading the meeting with Sharon Schmidt. He didn't know what he was going to say that could console his best friends wife. Thank goodness Lynda Beck would be there for him to lean on. He was always amazed at the inner strength of this small woman and how much he had come to depend and rely on that strength over their years together.

As he pulled up in front of his friend's house, he saw Lynda's car parked directly behind the big Lincoln Town Car that had been George's pride and joy. It had to be at least ten years old, but was absolutely spotless. Sharon often had complained that he wouldn't take his car out of the garage if it was raining or snowing. That left the big Lincoln in the garage for most of the winter and her without a car.

Lynda Beck met him as he walked up the steps and gave him an affectionate hug. She had obviously been crying, her blue eyes reddened from the tears.

The Sheriff asked, "Is she going to be alright?"

Lynda replied, "I just don't know Cubby," using a pet name that she had coined after Beck started to develop his rather substantial belly, "She's obviously upset and confused by it all, but she's not grieving like I expected. She's a lot tougher than I would be under the same circumstances."

"I doubt that. All you Scandinavian women are tougher than a boiled owl," he said affectionately."

"I guess I'd better go in and pay my respects. Is she lying down or anything?"

"Heck no, she's out in the kitchen. I tried to get her to sit down and relax a little, but she says she wants to stay busy. I don't think it's really hit her yet."

Beck walked through the large house to the kitchen, where he found Sharon Schmidt fussing at the stove. Sitting at the large kitchen table were two neighbor ladies with coffee cups in front of them. They were talking quietly and watching Sharon as she turned to see Beck enter the kitchen.

"Oh Tommy," she exclaimed. "I'm so glad you're here."

He stepped forward and put his arms around her and patting her gently on the back, felt hot stinging tears well up in his eyes. Sharon was trembling in his arms and suddenly started sobbing uncontrollably.

"I just can't believe it," she said, clinging to the Sheriff. "I just can't believe it," she repeated. "George was never sick a day in his life and then to have this happen with no warning. I just can't believe it."

Beck said, "I know, I know" soothingly with tears streaming down his face. "It's unbelievable. I couldn't believe it either when I found out about it."

Then, "Sharon, I'm sorry I wasn't here sooner, I was up in Lakeview and didn't get the message until an hour or so ago."

"Oh Tommy, it doesn't matter. There wasn't anything you could have done for him. And Lynda came over with one of your Deputies to tell me what had happened. She's been here ever since. She called the kids and got the message to them too. I talked to them and they'll be here anytime now."

"Well, you know how I feel. Of course I'll do anything I can to help you. Is there anything, anything at all that I can do for you now?"

Stepping back and brushing the tears from her face, she said, "Actually there is. They took him over to Decker's Funeral Home and I'd like to get his watch and rings before anything happens to them."

"I sure will," Beck replied. "Although I don't think you have to worry about Forest Decker keeping his personal effects or anything like that. He's as honest as the day is long."

"Oh I know that," Sharon said with a quiver in her voice. "It sounds crazy I know, but if I had them it might make it seem more like George had come home this afternoon. That's the first thing he'd do when he got here you know. He'd always take off that ruby ring and slip his watch off and lay them on the dresser. Said it was old habits. He didn't wear them when he was working and he didn't wear them around the house."

She paused and looked up at Beck and said, "I want those things back on the dresser when I go to bed tonight."

"I'll take a run over to the Funeral Home right now and get them for you. By the way, I'm told that he always carried a small note pad in his pocket too. Did he by any chance leave that here this morning when he left?" the sheriff asked.

"I know what you're talking about," she said. "That

danged little notebook had one of those spiral wire hinge thingies on it and I was forever asking him to carry it in any pocket but his shirt pocket. It was wearing holes in perfectly good shirts!"

Then hearing what she had said, continued, "I guess that won't matter anymore though will it?" and she started sobbing again.

As Beck turned to leave, Lynda gave him a hug saying, "That's the first time she's let herself go. I think she'll be alright now."

9

Brenda, running her fingers over Jeff's bare chest said, "We forgot to eat, do you know that?"

Rolling over, she stepped off the bed and started for the attached bathroom. "Me for a shower and then let's go get something to eat."

Jeff sat up on one elbow and admired Brenda's nude body as she walked away from him. She turned and looked back at him and with a coy glance at his bare body and said, "Unless of course, you'd like to come take a shower with me. It looks like there's room for both of us in there."

Some time later, after stepping from the oversized shower, they stood drying each other with large terry towels. Their bodies were flushed and red from their shower together, as well as from the rough material of the towels.

Jeff said, "If this is the kind of welcome home you give me when you stop by, I hope you stop by often!"

It had only been a just few minutes after the Sheriff had left, that they found themselves in bed together. And they had stayed there for a long time, enjoying their intimacy and the passion of the moment. Resting quietly until a short time ago, they had been talking in low tones about what was happening to them.

"Jeff, I don't know where this is going between us yet, but I know that we both have a strong attraction to each other. We need some time together to see if there's something more than ...." she paused.

And Jeff finished, "Sex! Yeah, I know what you mean, but what I'm feeling right now has nothing to do with sex! Well maybe some, after what we've just had together. But I've never experienced these kinds of feelings for anyone before."

"Where the heck are all my clothes?" Brenda exclaimed as she looked around the bedroom. She was wrapped in the large towel and she laughed as she found items of clothing scattered all the way into the front room.

"We sure must have been in a hurry," she said. "I don't even remember taking this stuff off!"

"I remember," Jeff said. "I don't think I'll ever forget it."

After dressing, Jeff said, "You know, I think I've got a couple of steaks in the refrigerator and enough lettuce and stuff to make a salad. How about if we just stay here and I'll grill the steaks out on the patio."

As an afterthought, "I think I could even find a bottle of wine around here someplace too. One of our suppliers gave me a couple of bottles last Christmas and I've never opened them."

Brenda thought about it for a second or two and then replied, "That sounds good to me, but as soon as we finish, I've got to go home. I've got some school work to take care of."

Jeff happily started the gas grill and soon had the steaks grilling. Brenda was busily tearing a head of lettuce and preparing the salads. When she finished, she stepped out on the deck with a glass of wine in her hand and stood watching Jeff fuss over the steaks.

As she looked around, she could see a small lake at the back of the property. It was difficult to see how large it was in the gathering darkness, but she could see what appeared to be a gazebo near the shore. As she watched, a flock of ducks went swimming past the shoreline.

"This is very pleasant here Jeff," she said. "No wonder you like this so much. Dad told me how you enjoyed the peace and quiet of the country."

"Yep," he replied, "This is where I do my serious thinking," he said with a soft smile. "I spend a lot of time out here watching the ducks and once in a while a swan or two will come sailing in."

"I've sat out in that gazebo on a lot of evenings like this and thought of all the world problems that I could solve if I were King." Then without thinking he said, "And I've spent a lot of evenings sitting out there thinking about you too."

Surprised, Brenda said, "Oh come on Jeff, we've only had a few days together. We hardly knew each other before a few days ago."

"Sorry if that surprises you, but unfortunately it's true. You're right, we hardly knew each other, but that doesn't mean I didn't want to know you. And like it or not, I thought of you often. I wish George had told me how much he wanted us 'to get better acquainted'"

"Well, I think we've gone a long way past 'getting better acquainted' now, don't you? I wish I'd known you before this too, I think I'd enjoy sitting out there with you in the evening."

Jeff grinned, "Well the night is still young. But right now, the steaks are done. Do you want to eat out here or inside."?

"I've got the table set inside. Let's go in."

Later, they walked hand in hand down to the gazebo and sat together for a short while. At last Brenda stood and said, "I've got to go home. I've still got papers to grade and lessons for the next couple of days to think about."

"Don't go. Spend the night here with me. The papers can wait and there's only one more school day left in the week. You can do your planning over the weekend. And why not bring your stuff out here and do it here anyway. I won't bother you," he paused, then with a lecherous grin, "much!"

"No! I don't want to start that. Not yet at least," she said with conviction. "I don't want to start something that could hurt us both."

"Brenda, my love," he said. "We've already 'started something'! And I, for one, have never been happier about anything. This has been the most unforgettable week of my life. I'd never believed all these wonderful things could happen to me. And you are definitely the best thing of all."

They had been walking back toward the cabin and she turned and allowed herself to be wrapped in his arms for a long passionate kiss. At last she pulled away.

"You're right Jeff," she said. "And that is exactly why I want to slow down a little. Too many things have happened at once, for both of us and I want to be sure that things don't change, for either of us, after the excitement wears off."

After giving him another kiss, she walked to her car and drove away.

Jeff stood in the driveway watching until her car was out of sight. Then he moved the Blazer into the attached garage and closed the doors for the night.

10

Sheriff Beck found Forest Decker in his office just off the entrance to the funeral home. Decker was busy working on his computer when he looked up to see the Sheriff enter.

Decker had bought this business two years earlier and was having a difficult time making ends meet. What it boiled down to and what Decker hadn't anticipated when he took on the large debt for this enterprise was, to put it quite simply, there just weren't enough people dying in this community for him to meet all of his obligations. This, in spite of the fact that his was the only funeral home in the area.

His first couple of years had been pretty difficult and he hadn't been sure if he was going to make it or not. Then about a year ago, his cash flow started to improve and he had been getting along pretty well since.

"Hi Sheriff," he said. "What can I do for you this evening?"

Beck replied, "I'm here about Doc Schmidt. I just ...." he stopped noting that Decker had suddenly turned very pale and a sweaty sheen appeared on his face. "What's the matter Forest? You look awful, are you alright?"

"Yeah, I'm ... It's just that ..." Decker stumbled along. "I seem to have eaten something that doesn't agree with me," he finally ended.

"Oh, well, I'm sorry to bother you like this," Beck said. "I'll only take a minute or two of your time. It's just that Sharon asked me to stop by and pick up Doc's personal effects. I guess she doesn't want them buried with him."

Decker seemed to relax and taking a couple of deep breaths said, "Sure, sure. I've got them right here." As he spoke he pulled open a desk drawer and came up with a large envelope.

"This is everything he had on him when they brought him in."

The Sheriff looked in the envelope and could see the ring and watch that Sharon had been worried about. There was also a billfold, a pocketknife, various bits of change and a folded piece of paper. He pulled the paper from the envelope and unfolded it. It appeared to be a prescription form. He looked up at Decker who was watching the Sheriff.

"That's apparently what he was doing at Walgreen's," Decker said.

"What do you mean?" Beck asked?

"Well, unless I'm mistaken, that's a prescription for heart medicine. And there was also a small bottle of nitro glycerin tablets in his pocket."

The Sheriff looked again in the envelope and seeing a small vial, picked it out and looked at it. It was filled with tiny white pills.

"I will be damned," he said. "I've known that old bird

for more years than I care to count and never knew he had health problems of any kind, let alone something like this!"

"Do you know when Mrs. Schmidt will be coming in to make the final arrangements?" Decker asked. He was wiping his forehead with a linen handkerchief and visibly trying to pull himself together.

"What do you mean?" Beck asked?

"I mean, will she be available in the morning? She'll need to select a casket and we'll have to discuss the funeral service, visitation and that sort of thing," Decker finished.

"And do you, by any chance, have any idea if Mrs. Schmidt will prefer cremation? I have to make arrangements for that type of thing with Ross's Crematorium down in Waushawa. He's the got the closest facility."

"Oh, yeah, I see what you mean," Beck said. "I imagine she'll have the kids come in and handle those details. They'll be here tonight, but I'll ask her about it when I take this stuff back to her. In the meantime, why don't you just figure on someone being here around nine thirty or so in the morning. If it's any different than that, somebody will let you know."

They were walking together toward the door when Beck suddenly stopped and asked, "Say, I just thought of something else I wanted to ask you. Doc carried a small spiral ring notebook in his shirt pocket all the time. Did you happen to find that when they brought him in?"

"No, no, I didn't see anything like that," Decker said wiping his forehead again.

"It'll probably turn up someplace," Beck said, and then looking at Decker said, "Forest, you better get yourself into bed and get some rest. You don't look good."

"Oh, I'll be alright. But I think I will go lie down for a while," Decker replied.

After the Sheriff left, Forest Decker returned to his desk and sat there for a long time with elbows on the desk, holding his head in his hands. Sometime later he walked down the steps to the 'preparation area' in the basement of the funeral home and began lifting weights that he had there.

Decker tried to keep himself fit and was in fine physical condition as a result. He was just under six feet tall and maintained a fairly consistent weight of one ninety or so. As he exercised, a heavy sweat formed, but it was from the exercise and not from an upset stomach.

The next morning Beck was sitting in his office going through Doc's lab notebook. He was having a hard time trying to decipher Doc's shorthand notes. He had returned the personal items to Sharon Schmidt the previous evening.

On his way home, he had stopped again at the coroner's office to look through George's desk, searching for the small notebook that Stoney had made reference to, but, once again had not been able to find it.

The Sheriff was having difficulty understanding Doc's highly personalized shorthand notes, as well as the scrawling handwriting. So far, it appeared that Doc believed all the victims had been in advanced stages of life, in other words, they were all older women.

The State Police were again in the area where his deputy had found the additional remains yesterday and were conducting a further search of the area. When Beck had informed the State Officer in charge of the latest search, about the death of Doc Schmidt, he was told that a state pathologist would probably be sent up to examine all of the remains, including these that had just been found.

Shortly after lunch, he received a phone call from Stony at the coroner's office.

"Sheriff, they've brought in the remains of that last victim," he said. "Should I do something with them, or what do you think I should do?"

"Just leave them for the time being," Beck said. "I think we'll have a state pathologist up here in a day or two. We'll let him look them over."

"Well," Stony said, "I've got them on the table now, but didn't know what I should do with them. I'll just cover them up until that guy gets here."

"That should be okay," the Sheriff said. "There should be somebody here by next week."

"There's one more thing you might be interested in knowing Sheriff," Stony said.

"What's that?" replied Beck.

"These bones we've got here are different from the others," Stoney said.

"Different? What do you mean different?" Beck asked.

"Well, for one thing, they're a lot larger than these others. I think these are a man's bones. And I don't think he was old like the others either," Stony continued. "And there's one other thing, I think this guy died as a result of a massive trauma to his head."

"Whaaat?" the Sheriff exclaimed. "What makes you think that? How can you tell....".?

Stoney replied, "The front of this guy's skull is badly fractured, just over his eye sockets. It looks like something hit him hard. The first thing that I could think of was ..."

11

Jeff had spent a restless night. He couldn't get Brenda out of his head. After she had left, his bed still held the sweet aroma of her earlier presence there. He tossed and turned for an hour or so, then gave up trying to fall asleep and got up and went into his 'guest' bedroom across the hall.

Jeff had felt that it was actually too small to be a real bedroom, so he had developed it into an office of sorts. Dwight had given him an old desk shortly after Jeff had finished his remodeling of the old cabin. It was big, cumbersome and old fashioned, but Jeff loved it. He had removed all the old finish and carefully restored it to its' original condition.

He had found an old credenza a year or so ago at a house sale, that more or less matched the desk. On this, he had placed a desktop computer with a printer alongside. He turned on the computer and as he was waiting for it to boot up, his thoughts turned again to Brenda.

Shaking his head, he stared at the screen and pulled up a list of Dynamics employees. He had been thinking about some of these men and was concerned that there were several that were reaching retirement age. A couple of fellows were already over retirement age, but chose to continue working. There were no mandatory retirement conditions to anyone's employment with the company.

Jeff was especially concerned with Bud Lyndaman. Bud had been with George since the company was founded and had been responsible for all the equipment repair and general overall plant maintenance for years. Lately he had been complaining about all those aches and pains that come with growing older. He had mentioned to Jeff a few days ago, that maybe he should start thinking about retirement.

The more he thought about it, the more he became convinced that Bud should have an assistant trainee, somebody that could eventually move into his position if he did decide to retire. He would be hard to replace and there didn't seem to be anyone in his small crew that would qualify to take over in his absence.

Sitting there before the computer screen, he was surprised sometime later to jerk awake. He had dozed off with his mind filled with the ownership of his new business. Leaving his computer on, he padded back across the hall to his bed and soon was sound asleep.

The next day, he was going through the morning mail when his secretary came in and asked, "Mr. Lawson, are you going to move out of this office today?"

Jeff's first reaction was to answer, "Helen, I've asked you a thousand times not to call me Mr. Lawson. My name is Jeff and I ..... what did you say? Move out of my office? Why would I ... Oh yes, I see."

It hadn't occurred to him that he would be using

George's office from now on. After thinking about it for a minute he said, "You know what, this office and George's are almost exactly the same. I might move some of his files in here but I think that'll be about it, at least for the time being."

It was obvious that Helen didn't think much of that idea saying, "Mr. Lawson, you're the owner of the company now and you should move into that office. Everybody will expect it."

"Helen, for the last time, don't call me Mr. Lawson. And why should I worry about what 'everybody will think'?" Jeff said with a smile.

Helen was an older, very dignified lady who had worked for the company for a number of years. She had streaks of gray in her brown hair and she was always carefully groomed and dressed. She had been George's secretary for most of those years and had also doubled as Jeff's secretary for the past two or three years. Jeff was uncomfortable with her showing such respect to him because of the obvious difference in their ages.

"Mr. Lawson," Helen said impatiently, "I know full well that your name is Jeff. But it was Mr. Gunderson all those years with him and it's going to be Mr. Lawson from me to you from now on," she finished quietly.

"And it *is* important what other people think. Mr. Gunderson's office is a symbol to most people here and it means something to all of us," this last said with her eyes watering slightly.

"I'm sorry Helen. Of course you're right. I hadn't thought about that. Maybe I can get a couple of the fellas from the plant to come in on Saturday and we'll get it done then. Would that be alright do you think?" he said feeling chastised by this very nice lady.

"Yes sir, but if you'd like, I can arrange to have it taken care of yet this afternoon while you're gone."

Confused Jeff asked, "What do you mean while I'm gone?"

"Oh, I'm sorry, I was supposed to tell you that when you first came in. Mrs. Dexter had called and said that you and she were supposed to go down to the county court house this afternoon. Something about some papers that have to be filed"

"Gad, I forgot all about that. Did she say what time I should pick her up?" Jeff asked.

"Actually, she said she'd pick you up, at your cabin a little after three." Helen had a slight smile as she said, "I was a little surprised she even knew where you lived."

Jeff, somewhat embarrassed at the inference replied, "Ahh, yeah well, George must have told her. Anyway," he continued, "would you remind me about quarter of three. Just in case I get busy and forget," trying to sound casual.

Helen with an open smile now said, "Yes sir, I'll be sure and remind you sir."

Trying to change the subject, Jeff said "All right, all right. Would you see if Bud Lyndaman is here today? Ask him to come up front will you. I want to talk with him. And ask Les to come see me when he gets in," he finished.

Helen said, "Mr. Noonan was here when I got in this morning. He's usually the first one in everyday. I'll tell him you want to see him."

As Helen turned to leave, Jeff said, "You know what Helen, I think you're right about changing offices. Go ahead and make the arrangements. I think we'll have Les move in here. After all, he's the company Controller now and his new position should have a certain amount of status too, don't you think?"

With a smile Helen replied, "I think that's a grand idea. He's such a hard working young man. And his wife is so sweet."

Well Jeff thought, that was a home run. He hadn't thought that Helen would be that enthusiastic about the idea. He sat there thinking about the afternoon meeting with Brenda. He glanced at his watch and it wasn't even nine o'clock yet. It was going to be a long day.

A short time later Bud Lyndaman stuck his head in the door and rapped lightly on the doorframe.

"Miz Parsons said you wanted to see me Mr. Lawson."

Jeff replied, "Yes, yes I did Bud, come on in and have a seat. How are you anyway, haven't talked with you for a while."

Actually, Jeff had spoken at length with him just a couple of days ago, concerning faulty parts they had received for one of the lathes.

As he sat down in the chair across from Jeff, he said, "Well, I haven't changed much since Tuesday, when we were talking about the bad spindle on number sixteen." He was looking at Jeff with a perplexed look on his face.

"Sure, sure," Jeff said, "I remember that, I just meant we haven't had much chance to talk about that fishing trip you had been talking about or anything like that," he finished lamely.

"Well, I really haven't had much time for fishing lately," Bud said. "With work here and all the remodeling my wife has me doing at home."

"Oh, I didn't know you were remodeling your house," Jeff said. "What are you doing, adding on or something?"

"No, no, nothing like that," Bud replied. "It's just a little bit of this and a little bit of that. Seems like every time I think I'm going to have some time on my hands, Jesse gets another idea for something she thinks needs to be done."

Laughing, Jeff said, "I think I know what you're talking about. I feel the same way about my place. I can always find something that needs fixing."

"Anyway Bud, I was wondering what your plans are. A couple of weeks ago you kind of hinted to me that you were thinking of retirement. Do you have any plans in that direction these days?"

Bud smiled and said, "Now boss, when I mentioned that to you, you were just another guy in the plant. These days, you're the owner of the company and I have to be careful what I say to you. You might just take it the wrong way."

Jeff laughed at this saying, "Oh, you don't need to worry about that Bud. Nothing has really changed around here except I guess I'm going to get a different office. No, I'm just wondering if you shouldn't have somebody that you could train to take your place, if, down the road in a year or two, you might be ready to take life a little easier."

Bud sat thinking about what Jeff had said. There was no expression on his face to indicate what he was thinking.

Jeff said quickly, "Bud, I want you to understand, I'm not suggesting retirement or anything like that. I'm just concerned that there doesn't seem to be anyone in your crew that would be able to handle your job."

Before Jeff could say anything further, Bud said, "Well you shore are right about that. I've thought about that myself over the last few months. Those are all real good boys on my crew, but you have to tell them every damned thing to do. They just never see things that have to be done!"

Jeff was about to speak when Bud asked "What have you got in mind? You want to hire some college boy to come in and learn the ropes?"

"No, I don't think so," Jeff said. "What I have in mind is more of an apprentice type program. We'd bring someone on board that could learn our business, somewhat like learning a trade,"

Then, "You don't know of anybody that we have now that might fill the bill do you?"

"I'm afraid not Mr. Lawson," Bud replied. "There's a lot of really good men out there in that plant, but I don't know of any that would qualify for what you're thinking."

"Okay Bud," Jeff said. "We'll start looking and in the meantime if you think of somebody that might work out, let me know."

Bud stood and reached across the desk to shake Jeff's hand saying, "Thanks boss, I think you'll do a bang up job with this company and I'd like to stick around for a while yet and help you make it go. If there's anything I can do to help you, just let me know."

Jeff stood and shook the knarled hand of the old maintenance chief saying, "Thank you Bud, that means a lot to me. And if you have any problems I can help you with, come and see me anytime. I'll do the same with you."

Later that afternoon, Helen stuck her head in the door

saying that she had the men from the plant outside and would Jeff please leave so she could get all this moving done, "before we have to start paying these guys overtime!"

Jeff smiled and picking up an old battered briefcase, pushed away from his desk and walked out of his office. Waiting outside was Les Noonan with a large box of files in his arms. Obviously, Les wanted to get moved into his new office today too.

As he walked by, Jeff said, "Gotta match Les?"

Noonan grinned and said, "Sorry Boss, I don't smoke."

As Jeff got in his Blazer, he was struck by the reference made by Lester Noonan and Bud Lyndaman earlier, when they each addressed him as 'Boss'. He hoped he could live up to their expectations and carry on a tradition that would be received as well as George Gunderson's had been.

12

Sheriff Beck was about to leave and go home to change for visitation hours at the funeral home when Jeff Lawson walked in his door.

"Hi Sheriff," he said. "We were just down to get some papers filed here with the Registrar and as long as we were here, I thought I'd stop by and see how your investigation is going."

The Sheriff noted the 'we' and wondered aloud, "We? You said we! Who's we?"

Then, "Oh, you're here for George Gunderson. Did he come down with you? I haven't talked to him in a long time."

Jeff said, "Actually, Bren ... I mean Mrs. Decker came with me."

Remembering Gunderson's comments a couple of days ago, Jeff couldn't help wondering when he had ever had a conversation that amounted to anything with Beck.

Beck volunteered, "Last time I spoke with George was when that fella got injured in your plant up there. George wasn't too pleased with my report on that deal. If

I remember right, there was a machine guard that wasn't installed right and some state inspector came in later and shut down the whole plant till everything was fixed and inspected."

Beck spread his hands saying, "Old George really got after me, but I told him I didn't turn that report over to anybody. He was the only one that got a copy. I don't think he ever did believe me."

"I remember that. That was two or three years ago. Jerry Dobbs, he lost a couple of fingers working on the big brake press. He still works for us," Jeff said.

Understanding now why George didn't like Beck. George could hold a grudge sometimes he thought.

"Yeah," Jeff continued. "That was an O.S.H.A. inspector that just happened to come by for a routine inspection. Usually they give you anywhere from thirty to ninety days to correct a problem, but because there had just been an injury, he shut the whole place down."

"Well anyway, I always liked Gunderson," the Sheriff said. "I hope he doesn't blame me anymore, for that."

"I'm sure he doesn't," Jeff said, trying not to grin at the thought. "I was just wondering if there was anything new on those bones I found."

"No, nothing much," the Sheriff answered. "We've found remains of another person though. Somehow, we just plain missed them."

"Really? Was it another woman," Jeff asked surprised at this information.

"Not this time," the sheriff said. "Appears to be a man in his late thirties to mid forties. We think he's been out there longer than any of the others we've found. He was probably out there last fall when you sat by that stump during deer season."

"This isn't making any sense," Jeff said. "If this guy is one of those sexual predator types, that we hear so much about these days, why would he kill a man too?"

Shaking his head he asked, "Have you been able to tell how these people were killed?"

"No, not really," the Sheriff hedged, then after thinking for a few seconds he shrugged and said, "I'm going to share some information with you that I haven't told anybody yet. And I'd appreciate it if you kept it to yourself. Those women were all old ladies, probably in their seventies at least. That's what Doc was looking into the other day."

Jeff's expression showed his surprise at this information and before he could answer, Beck continued "I'm probably breaking my own rules here, telling you this, but I don't have anyone to share this with anymore and I sure do need somebody else's thoughts on the matter."

Jeff said, "What about the coroner, Doctor Schmidt? Didn't you tell us the other night that he was on to something? What was that? Have you talked with him lately?"

The Sheriff looked at Jeff painfully, with tears forming in his eyes, "No, I haven't. Doc had a heart attack and died before he could tell me what he was looking for."

As Jeff stepped toward him, the Sheriff held up his hand saying, "I've got to go now too. I was just leaving when you came in. They're having visitation at the funeral home this evening and me'n my wife should be there early. So, I'd like to get going now, but I'd like to come down and talk with you again in a day or so if you wouldn't mind."

Jeff replied, "Of course, of course. Come down any

time. I'll help any way I can. I take it, you and Doctor Schmidt were friends," he finished.

The Sheriff nodded his head, afraid to speak, finally saying, "I'll be in touch. Thanks for coming by this afternoon."

Jeff turned and started out the door and stopped suddenly and turning to the Sheriff asked, "This friend of yours, the coroner, his death doesn't have anything to do with these others does it?"

The Sheriff had started for the door and stopped gaping at Jeff, thinking about what he had just asked. Then shaking his head, "No, no, I don't think so." Then with finality, "No, I'm sure it didn't."

Jeff turned and with a wave of his hand left the Sheriff standing in his office with a thoughtful look on his face. Finally shaking himself, he continued out the door with Jeff's question still ringing in his ears.

Jeff left the courthouse and was looking down the street where Brenda had parked her Chevy. She didn't seem to be in the car and as Jeff walked up to place his briefcase in the back seat, she called from across the street. She was standing in the door of a ladies dress shop, waving and calling, "I'll be there in a minute Jeff, they're just writing up the bill. I'll be right there," she repeated.

Jeff leaned against the car thinking about his conversation with Sheriff Beck. This was one of those times when he wished he'd never quit smoking. He had given up cigarettes before he got out of the Army, but whenever he wanted to do some serious thinking, the old cravings came back.

He didn't hear Brenda walk up until she poked him in

the ribs and said with a devilish grin "Hi sailor, looking for a good time?"

He jumped slightly and turned saying, "Ahh, no thanks lady, I've already got a girlfriend. And she's more than I can handle."

Laughing, she poked him in the ribs again saying, "That's what I like in a man. Faithful to his woman."

Then, "It's not dinner time yet, but I know of a pretty good place down the street where we could get a drink or two and eat when we're ready."

"Okay, sounds good to me. Is it too far to walk? I feel like stretching my legs."

"Just let me put this stuff in the car first." And a few minutes later they were walking hand in hand down the street.

At that moment, Sheriff Beck drove slowly past and noticing the two, couldn't help thinking again about what Quint Mason had said concerning George Gunderson's interest in Jeff as a potential son-in-law. It sure looked like George was going to get his wish.

It was a neighborhood type bar that Brenda led him to. They paused for a moment after the bright sunlight outside, waiting for their eyes to adjust to the dark interior. They moved to a back booth and when Jeff started to seat himself across the table from Brenda, she said "Come on, sit beside me. I won't bite."

Jeff slid in beside her. Just then, an older man wearing a white apron approached carrying menus and table settings.

"Afternoon folks," he said. "You planning to eat with us today?" Before they could answer, he continued, "The specials are here on the menus. Can I get you something to drink before you order?"

Brenda looked at Jeff, and then looked up saying "White Zin for me. What do you want hon?"

Jeff glanced at the bar keeper, then asked, "Do you have Famous Grouse scotch?" The bar tender was nodding and Jeff said "On the rocks with a dash of water, OK?" With that the bar tender went back to prepare the drinks.

Brenda said, "I know this place is kind of dumpy by some standards, but Dad used to bring Mom and I here every time we were in town. Mom always got a kick out of coming in here and I guess I did too."

Looking around, "I think she always felt at home in this old joint." She was dabbing her eyes with a napkin as she said this last.

Jeff said, "You must have been very close with your mother. I remember that George took her passing pretty hard too. I worried about him for a long time after she died."

"You're right. If mom was still alive and well, I'm sure he never would have sold the business. He's just lost his enthusiasm for work. The one saving grace for him has been you. He knew how much you had become a part of the business."

She was interrupted by the bartender returning with their drinks. After placing them on the table, he stepped back asking, "Are you folks in a hurry, or, would you like a little time before ordering?"

Jeff looked up and said, "Yeah, please. We'll order later."

The bartender said, "Okay, we'll be getting the courthouse crowd in here shortly. Friday night you know.

I'll have a couple of waitresses come on in a few minutes and one of them will take over your booth then." With that he returned to the bar area.

Jeff turned to Brenda saying, "How long had your folks been married anyway? George never said."

"Not quite forty years," she said. "They married late, at least what was considered late in life in those days. Dad was thirty-four or so and mom was a year or so younger. I came along late too. Dad was forty four when I was born."

"It must have been great, growing up and having somebody like George and your mother so close. I never had that as a kid."

"Did you ever want to know about your parents," Brenda asked.

"Nope, never did," Jeff replied, then, "Well, maybe when I was in the orphanage, but later I began to think about it and decided that if, whoever they were, they hadn't had any interest in me or my life, I sure didn't care to know about them," he finished bitterly.

Brenda touched his hand, saying, "That must have been terrible growing up that way."

"Oh, it wasn't so bad. This couple took me in when I was seven and more or less raised me," Jeff said. "They got a payment from the state every month until I turned eighteen and of course the money stopped coming in then. So, I got a job with a local paper mill until I decided to join the army."

Jeff took a sip of his drink and was about to say something, when a voice beside him said, "My, my, what you see when you don't have a gun!"

Turning, he was looking into the smiling face of his

friend Dwight Sutherland. Standing slightly behind him was his wife Donna.

Surprised Jeff said, "My gosh Dwight, what the heck are you doing down here? There aren't any cows being sold here today."

"Came down to see the County Agent. I didn't expect to see you here either," he said glancing at Brenda with open curiosity.

"Well, come on, sit down and join us," Jeff said. "You'll just keep standing there until I introduce you anyway. Jeez, seems like a person can't get away with anything anymore."

After Dwight and his wife were seated and Jeff had made the introductions, Donna, smiling, was looking from Brenda to Jeff with obvious interest. Finally she couldn't stand it any longer and said, "What's going on here, Jeff? Why do you have to run off to the big city to see your girl?"

"Oh, you're mistaken Donna," Jeff replied straight-faced. "Mrs. Dexter is a business associate and we were just discussing a business proposition."

Donna was temporarily crestfallen, but then said, "Oh, I remember you Brenda. You were Brenda Gunderson in high school. I think you were a year ahead of me as I recall." Glaring at Jeff, "Business proposition eh? Huh!"

They sat together enjoying drinks and friendly conversation for some time, when Dwight finally said, "Let's go Donna. I've still got a lot of work to get done at home and it's going to be dark before we get there."

Jeff said mockingly, "Oh my, do you have to rush off? Why not stay and have dinner with us. You know we'd just love to have you join us."

Dwight looked at Donna saying, "Well maybe we could, you've got a baby sitter and I don't have anything so important to take care of that can't wait till tomorrow." Glancing sideways he winked at Brenda.

Jeff was squirming in his seat at this unexpected development when Donna said, "Oh don't worry Jeff, he's just trying to be funny. He's got a new hired hand and he wants to get home and start bossing him around."

Jeff visibly relaxed as the Sutherlands were leaving. Donna turned back and said to Jeff, "You bring Brenda out to the farm this weekend. We'll grill some steaks or something," then speaking to Brenda, "You make sure he brings you out. No excuses."

Then she turned and hurried after Dwight.

After Sutherlands had been gone several minutes, a waitress approached and asked if they were ready to order. Jeff ordered a second round of drinks and the special of the day. Later, as they stepped outside on the sidewalk, it began to sprinkle and when they had gone only a short way, it started raining in earnest.

They began running trying to beat the rain, but it started coming down harder. Finally reaching the car, Brenda couldn't get her remote to work and finally had to unlock the door with the key. By the time they were inside, they were soaked and shivering. Brenda had just started the car when the rain stopped as suddenly as it had begun.

Brenda looked at Jeff saying, "You were the one that wanted to 'stretch your legs'. This is all your fault."

Jeff looked at her and laughed out loud. "You aren't going to blame me for an act of God are you? But I have to admit, it was my idea to walk. How about turning on the heater and see if that won't make us feel better."

"Let's give it a few minutes for the engine to warm up, shall we," she said caustically. "It'll only take a few minutes. And I can't drive this way anyway" pointing at the windshield which was fogged over from the defrosters and the weather.

"What did the sheriff have to say?" she asked trying to change the subject.

"Oh not much. He did say he's got a few ideas, but he was pretty upset over the death of his friend. Do you remember him mentioning a Doc Schmidt when he was at my place?"

"Yes, of course. He's the County Coroner that he mentioned, right?" she asked.

"Was," Jeff said. "Was the County Coroner. He had a heart attack yesterday and died. Apparently the Sheriff and his wife were pretty close friends with the Schmidts."

He thought for a minute, and then said, "He asked if he could come down and talk with me again next week. I think he needs someone to bounce his thoughts off of and I've been elected" he finished.

When the windshield had cleared up, Brenda put the car in gear and headed back to Lakeview. It was only twenty-five miles or so, but it seemed to take forever. Even with the car heater on, they were both cold and uncomfortable.

Finally, turning into Jeff's driveway, Brenda said, "Jeff, I'm going home and jump in a hot bath and get into some dry clothes, so please don't ask me to come in. Call me and let me know about our visit with your friends this weekend, okay?"

Disappointed, Jeff said, "Brenda, my darling, the Sutherlands are now your friends too. And are you sure about not coming in?"

"Yes I am," she said. "So stop looking at me with those hound dog eyes and get in the house. It looks like it might rain again any minute."

Leaning across the seat, she kissed him saying, "I'll talk to you tomorrow."

As he ran to his front door, Brenda was backing out of the driveway and with a quick toot of her horn, she was gone. Jeff tried to open the door, then remembered that he had locked it as the sheriff's had advised. While fumbling for his key, the rain started again and was pelting down on the small roof over his front porch.

13

After a hot shower and wrapped in an old terry robe, Jeff came out into the main room of the cabin. Turning on the television to a local station, he heard a newsman telling about the death of Doctor George Schmidt. Because of the weekend, the funeral service wouldn't be held until Monday. Jeff watched with interest for some time and when the news turned to other matters, he started channel 'surfing'.

Finding nothing of interest, he finally changed to an all sports channel, but quickly losing interest he switched off the television and was about to go back to his 'office' when he heard a car in his driveway. Going to the window, he was surprised to see George Gunderson getting out of his car.

"Hope I'm not catching you at a bad time" George said as he approached. Jeff had stepped out on the porch to meet him.

Shaking hands with Jeff he said, "I just ran into Bud Lindaman down at the Log Jam," interrupting himself as he looked around the main room of the cabin. "Say, this is really nice. I don't think I've ever been out here before."

"Thanks and no you haven't. If you recall, I invited you several times but you were always afraid I'd poison you or something," Jeff said with a smile. "And what were you doing at the Log Jam anyway?" The Log Jam was a local tavern.

George laughed, saying, "If I was afraid of being poisoned, I sure wouldn't be eating at the Log Jam either. Actually, I just stopped in for a sandwich and a beer when I ran into Bud and his wife. He was telling me about the conversation you'd had with him today."

"Come in, sit down, sit down," Jeff said. "Can I fix you a drink, I've got beer if you'd prefer," Then, "I hope Bud isn't afraid I'm trying to force him to retire, cause that sure isn't what I've got in mind."

"What kind of booze have you got?" George asked. "I'd like scotch if you've got it."

As Jeff stepped into the kitchen area of the big room, he said "No, I don't think Bud took it that way at all, but when he told me what you were thinking about, I had an idea and I thought you might be interested in it."

Jeff was rummaging in a cupboard looking for a bottle of scotch. He finally came out with a bottle of Jack Daniels and turning to George asked, "I'm afraid I don't have any scotch George, how about some bourbon?"

"That'll be fine, but have you got anything to cut it with, other than water I mean," George replied. "How about a coke, that'd do it."

It took Jeff a couple of minutes to fix the drinks. He grinned and said, "I guess I should stop at a liquor store and pick up some scotch. I'm starting to develop a taste for it lately."

Handing him his drink, George looked at him curiously, but didn't say anything.

"What you and Bud talked about, seems to make a lot of sense to me," George said. "That workforce is starting to grow a beard. Most of those guys have been there for a long time. And incidentally, you don't need to worry about Bud, he's all for the idea."

"That's good to hear," Jeff said. "What's your thinking on the idea?"

"Nothing to do with the program itself, I was thinking of somebody that might make a good trainee to work with Bud," George replied.

"Oh, who do you have in mind?"

"Well," George said, "The more Bud talked about it, the more I got to thinking that young Red Waters would be an ideal candidate for that sort of thing. What do you think?" he asked taking a sip of his drink.

"He'd probably work out okay." Jeff said. "But, do you think the other guys might have a problem with him?"

"Why would anybody ... Oh I see. That business with his pa and the Raeford brothers, right?" George said, "You know, if you go back far enough in our old personnel files, you'd find that they both worked for us at one time."

"They were just plain mean. Seemed like they were always picking fights with the other guys and worst of all, drinking on the job. With all that power equipment out there, it was no place for a drunk, so I called them in one morning and told them to get out and not come back!"

Then, "No, no, I don't think there'd be any animosity at

all with the rest of the fellas in the plant. They were happy to be rid of the Raefords too."

"I've seen that one brother, I don't know which one, just sitting in that old empty storefront downtown every now and then. He looks like a dirty old hippy most of the time," Jeff said.

"That would be Jeremy. Only got one arm these days. He fell into a saw or something over at the sawmill. He was drunk'rn a skunk," George said. "Sure didn't surprise me any, when I heard about it. I'm just happy to have gotten rid of him and his brother when I did."

"Let me think about this for a day or two. I like Red and he'd probably work out okay, but I was hoping to find someone with a year or two of college," Jeff said.

George snorted "Well, if he works out, send him to night school over at that Business College you took all those courses at."

Surprised, Jeff said, "I didn't realize you knew I was taking classes over there. How'd you ever find that out, you old Devil?"

Smiling at his old friend, he said, "You weren't spying on me were you?"

George said a little smugly, "I try to know everything about the people that work for me."

Then "Actually, Helen Parsons told me. She's very fond of you Jeff, but she was afraid you were trying to prepare for another job with some other company. But, after three or four years of those classes, we decided you were just trying to get an education. That's another reason I know you'll make a success of Wildwood Dynamics."

"Okay George," Jeff said a little embarrassed at George's comments, "I'll give Red a call and ask him to come in and see me next week sometime. You're right. If he's as good as we both think he is, it'll be in our best interests to send him to school. At the same time, he's got to want to go! But, from what Birdie tells me, he'd jump at the chance."

George, laughing said, "That Birdie, she must be cleaning dust out of every house in town. She's sure a good girl. Just because she got pregnant before she should have doesn't change that. She and Red were going to be together anyway," and then "Just like you and Brenda. They were meant for each other."

Jeff didn't know what to say to that. George finished his drink and stood up saying, "Let me know when you get some decent booze in the house and I'll stop by again and help you drink it."

"I'll sure do that. And if it needs to be said, you're welcome here any time. And I'll be sure and have your favorite scotch on hand next time," Jeff finished.

George laughed out loud as he was walking towards the door "And how in the world could you possibly know what my favorite scotch is? Until tonight, we've never had a drink together, so how would you know that?

Never mind," he continued out the door, "I can guess how you know and you don't need to explain."

With a wave of his hand he headed to his car and turned saying "If you get a chance to talk to Red, I'd be interested to know how that goes."

14

Sheriff Beck had struggled with his emotions all evening during the visitation hours. He marveled at Sharon Schmidt as she met the many visitors that had given up their cocktails and normal Friday night activities to stop by and offer Sharon their heartfelt sympathies. Young Sharon, Doc's daughter, seemed to be in a state of shock and mumbled her thanks to those that offered condolences.

His son Jack, on the other hand, seemed to be taking the situation in stride. Whenever it appeared his mother was faltering, he seemed to be right there offering his young strength and fortitude. His wife, Emily, simply sat by young Sharon most of the evening, trying to give her support.

Beck had stepped up to the casket when he first entered the visitation and had stood there with tears flowing down his cheeks in unashamed remorse at seeing this waxen image of George Schmidt that he had just spoken with on the phone only two days earlier.

As he stood there, he bowed his head and said a short

prayer for his old friend. His wife Lynda was clutching Beck's arm and was also having trouble controlling her emotions.

"Come on Cubby" she said now. "We've got to get back out in front and give Sharon some time with Jack and young Sharon."

The Schmidt's, Sharon, young Sharon, Jack and his wife Emily were standing off to one side, waiting for Beck and his wife to move back to the vestibule of the Funeral home.

Beck stepped forward and said to young Sharon, "You know, when you were born, I wanted you named Jill," gesturing toward her brother. "You know, Jack and Jill, but Doc was so enamored with his Sharon here," he said gesturing at her mother, "That he wouldn't discuss any other name. He was right as usual, it is a pretty good name after all."

Giving Sharon, the mother and Jack's wife a hug, he turned and shook young Jack's hand saying "You're the main guy now. We'll be there if you need us, but you're the main man from now on."

With that, he turned, followed by his wife, and moved out into the vestibule. He never looked at his old friend again.

As they sat waiting for visitors, Forest Decker stepped into the waiting area. He was wearing an old sweatshirt that was presently sweat soaked, and running shorts.

He stopped and said to the Sheriff, "I'm sorry folks, for my appearance. I assure you the next time you see me this evening, I'll be in more acceptable attire. I've just been out on my run and the time seems to have gotten away from me," he apologized.

"I'll be back in twenty minutes. Does everything seem to be in order so far," he asked. "I hope the arrangements are satisfactory," he finished.

"Everything seems to be okay with me," Beck said, surprised at seeing a funeral director dressed so casually. "I assume everything is okay with the Schmidt's too," he finished a little peevishly.

Lynda poked him in the ribs and glared at him. Beck said, "Sorry Forest, I'm pretty upset with this whole thing." Then, "How far do you run anyway? You look like you've been at it for some time."

Decker replied, "Well, I try and run anywhere from three to five miles a day. Of course, with this kind of obligation," waving his hand around the funeral home, "I'm lucky if I can get that many miles a week."

Beck observed, "You seem to be very fit, Decker. Maybe I'll send some of my overweight deputies over here to run with you once in a while."

Decker laughed uneasily, "Sure Sheriff, anytime. Just give me a call a day or so ahead of time."

"I'm glad to see you've recovered from whatever was ailing you yesterday, when I was here. You look like the picture of health today," the Sheriff said.

"Oh sure, sure, I'm feeling a lot better. Well," he said, turning to leave, "I've got to get showered and changed. I'll be back in just a few minutes."

With that he left the Becks sitting looking at each other.

The next morning, Beck was back in his office going through what little information that had come in since yesterday. Stony had sent over a number of snap shots of the latest victim.

As he sorted through them, he saw the cracked and broken pieces of the skull that had led Stoney to believe this person had been bludgeoned to death. He was surprised to find two or three photos of Doc included with the group of pictures.

Whoever had taken these pictures had opened the car door, giving a full side view of Doc sitting behind the wheel. He sat with his head bowed and hands in his lap. He was wearing a white shirt, tie and slacks. When he was working, he normally wore a white lab coat and seldom wore a suit or jacket.

Beck felt tears beginning to sting his eyes as he sorted through several photos, taken from different angles of his friend. He took out a handkerchief and dabbed his eyes, then opened another envelope that had been sent over from the state photo lab.

These were the snap shots that young Lawson had taken of the first victim. There didn't seem to be anything there that he didn't already know, so he laid them to one side and picked up the shots of Doc again.

Something was bothering him, but he was having difficulty concentrating on what it might be. He'd have Irma look them over on Monday and maybe she could see what was bothering him.

As lunchtime neared he put all the photos in an oversize envelope, marked 'Evidence' and placed them in the file drawer of his desk. Locking it, he left the office, still troubled but unable to understand what was bothering him.

He stopped by the dispatcher's desk on his way out and asked Johnnie, the weekend dispatcher, if anything was happening that he should be aware of. When Johnny assured him that everything was under control, Beck left the office and walked to the parking lot.

He unlocked his car and slid in the seat behind the wheel. Fastening his seat belt, he started the engine, but sat there with the motor running for several minutes, still thinking about those pictures of Doc. Finally, shaking his head, he put the car in gear and drove away.

15

Even though it was Saturday and the plant was shut down for the weekend, Jeff had gone into his office that morning. As he stepped into his office, he was surprised to see Lester Noonan sitting at his desk. Les was looking curiously at Jeff, finally saying, "I guess you forgot we've both been moved since yesterday, eh boss?"

Jeff was too embarrassed to admit that he had indeed forgotten about the move and said, "Oh no, no, nothing like that. I thought I saw you in here and was wondering what brought you in on a weekend. Your wife is going to have my hide if she thinks that you're going to leave her home alone on weekends!"

Les smiled and said, "That's a fact. She was complaining about that just this morning. Of course, I blamed you and told her you insisted that I spend Saturdays in the office."

Jeff was thunderstruck at this comment and exclaimed, "Okay, that's it. You're fired! I can't have anybody working here who's going to blame me for their divorce!"

Les laughed out loud at this, saying, "Okay, okay, I really didn't blame you. My lovely bride wasn't even out of bed when I left this morning. I'm just trying to get things settled and organized a little, before coming in here on Monday."

Jeff said, "Seriously Les, I don't believe in overtime or weekends spent in the office unless it's something really important. I feel that we've got all week to get our work done," he paused then emphasized, "during regular office hours! So, try not to make a habit of staying late every day. I really would prefer that you spend your free time with your family," he finished.

At this Les beamed and said, "Actually, I really don't have a family as such," he paused than said, "yet! But that's going to change in about six months and I'm sure things will be different after 'short round' arrives."

"Short Round?" Jeff said. "That's what we used to call artillery rounds that fell short when I was in the army."

Les, laughing now said, "That's what my dad told me too. That's what he's called Myra since the first time he ever met her. When she asked him about it, he told her, that was what they called people that were 'vertically challenged' when he was in the Marine Corps. So, she's been 'short round' ever since and, for the time being at least, that's what we're calling the baby, at least till we know if it's a boy or girl."

Jeff smiled at this and said, "That's wonderful Les. I'm happy for both of you. One more reason not to leave her alone on weekends anymore. As a matter of fact, sometime real soon, before cold weather sets in, we'll try and get together out at the cabin and have a cookout. Sound good to you?" he finished as he turned and walked out of his old office.

"Sounds like a winner," Jeff heard him say. He was

smiling to himself at the idea of calling Myra Noonan 'short round'. But in retrospect, it fit the tiny little wife of his new controller. She was only five foot three or four and pretty as a little doll. Jeff had only met her once and was quite taken with the friendly young woman.

Les had left and been gone for a couple of hours when the phone on Helen Parson's desk purred softly. Leaving his desk, Jeff stepped into her office and answered fully expecting it to be a wrong number. He was surprised to hear Brenda say, "I saw Les Noonan and his wife a little while ago and he told me that you had just read him the riot act about working on Saturdays. Doesn't that apply to you too?"

"I didn't read him the riot act," Jeff said defensively, "And how do you know Les anyway? They've only been here a few months."

"Well, Mr. Smarty Pants, Myra Noonan is an elementary school teacher and has the room right next to mine. And besides that, his aunt is Helen Parsons. So what do you think of that?"

Jeff was surprised beyond words, but tried to cover it up with a weak "Oh sure, I knew that" he mumbled.

"Sure you did. Back to my original question. Are you going to spend all day in there or are you going to leave pretty soon?"

"Actually, I was just getting ready to leave. What have you got in mind?"

"As soon as you get in the car I'll tell you. I'm sitting in your Blazer right out front."

Jeff left the building so quickly that he had to return and lock the front door before he could get to the parking lot. He looked at the Blazer sitting empty, and then realized that Brenda's Chevy was parked right beside it. She had that great smile and was waving at Jeff's confusion. She had the window turned down and said, "Actually, I should have said I'm sitting **Next** to your Blazer. Anyway, get in your car and follow me."

"Where are we going," Jeff asked

"My place. Dad's coming over for lunch and I thought you'd like to visit with him."

The disappointment Jeff felt at this bit of information was crushing. When she said 'my place' he had a sudden vision of a quiet afternoon with Brenda and hopefully taking up where they had left off a day or so ago.

Seeing the look on his face, "She said, Oh don't look like that. Dad will only be there for lunch. He just wanted to get out of his house for a while, that's all."

"Sorry," he said, "I didn't realize I had 'that look on my face'. George is no problem. I'll enjoy talking with him again. Did you know he stopped by my place last night?"

"Sure I know." she said, "I drove back and forth past there three or four times last night before I finally gave up and went back home."

"What," Jeff exclaimed. "Why didn't you stop? George would have understood."

"Only too well I'm afraid," Brenda said. "Remember Jeff, he's my father and there's limits to what I'm willing for him to know just yet."

With that she backed out of her parking place and drove away. Jeff hurriedly got in the Blazer and fumbling for his keys finally got it started and drove quickly out of the parking lot. But Brenda was already out of sight. Jeff drove after her but never saw her car again until he pulled into her driveway and her garage door was just closing.

Jeff was just getting out of his Blazer when George Gunderson pulled in behind him. He was driving a two-year-old Cadillac CTS that hadn't been washed since the day he drove it away from the dealership. Jeff was never able to understand how George, in all other respects, maintained such an orderly life and didn't bother with the basic care of his personal automobile.

"Hi George," Jeff said. "I see you just ran your car through the local car wash. I don't suppose you've had the oil changed yet either. As a matter of fact, have you **Ever** had the oil changed? How many miles have you got on that heap by now?"

"Heap!" George exclaimed as he walked up to shake hands. "Heap!" he said again. "I'll have you know that's no heap. That is one fine automobile. I've got almost twenty thousand on it and I haven't had one bit of trouble with it."

As they walked toward the house, Jeff laughed and asked, "What color is that anyway? I don't remember what it looked like when you first got it."

George didn't respond at first to the good-natured ribbing. He just smiled and said finally "It's about time I got a new one anyway, and if you remember, this is a company car and it actually now belongs to you!"

"What! Oh no you don't. You're not going to pawn that thing off on me. You've probably been smoking those stinky cigars of yours in there too haven't you?"

Laughing they walked on into the house where Brenda was waiting for them. Later, after a couple of drinks and lunch, Jeff, Brenda and George sat and visited in the room that Jeff now simply referred to as the 'Big Room'.

It was nearly three o'clock when George, looking at his

watch said, "I've got to get going," and with a grin glanced at Jeff saying, "I've got to get down to the Cadillac dealer before they close this afternoon."

And a short time later he was gone leaving Jeff alone with Brenda. They spent a lazy afternoon talking about a hundred different things and just enjoying the day and each other's company.

If Jeff had thought he was going to take Brenda to her bed, he was disappointed, as she had carefully explained that she wanted their relationship to blossom on something other than their physical attraction to each other.

As evening drew near, he suggested they go someplace for dinner. They ended up at the Log Jam and had beer and hamburgers. Very unromantic, but still very enjoyable.

When Jeff brought her home, he asked, "Would you like me to walk you to your door and give you a goodnight kiss, or, will a simple handshake do?"

She laughed and said, "I've got to go to church in the morning and I don't want to go with a guilty conscience, so let's just say goodnight here."

As Jeff drove home to his cabin, his mind was in turmoil. What was going on here with this woman? He was completely at her mercy. His mind was filled with the images of her in his bedroom just a day or so ago and it was those thoughts he couldn't get out of his mind.

He was totally, completely enamored with her and he had to admit, he had never had such deep feelings for anyone in his life until now. He was sure he was in love with this woman, and he thought she was falling in love with him too. So why was she suddenly so standoffish today and this evening?

He stopped at the only party store in town and bought

two bottles of Famous Grouse and two bottles of Sutter Home White Zinfadel. When he got to his cabin, he opened a bottle of scotch and put both bottles of wine in his refrigerator. Fixing his drink, he sat on a couch and watched television for an hour or so before going to bed. Later, he couldn't remember what he had been watching on television.

16

Sheriff Beck had been preoccupied most of the day with the Schmidt family. They had asked he and Lynda to join them for an early dinner before going to the funeral home for tonight's visitation. It was a solemn affair, with Sharon trying hard to be at ease with the situation.

Young Sharon was withdrawn and uncommunicative, while Jack carried the conversation for all of them. The family minister and his wife had stopped by to offer condolences and Sharon had insisted that they stay and join them for dinner. The minister would lead the protestant service on Monday morning and so he had spent some time with Sharon getting some background information on Doc for his sermon.

It was another difficult night at the funeral home. However, this time Forest Decker was there to meet the mourners and unlike the previous evening, was dressed appropriately in a dark suit as were his three assistants. Once again, Beck was impressed by the physical appearance of the mortician. The sheriff guessed his height to be six feet and close to two hundred pounds.

"I wonder what this guy did before he became a funeral director," Beck thought. "He looks more like a football coach, or, even a football player, than a mortician."

Something was bothering Beck about this guy, but he decided it must be his profession. Beck hated funerals and funeral homes. He hated the putrid, overly aromatic smell of all the flowers that always accompanied such rites. And tonight was no different. The strong odor of all those flowers was wafting through the room and was almost making him nauseous.

"God help me," he thought. "When my time comes, I'm going to have to tell Lynda, absolutely no flowers! Maybe I should consider cremation. That doesn't have all this hoop-tee-doo anyway."

He decided to step outside and get some fresh air and get away from all those flowers.

Stony had just parked his car and was walking across the street toward the funeral chapel and seeing the Sheriff gave a friendly wave.

"Hi Sheriff," he said as he approached. "I thought I'd best come by tonight and pay my respects because I'm going home tomorrow and I'm not sure when I'll get back."

Beck replied, "Where's home Stony?"

"Chicago," Stony said. "North side. That's how I happened to go to Northwestern. Right now, I'm not sure what my status is, so I need to stop by the school on Monday morning to talk with a counselor."

"Listen Stony," the Sheriff said. "If I can help you in any way, just let me know. I'll be happy to send a letter down to the school if you want me to. You've been a big help to Doc and I know he thought very highly of you and I'll put that in letter form if you want me to," he finished.

"Gee thanks Sheriff, that means a lot coming from you," Stony said. "I don't know what I'm going to find out when I get down there, but I'll be sure and let you know."

"By the way," he continued. "I was hoping to run into you tonight. I've got a couple more of Doc's notes that I found in the examination room desk. I was looking for that small note book you asked about, but that wasn't there," he said.

"Thanks Stony, but if they're anything different than what I already have, I doubt if they'll help me much. Why don't you give them to me before you leave and I'll look them over Monday."

Later that evening, as he was having a glass of cranberry juice, liberally laced with vodka, he opened the envelope that Stoney had left for him. He was surprised at how many loose-leaf sheets there were. A cursory glance at the material, however, convinced him that these notes probably dealt with other cases. With that, he returned them to the envelope and laid them on his dresser bureau, where they would remain until Monday morning.

17

Jeff had been working in his yard early Sunday morning. His thoughts were still preoccupied with the events of last night. Or, more accurately, the nonevents of the night before. He couldn't understand what was going on with this woman that he was so deeply enthralled with.

When he was sixteen, he had suffered a bad case of teen infatuation with Jennifer Steiner, another sixteen-year-old classmate. He remembered how she had suddenly matured that year, developing wondrous curves and breasts. She was very much aware of the impression she was making on, not only Jeff, but also all the boys in her class.

Thinking back, Jeff was aware now, that Jennifer Steiner was a teaser. She loved the attention and ultimately ended up going steady with a senior class football player. She never finished high school, having to leave early to have her baby!

Brenda was certainly no Jennifer Steiner, but the image of those frustrations of his teen years came back to him now and he just didn't know what to think about his relationship with Brenda. She seemed to have a lot of the same characteristics that had driven him crazy as a sixteen-year-old kid.

He found himself sitting in his gazebo watching a flock of Snow Geese float by. They had suddenly arrived just this morning and he hoped they would stay for a while and not take off on their southern migration right away.

He was suddenly jarred back to the present when his cell phone rang. It was Donna Sutherland. "Where the heck are you anyway, I've been trying to call you at home for the last hour."

Without waiting for an answer, she continued, "Remember you and Brenda are supposed to come out here today. Why don't you try and get here around two thirty or so. Dwight's going to put on his barbecuing apron and grill steaks. Beer or booze first though."

Donna just kept chattering away, not giving Jeff a chance to speak at all. "Right now I'm trying to get everybody ready for church. We should be home around eleven. We'll see you this afternoon. Don't be late."

Before Jeff could answer, she had disconnected. Other than saying hello and grunting a couple of times, Jeff had never said a word during the conversation.

Finally, leaving his gazebo and walking to the house, it suddenly dawned on him, that he didn't even know Brenda's phone number! Other than the short conversation yesterday, he couldn't ever remember talking with her on a phone.

"Oh brother," he thought, "What if she has an unlisted number?"

When he finally found a telephone directory that had been stuffed in a magazine rack by the TV set he was relieved to find her name in the book. He was surprised to see that the listing was still in the name of William Dexter. "I wonder why she never changed that," he thought as he dialed the number.

"Hi," he said when he heard her voice. "You sound sleepy, I thought you were going to church this morning."

She said, "I'm just getting ready and I'm about to leave. If I sound sleepy it's because I am. You kept me awake all night."

"What ... I kept you awake!" Jeff said in surprise. "How did I keep you awake. I wasn't anywhere near."

"Oh yes you were," she replied. "You just didn't know it, that's all. What's up? I've got to leave or I'll be late."

Jeff said, "Can I pick you up after lunch, say two o'clock.? Donna and Dwight have invited us out there at two thirty. They're having a cookout."

"Okay," she said. "Am I supposed to bring anything?"

"Nope, just your wonderful, beautiful self," Jeff joked.

"Jeff, I've got to go. Bye now, I'll see you around two." And with that, the line went dead.

It was exactly two o'clock when Jeff pulled into Brenda's driveway. He was getting out of the Blazer when she came out of the house. Turning, she locked her front door and started toward Jeff. She was dressed casually in slacks, white blouse and tennis shoes. She was carrying a white sweater folded over one arm.

She smiled as Jeff hurried to open the door for her saying, "Wow, such service. I've been opening my own doors for so long, I'd almost forgotten what it was like to be with a real gentleman again."

"I don't always open doors for beautiful women," Jeff said with a grin. "But you're a special case, so I make exceptions for you."

Stopping, she gave a Jeff a kiss before climbing in the Blazer. Once they were both in the car, Brenda complained, "You're a big shot owner of your own business now. Don't you think you could have something besides this old truck for a company car? Something a little easier for women to get in and out of?"

"And besides that," she continued. "This thing has bucket seats! How am I supposed to snuggle up to you in this thing?"

Jeff laughed out loud at her saying, "Pardon me, but this is no truck! It is a top of the line Sport Utility Vehicle and it's only three years old. It's hardly broken in, so if you want to snuggle, we'll have to use your car next time.

"And anyway, before buying a new car, I'd have to talk with Les Noonan to see if we can even afford a company car."

The lighthearted conversation continued until they approached the Sutherland farm. It was a typical two-story farm home with half a dozen out buildings and a very large barn.

There were a number of beef cattle scattered across the fields beside the long tree lined driveway leading to the house. As they neared, they could see, what could only be described as an open sided circus type tent set up in the spacious back yard.

Several cars and a couple of pick up trucks were already parked on the driveway next to the house. Jeff recognized the fellows he played poker with regularly and their wives.

"I didn't expect this," Jeff muttered as he helped Brenda from the Blazer. "The way Donna talked it was just them and us," he finished.

"It's okay," Brenda said. "What have you got there?" Indicating the paper bag Jeff had picked up from the back seat.

"Well, when I thought it was just you and I, and not the whole county, I thought I'd bring a bottle of your favorite wine and what has become my favorite scotch these days," showing her the bottles in the sack.

The afternoon was a picture of total chaos. It seemed that everywhere Jeff looked there were kids running around, kids of all ages. Donna greeted them and immediately took charge of Brenda and began the introductions.

Jeff handed the paper bag over to Dwight who immediately passed it straight back, saying, "Hey man, we're just simple farmers here. We mostly drink beer, not this high priced stuff. Go put this back in your car and you and I'll drink that Wednesday night."

"Wednesday night," Jeff asked. "What's Wednesday night?"

"Well, I'm sure you've been just awfully busy with all your entrepreneurial enterprises and other, more pleasant activities lately," leering at Brenda as she was being whisked away by Donna, "But you're the host for poker Wednesday. Remember?"

"Oh, poker, sure, sure," Jeff said. "I wouldn't forget something as important as that. After all you and the boys always seem to donate to my lifestyle and you do it so willingly," he finished laughing.

But thinking to himself, "Dang, I did forget all about that!"

Looking around the spacious back yard he commented, "My gosh, what is this, 'fertile valley' or something? Do all these kids belong to these guys?" He had started to return the paper bag to the Blazer and Dwight was walking along with him.

"Yep," Dwight replied, looking around "Only two of them are mine though and they're probably the youngest ones here. Our little guys are both a couple of pistols!" This last with fatherly pride.

Later, Jeff did get the chance to sit with Brenda at a picnic table under the cover of the tent, while they enjoyed the steaks that Dwight had grilled. Dwight and Donna sat across from them and the two women were caught up in conversation, while Jeff and Dwight attacked their steaks.

Jeff said, "My gosh Dwight, you must have cleaned out your freezer and then some to grill this many steaks. There must be thirty people here, counting all the kids."

Picking up a bottle of beer he continued, "And by the way 'poor country folk that doesn't drink that high priced stuff', this is pretty darned good beer and I don't think it came from Wisconsin either!"

"Nope, but it's not imported either. I found out that this comes from the oldest brewery in the U.S. of A. Out in Pennsylvania somewhere."

Then, "As far as the steaks are concerned, just the grown up folks got steak. All the kids got hamburger and hot dogs," he laughed.

As the sun dropped lower toward the horizon, the air became noticeably cooler. Brenda sent Jeff to the Blazer for her sweater and soon after asked Jeff if they could leave. Everyone seemed to be loading kids in their cars and fixing car seats for the littlest ones. The day was over and all were thanking Dwight and Donna for a wonderful afternoon. Donna gave Brenda a hug and told her how happy she was that she had been able to join them.

Then she took Jeff by the arm and pulled him away and looked up at him saying, "Jeff Lawson, if you don't marry that girl I'll never forgive you. She's wonderful and just perfect for you. Now you bring her out here again, and do it soon too," she finished, giving him a hug.

Jeff laughed and replied, "Well, I agree, she's pretty special alright. But, come on Donna, we've only really been seeing each other for a week or so. Things like this take a little time you know."

Donna wouldn't hear any arguments. She gave him a hug again and stood and waved as they drove away.

"I like your friends," Brenda said as they were driving back into town. "And those little boys of theirs are just darling. How big is their farm anyway, do you know?" she asked.

"I think Dwight told me it was section and a half. How much is that? Isn't a section something like a square mile or so? I don't know how many acres that is, but it's a big operation. He's got two or three hired hands."

Later as he pulled in her driveway, she said, "I hope you don't want anything to eat. After that meal this afternoon I might not eat again for a week."

Smiling at Jeff she continued, "But if you'd like to come in and have a night cap, I could handle that okay."

As they entered the 'Big Room,' Brenda stepped behind the bar and came up with a bottle of brandy. Holding it up for his approval, Jeff nodded and she placed a couple of wine glasses on the bar.

"I know you're supposed drink this stuff in a brandy snifter, but I don't have anything like that, so these wine glasses will have to do."

They sat on the large couch with the stereo playing

softly as they sipped their drinks. Brenda sat with her legs tucked under her at one end of the couch.

Finally she spoke saying, "Jeff, I'm going to be gone a couple of days. I've got to go down to the Twin Cities and attend some teacher's conferences. I'll be leaving early in the morning, so I'd like to make an early evening of it tonight too. Do you mind?"

Once again, Jeff had the feeling that Brenda was pushing him to one side. He couldn't understand why she was being so stand offish.

He took a thoughtful sip of his brandy, then said, "Would it make a difference if I told you I'd like to stay here with you, make love all night and watch the sun come up in the morning from the dinette in your kitchen?"

"Jeff, I'm really sorry, because I'd like nothing better, but," she hesitated, finally blurting, "Jeff, I've had a visitor for a few days and I'm not very good company right now." She wasn't looking at him and her face was suddenly flushed with embarrassment.

"Visitor?   I haven't seen anyone .... " suddenly understanding what Brenda was trying to tell him, he laughed with relief.

"Darn you Jeff, it's not funny," she stormed. "You dodo. It's a very unpleasant time for me."

"Oh no my sweet," Jeff grinned. "I'm not laughing at you. I thought you were pushing me away the past couple of days because you were unhappy with my company for some reason. And you've had me on pins and needles now for a couple of days." He sat mentally calculating the time...

"I can see what you're thinking, or, counting! Don't worry, I'll let you know."

Then with a sly smile, "Maybe by Wednesday night?" She said making it a question.

Later that night as Jeff drove home with his head full of wild thoughts and looking forward to Wednesday night, he suddenly remembered .... ***Poker Night!*** Oh no, how was he going to get out of that?

18

It was Monday evening, before Beck could get to his office. He had spent all of the previous day with the Schmidts and also eight hours or so at the funeral home too. The sheriff had been amazed at the number of people that had come and gone over the past few days. Old friends of Doc's, as well as many of his patients that he had cared for in his lifetime.

Earlier in the morning at the church service, the minister had spent some considerable time eulogizing this long time member of his flock and again this morning at the funeral service itself, he had actually broken down during his sermon. All this combined to put a tremendous strain on the sheriff's emotional condition.

After returning to the church hall after the cemetery service, the church ladies had supplied a luncheon for family and friends. This had taken most of the afternoon and by the time the last person had left, Sharon seemed exhausted.

Beck and his wife had stood with Sharon and the family saying goodbye to all those that had attended the luncheon. After the last of the visitors had gone, Sharon turned to the Becks and said, "I don't know about you folks, but I could use a drink! Let's go back to our place and see what we've got."

So, the late afternoon was again spent with Sharon and the family while they tried to unwind from the stress of the past few days. Knowing he would have to go to his office as soon as he could, the sheriff only had a weak vodka and grapefruit juice. As he sat at his desk now, he was aware of the sour taste the juice had left in his mouth.

He spent most of the next couple of hours going through various reports and a number of 'housekeeping' procedures that required his attention and were necessary to maintain a smooth running department.

At last he felt he was caught up enough to return home and try and get a good nights sleep. He was worn out from the steady pressure of the weekend and was looking forward to getting back to a more normal routine.

As he prepared to leave, he stopped at his office door and returned to his desk. Unlocking the file drawer he retrieved the envelope with the photos of the victims. He also picked out Jeff Lawson's camera that he had placed in the same drawer with the photos.

Then picking up Doc's lab notebook that he had left on his desk, he finally left his office. A short time later, at home, he placed the envelope, camera and notebook on the bureau with the other papers that Stony had given him. He planned to look them all over again in the privacy and comfort of his den in the morning.

But, the next morning, before he had even finished his first cup of coffee, he received a call from Rhonda.

"Good morning Sheriff Beck," Rhonda said cheerily.

"I have a message for you and didn't think it would wait till you came in this morning."

"How can you be so chipper at this time of night?" he growled. "It's not even daylight yet."

"Sheriff, this might be the beginning of your day, but, it's getting pretty close to the end of the day for me. If you remember, I was here when you were leaving last night!"

"Yeah, yeah. I know all about it," Beck laughed. "What time did you start anyway? What time is it now?"

"It's ten minutes till six and if Irma isn't here in ten minutes, I quit," Rhonda replied. "These twelve hour shifts are killing me and I'm only twenty six years old," she complained.

"Yeah, I know," Beck said. "I've had an ad in the paper for a few days and I've had a couple of people send me their resumes, but I haven't had time to talk with any of them yet," he apologized. "I'll take care of it just as soon as I can, but in the meantime, we'll just have to try and make the most of a bad situation."

"I know Sheriff, I'm not really complaining, but I sure would like a day off one of these days."

"Thanks Rhonda," Beck said, "Now what's the message that couldn't wait a couple of more hours?"

"Well, it's Deputy Conway," Rhonda replied.

Beck groaned inwardly. Dan Conway was a rookie deputy and although only with the sheriff's office for a few months, had already been dubbed 'Deputy Fife' by his fellow deputies. If he weren't so shorthanded, Sheriff Beck probably would have Conway on a desk or tucked away in some innocuous position, if with the department at all!

"Alright," Beck asked, "What has Mr. Conway done now?"

"It seems he started chasing, what he thought was a drunk driver last night," Rhonda hesitated, but Beck could hear withheld laughter in her demeanor, "And when the driver wouldn't stop, Deputy Conway," Rhonda hesitated again.

"Well sheriff, Deputy Conway rammed his car into the side of the drunken driver and in the process, rolled the patrol car upside down!" Saying this last with barely held laughter.

"Oh for crying out loud, what next?" Then he asked, "Was Conway hurt?"

"No, he's okay, but the so called drunken driver," Rhonda was no longer trying to keep from laughing. "The drunken driver was Quint Mason, town marshal of Lakeview!"

She continued, "It turns out that Mason was driving somewhat erratically because he was driving with his lights out, checking the doors of the downtown businesses."

"Mason never saw Conway coming, because in his excitement, he forgot to turn on his flashers. And before you ask, Mason is okay too, but it sounds like the Lakeview patrol car was totaled!"

"Oh my God. That idiot! Have you sent anybody down there yet?"

"Yes sir, we've got two patrol cars there now and a couple of wreckers on the way," she finished.

"Alright," Beck said tiredly. "As soon as I can get dressed I'll head on down there myself and see if we can keep this thing from getting out of hand. You get a message to those folks down there that I want one car to stay there and Conway is not to leave till I get there!"

Sheriff Beck was a patient man, but Deputy Conway

would exhaust the patience of Job and the Sheriff was at the end of his rope with this troublesome officer. There didn't seem to be any alternative with this guy, but to let him go. Driving to Lakeview, he began getting the germ of an idea and the more he thought about it, the better it sounded to him.

Arriving at the scene of the accident, a wrecker had up righted the patrol car and was loading it on a flat bed. It appeared to Beck that Rhonda had been right, the Lakeview patrol car appeared to be a total wreck. Quint Mason and a county deputy were standing beside it, while the deputy was writing on a clipboard. Conway was not in sight.

Quint looked up as Beck approached. With a slight wave of his hand he stepped forward to meet Sheriff Beck and motioned for them to step away and out of earshot of the deputy.

He spoke first saying, "Now Sheriff, I don't want you to get all upset with Deputy Conway. He thought he was doing the right thing. I wasn't paying any attention to how I was driving and never did see him until it was too late."

"Okay Quint, I'll read the report later," nodding toward the deputy. "Just give him all the details you can think of."

"Where is Conway? I left instructions that he should stay on scene till I got here."

"I think he's over there in the patrol car," Mason responded. "Listen sheriff, take it easy on him. He's pretty shook up and he's afraid you're going to fire him. I told him that once you had all the facts, he'd be in the clear."

"Well, we'll see about that," Beck replied. "From what I see here," he paused. "Well, we'll see" he said again as he turned toward the patrol car.

As he neared the patrol car, Conway opened the door and stepped out and started to speak to the sheriff. Beck motioned him back in the car and got in the drivers side and sat there shaking his head looking at Conway.

"Too bad," the sheriff was thinking. "He sure looks like what a law enforcement officer should look like." Conway was a good looking, dark haired very fit young man. His enthusiasm was commendable, however, in Beck's mind, he was little too much of an 'eager beaver'. Something would have to be done about that.

Finally, Beck asked, "Conway, what time does your shift end?"

"I'm off at eight sir," the young office replied with a slight quaver in his voice.

Sheriff Beck said, with unusual formality, "Deputy Conway, you are relieved from further road patrol, pending a full review of the circumstances surrounding this incident. Until said review can be presented for consideration and possible disciplinary action, you are, until further notice, assigned duties as a department dispatcher. Do you understand?"

"Yes sir," Conway said quietly. "Sir do you think I'll be able to get back on the road anytime soon?"

"Conway," the sheriff replied solemnly. "These things generally take a lot of time to get resolved. For the time being, I wouldn't get my hopes up."

"And today, I want you to spend a couple of hours with Irma. We'll work out the details of the assignment in the next couple of days. Two hours of overtime are approved." He finished.

With that he got out of the patrol car and walked back

to Mason and as he drew near, his deputy seemed to be wrapping things up.

"Quint, have you got a ride back to your office. I'm going that way if you don't."

"I'd appreciate that sheriff," Mason replied. "But my office is just down the street here a couple of blocks. I can walk that without any problem."

"Come on, hop in," the sheriff said. "I'm going right past there."

As they drove away, Beck said, "Sorry about the loss of your patrol car Quint, but the county has pretty good insurance, so you should have a replacement in a week or so. In the meantime, I'll arrange for you to use an unmarked Sheriff's Department car. I'll get it down to you this afternoon, okay?"

Before Mason could answer, Beck continued, "Say Quint, were you gone for the weekend? I just wondered because my office had a call from someone down here Sunday afternoon about some vandalism that happened here. One of our patrolman covered it for you," he finished.

"Oh, yeah," Mason acknowledged. "I was gone all weekend. I just got back a few hours ago. That's why I was out at this time of day," he said. "Trying to get caught up on ...." he stumbled, finally saying, "things."

"You know Quint," Beck continued. "I get reports from all over the state. Once in a while, as a matter of courtesy, other county officers send me accounts about citizens from here in my own county. I do the same for them when I have something I think they should know. Did you know about those reports Quint?"

Mason sat looking straight ahead, sat without comment.

"Quint," Beck said softly, "Maybe you should stick around home a little more. It's just too easy to get yourself in trouble when you're off your own turf, don't you think so," he said looking at Mason.

"Here's my office Sheriff," Mason mumbled. "I appreciate the lift. I'll talk to you later."

As the Sheriff drove away, Mason stood on the sidewalk watching him leave. He bowed his head and turned to unlock his office door and stepped inside out of sight.

Beck was thinking, "I hope he gets his head on straight pretty quick. Those guys down in the city aren't going to put up with much more of his shenanigans and neither am I."

Beck was well aware of Mason's 'business trips' out of town. They usually involved excessive drinking and carousing with young women half his age. It was inevitable that, sooner or later, he was going to get rolled, beat up or both. According to information the Sheriff had received, over this past weekend, Quint had been picked clean by a young redhead that he had introduced earlier in the evening as his 'niece'.

It was an unfortunate choice on his part, to do a good deal of his drinking in a bar commonly frequented by off duty police officers. He was often involved in drunken conversations, trying to impress 'his fellow law officers' of the importance a small town marshal like himself had in solving local crime.

According to the latest report Beck had just received, Mason had discussed at some length, the investigation he was currently involved in concerning the bones of several young women recently discovered.

19

Beck decided, as long as he was here, he'd stop by Wildwood Dynamics and have a talk with young Lawson. He had just learned over the weekend, that old man Gunderson had sold the business to Jeff. Beck thought he could use his visit to congratulate the young man and maybe have a chance to talk some more about the case. Too many things seemed to be happening at once for him to stay focused. Maybe talking with Lawson would help.

Jeff was on the phone with George Gunderson when Mrs. Parsons stuck her head in his door and motioned to him. He held up a finger and said, "Hold on just a minute George, Mrs. Parsons is yelling at me."

Mrs. Parsons took immediate umbrage to that, "Don't you dare tell him I yelled at you!" she exclaimed with a shocked look on her face. "But if you can spare a minute, the Sheriff is out here and wants to see you."

Then, "And I hope he's got a bunch of unpaid parking tickets with your name on them," she harrumphed.

Jeff grinned and said, "Okay, send him in, but if he takes his handcuffs out, call our attorney right away."

Jeff was still talking with George when the Sheriff came into the office. Jeff motioned him to a chair and continued talking. "No, I haven't had a chance to talk to young Waters yet. Birdie will be at my house in the morning and I'll ask her to have Red come in and see me."

He paused listening and then, "No, that's okay George. I know, I know …" Paused again, then, "Okay, well if you run into him, ask him to come in anytime tomorrow."

Another pause, then, "Yeah, she said she'd be home later today. I talked with her last night and she thought they'd be done by two or two thirty." Another pause, then, "Yep, Okay George, I'll talk to you later. Thanks … goodbye."

Hanging up and turning to the Sheriff he smiled and said, "What's the charge officer? Do I need a lawyer?"

Beck laughed. He liked this young man and his easy way. He said, "Nope, not today. I just heard that you had bought the business from George and I wanted to stop by and tell you, congratulations."

Jeff said, "Thank you Sheriff. I'm still trying to get used to the idea, but I'm pretty excited about the whole thing.

Beck was pulling Jeff's camera out of a sack he had carried in and also the large envelope of pictures. He laid the camera on the desk and started to pull out the photos Jeff had taken. Jeff picked them up and was looking through them with interest.

"These turned out pretty good considering how much I was shaking," Jeff said. "I didn't really look at those bones very closely while I was taking these. I just started snapping away."

"The state boys took pretty much the same stuff, so I guess we won't need these."

Jeff was pawing through his desk drawer and came up with a magnifying glass. He was studying one picture in particular.

Finally, he said, "I guess you know that this lady had broken her leg at some time or another don't you?"

Sheriff Beck was surprised and said, "Yes, I knew that. Doc told me. What do you see there that indicates that?"

Jeff was still studying the photo and said, "I thought at first this was just a twig or something laying on this bone here," he was pointing to a picture. "But when I look closer I can see what appears to be a couple of screws in the bone, and look here," he said. "See this dark spot at the end of the bone. I'll bet that's one of those titanium rods they use for a compound fracture."

"Well, I'll be," the Sheriff commented, looking at Jeff. "I looked at all those shots and never noticed that kind of detail. It's probably all in Doc's lab notebook, but I just haven't had time to study it."

"Do you still want to give these back to me or do you want to keep them. I really don't have any interest in them and," Jeff paused as he was sorting through the photos.

"Who's this? This isn't anybody I know and I didn't take this picture."

It was a picture of George Schmidt. The Sheriff reached for it saying, "That's a picture of Doc. That's the way they found him the other day. I didn't mean for that to be mixed in with those shots of yours."

But then he handed it back to Jeff and said, "Say, would you take a look at that picture. Is there anything that strikes you as peculiar, or unusual about it? I feel like I'm missing something here."

Jeff studied the picture for several minutes, finally looking up, saying, "I'm sorry to disappoint you Sheriff, but I'm afraid I just don't see what's bothering you. Of course, I never knew Doc, so if there was anything about him in particular, I probably wouldn't see it anyway."

"I know," Beck said. "I don't know what it is that's bothering me, but I just can't seem to put my finger on it. Maybe it'll come to me, probably in the middle of the night. And won't my wife love that!" He laughed.

As Jeff handed the photo back, he suddenly stopped and looked at it again. Then he said, "I don't know how important this is, but there is one thing I noticed. It's really just a minor detail."

"What," Beck said, "What do you see?"

"Actually, it's what I don't see," Jeff said as he handed the photo to Beck. "But your friend Doc, didn't have his seat belt fastened. Does that help you?"

"Hmmm," the Sheriff said, "I don't think it means anything, but I didn't notice that. That's probably what's bothering me."

He sat silently looking at the picture for several minutes. Then, with a start, "Sorry Mr. Lawson, it's just a feeling I have. Doc and I go back a long way and I just don't feel right about this," he said indicating the photo.

"I guess you're busy enough without me coming in here wasting your time like this. I think I will take those pictures of yours back with me and compare them with the state snapshots."

Standing up to leave, he reached across the desk to

shake hands with Jeff. Jeff quickly stood up and extended his hand to the Sheriff.

"That's absolutely no problem Sheriff. I wish I could give you more satisfaction on the picture of your friend there. You're certainly not wasting my time. I'm interested in all this too and I'll be glad to help anyway I can. Feel free to stop by any time. And by the way, it's Jeff, not Mr. Lawson," he said with a smile.

Beck laughed and as he turned away to leave he said, "Okay Jeff, and you can just call me Sheriff!"

Jeff laughed at this and was about to sit down again, when Beck turned and said, "I didn't mean to eavesdrop on your conversation a minute ago," gesturing toward the phone. "But I was wondering if you were talking about that young Indian boy, Red Wing Waters."

"Why yes I was," Jeff answered. "I'm hoping to bring him into the company as a sort of apprentice to work with our maintenance foreman here."

"Good," the Sheriff said. "I've heard some good things about him. I hope he works out for you." Then with a wave of his hand he left.

Jeff remained standing for a few minutes, wondering how the sheriff could have any information about Red. Then with a shrug, he sat down again and continued working on a pile of paperwork on his desk.

20

As the Sheriff was leaving Lakeview, he couldn't help thinking about the pictures that Stony had given him of Doc. He mentally kicked himself for not noticing the seatbelt thing. He should've seen that right off. Doc had been a real bug-a-boo about seat belts. He wouldn't drive out of his driveway without hooking up. And he made sure that anybody that was with him do the same. He always said he'd seen too many accident victims that hadn't been hooked up.

Beck didn't know what to think about that. He decided to swing by the Walgreen's Drug Store on his was back to the office and talk with Sam Bell, the local druggist. According to Stony, the druggist had called him to the scene. Maybe, he had unhooked Doc's seatbelt when he was discovered in the car.

A short time later Sam and Beck were standing in the parking lot behind the drugstore. "He was right over here Sheriff," Sam was saying. "One of the kids in the area came in the store and told me there was someone out here in the parking lot and he looked like he was dead."

Sheriff Beck was looking around the parking lot. He finally said, "Why do you suppose he parked way back here. He could've just about pulled right up to the front door. If he were having a heart attack, why would he park way back here? Wouldn't he want to get help as soon as he could? Were there a lot of other cars in here that afternoon too?" Looking around again, Beck saw only a few cars parked here today.

"Actually, there were only two or three cars back here that day. And they mostly belonged to the store employees," Sam answered. "That's my car parked right there" motioning toward a Nissan Spectra, "And that one belongs to Nedra, and that one is Tanya's. That's pretty much the way it looked the other day Sheriff."

"Had Doc been in the store to get a prescription filled that day?" Beck asked. "He had a bottle of Nitro Glycerin pills and a prescription in his pocket."

"Nope, to my knowledge he never had a prescription filled, or, for that matter even bought a bottle of aspirin from the store. He used to stop by and get a paper now and then, but that's about it. If he had nitro pills, he probably had them in his own medicine supply at his office."

As an afterthought, Sam said, "I sure filled a lot of his prescriptions though, but they were all for his patients, not for him."

Beck stood there thinking, finally saying, "Sam, did you find him in the car yourself, or did someone else?

"No, the kid just told me about him and I came out here to see for myself and that's when I found him. I checked for a pulse, but he was gone."

Beck pulled out the picture of Doc and showed it to the druggist. "Sam, is this the way you found him. Other than trying to get a pulse, did you move him or change his position in any way other than what this shows."

"Yep, that's pretty much the way he looked. I did open the door, but other than that, I didn't change anything."

Beck hesitated and then said, "Sam just for the record, did you unhook his seatbelt to take his pulse."

"Nope, didn't really do anything, just ran back to the store and called your office."

Then, "Sheriff I'm sorry but if that's about it, I've got a bunch of prescriptions to fill yet this afternoon, so I should get back inside."

"Okay, thanks Sam. You've been a big help," Beck said as the druggist hurried away toward the store.

As Beck was leaving, Forest Decker jogged past in front of the store. He was unaware of the Sheriff's car parked, as it was, in the rear parking area. He was dressed, as he had been at the funeral home a few nights ago, in sweatshirt and running shorts. Beck watched a little enviously as the well-conditioned young mortician disappeared downs the street.

He was thinking, "Maybe I will have my guys come over here and run with him a couple of times a week. It sure wouldn't hurt any of them to get in better shape."

Back at his office, he became involved in the day to day activities of his office and wouldn't get a chance to get back to the file on "The bones case" as he'd come to refer to it, until much later in the afternoon.

21

Jeff left his office a little after one o'clock to grab a sandwich at the local cafe. As he sat at a side booth eating his sandwich and drinking a coke, his thoughts drifted, as they often did lately, to Brenda. He was wondering what she was doing, when she'd be back from her conferences and how soon they could be together. He was thinking, that maybe he would take her to a nice dinner someplace and maybe they could catch a movie afterwards. Before Brenda came along, Jeff had spent a lot of his nights going to movies.

His thoughts were interrupted by the sight of Quint Mason walking up and sitting down at the counter. Jeff was struck by the marshal's pasty appearance. He ordered a bowl of soup and sat there sipping a cup of coffee that the waitress had placed before him. His hands were shaking so badly that Jeff was afraid he'd spill coffee over the front of his shirt.

Jeff was thinking that the last time he had seen anybody in that condition, was after an overnight pass when he'd been in the army. His friend Dwight had looked and acted a lot like that after having had way too much 'fun' the night before. In his case, it was a bottle of cheap whiskey!

Jeff finished and after leaving a dollar on the table for a tip, walked to the counter to pay his bill. He said, "Hi Quint, what's new?"

Mason looked up in surprise and recognizing Jeff said, "Nothing much. How about you? I hear you're the new owner of the lamp factory now."

Then he growled, "I also hear you're getting pretty chummy with our fat Sheriff too. What's that all about anyway?"

"Now who's spreading those kind of stories? I hardly know the Sheriff," Jeff paused, not liking the way Quint had asked the question. "He just stopped by our plant a little while ago to get some follow up answers to those bones I found the other day."

"Is that so," Mason said. "What kind of information did he think you'd have anyway?"

"Nothing important. He just happened to be in town on other business and stopped by," Jeff was getting irritated at the sarcastic manner of Mason's probing. Paying his bill, he turned away, leaving Mason glaring after him.

Returning to the office, Jeff noticed a beige Accord parked in the visitor's parking area. The car looked familiar but he couldn't remember where he'd seen it before. He suddenly remembered it had been parked in George Gunderson's driveway the evening that he had accepted George's offer to buy the business. The car belonged to Red Waters. Red was waiting in the lobby when Jeff walked in. He had been paging through one of the company's trade journals that had been placed in the lobby for visitors while they waited.

"Hi there Red. How are you doing today? Did Birdie talk to you this morning?"

"What?" Red said, "No, I haven't seen Birdie since she left to go out to your cabin this morning. Mr. Gunderson stopped by my shop this morning and told me that you wanted to see me."

"Okay, I had told Birdie I wanted to talk with you too and I thought" .... He paused thinking, George is pushing this kid. I wonder how much he's been told. "Did George tell you why I wanted to see you?" he asked.

"No sir, I just figured you must have been having a problem with one your lawnmowers here. Isn't that it?"

"Nope, come on in my office. I want to talk with you about something."

Earlier that day, he had found Bud Lyndaman on the shop floor working with his crew. He had taken Bud to one side saying, "Bud, I think I've got a candidate for that position we spoke about a few days ago. Do you know a young Indian named Red Waters?"

"Sure, I know Red. He's a real good young man. If you're thinking about him we'll have a real winner if you can get him to come with us."

"Any reason that you know of, why he wouldn't want the job" Jeff asked.

"Well you know" Bud said, "He's got a pretty good little business there, but I'm not sure how much money he makes at it. The other thing is what happened to his dad. You know that story," Jeff nodded.

Bud went on, "Well, I think he believes a lot of folks think he's a lot like his old man and they all kinda look down on him. I don't think so, but I can understand how he would feel that way."

"Alright then," Jeff said "If I'm hearing you right, you or your people won't have a problem with this if I can get him to come on board. Is that right?"

"Yes sir," Bud answered. "I'll be happy to have him and the sooner the better."

Now, here was Red sitting across from him. "Red," he started." How's your business doing? Is it doing pretty good, or, are you struggling a little bit with it?"

Red opened his mouth to answer, but no sound came out. He sat looking at Jeff for several seconds, finally saying, "It's doing okay. We're not getting rich, but we get along."

Jeff smiled and said, "Red, I'm sorry if it sounds like I'm prying, I don't mean to be sticking my nose into your business. I'm interested because I think I can offer you something a little better. But that's up to you to decide."

Now Red was interested, "What have you got in mind?"

So Jeff outlined the apprentice program he had in mind and went on to say that if he proved his worth, he would send him down to a vocational training school in the area for evening classes.

He finished by saying, "We'd start you out at twelve dollars an hour for the first ninety days and if Bud is happy with your work, wages would increase a couple of dollars an hour, with occasional merit increases after that."

Jeff finished by explaining the benefit package that he'd be entitled to after his ninety-day training period. He was looking at Red as he explained all this and the young Indian's face never changed. Jeff was beginning to wonder if Red was even hearing him or if he had tuned him out for some reason.

With a large smile, Red said, "That sure sounds like a great job Mr. Lawson. But, I don't dare say yes, without first talking with my wife. This would be quite a change for us, and I'm pretty sure Birdie won't have any problem with this. She might even see it as a way to give up a few of her housekeeping customers. I want to thank you Mr. Lawson and I'll let you know tomorrow, if that's alright with you."

"That'll be fine Red and by all means talk it over with Birdie." Then Jeff said with a grin, "But if this means she won't be coming by and keeping my house straight every week, I may have some second thoughts here …. I'm just kidding Red, I'll look forward to hearing from you tomorrow."

As Red was leaving, his phone buzzed. Normally, Helen would screen his calls, so this must be someone she just automatically put through. He was delighted to hear Brenda's voice on the line.

"Hi you," she said. "I just got home and wondered if you'd like to come here for dinner tonight?"

"Hello, I'm glad you got home safe and sound. How was your conference?" he asked.

"It was okay, very boring like most of them that I've attended. Lot of the same old stuff. That's why I left before the end of the last session. I've heard it all before" she finished.

"I thought maybe we could have dinner over at Gina's and take in a movie afterward," Jeff said.

"How are you ever going to find out if I can cook if we keep going out to eat all the time," she replied. "Besides, all I've done for the last two days is eat restaurant food. And if it's a movie you want, I've got tons of CDs right here.

Doesn't that sound more interesting," she said in that soft voice of hers.

"I have to admit, it really does. What time do you want me there," he asked.

"Oh, anytime in the next fifteen minutes will do," she said with a smile in her voice. Then, "Why don't you just come by when you leave the office this afternoon."?

Jeff glanced at his watch; it was just past two thirty. He groaned, "I might just be there in fifteen minutes. I'm the boss these days you know and I can come and go as I want."

After a pause with no response from Brenda, he said, "I'm sorry, I'm just so anxious to see you that I forgot I've got a meeting with Les and one of our suppliers at three thirty. We should be wrapped up by five. Is that too soon?"

"That will be fine Jeff," she answered quietly. "And fifteen minutes really would have been wonderful too. I'll see you at five. Bye, bye love" and with that, the line went dead.

22

L ike young Lawson had done, Sheriff Beck was scanning the photos that were scattered over his desk with a magnifying glass. He had looked at Jeff's snapshots and then the pictures taken by the state photographer. The set of pictures supplied by the state officer of the first discovery, were not quite as clear as the shots that Jeff had taken. But, the screws and rod that Jeff had seen were visible in all the pictures and Beck was kicking himself for not seeing them sooner.

He pulled the snapshots of Doc out and was scanning these too, with the magnifying glass. After several minutes he laid them back down and sat there thinking. Something had been bothering him about these photos since the first time he'd laid eyes on them. It was maddening not to be able to understand what it was.

The seat belt thing that Jeff had noticed nagged at him, but in the back of his mind he knew that wasn't what was bothering him. There had to be something else. Picking them up, he began scanning the photos again.

And suddenly, there it was! He had been looking at

these snapshots for days and the thing that was bothering him was right there in plain sight. Beck stood up so quickly that his chair slid back and crashed into the small refrigerator behind him. With the magnifying glass he looked closely at Doc's shirt pocket and there was the clear image of a small spiral hinge note pad protruding above the top of the pocket!

The Sheriff pulled his chair back in place and sat down. What did this mean? He had been told about the notebook by Stoney, so it wasn't likely that he had taken it from Doc's pocket. It hadn't been returned to Donna with his other personal effects. He would interview the deputy on the scene in the morning, but he could think of no reason to believe his deputy would remove something like that without mentioning it in his report.

That left Forest Decker. The Sheriff was remembering how nervous he had been when he'd been asked about that notebook. Beck sat for several minutes reviewing all those details and finally came to the conclusion that Forest Decker was *lying*!

But why? Why would Decker deny knowing anything about the little note pad? Where did he come from anyway? What was his background and training? Where did he go to college? At the moment, Beck had only questions and no answers. As he sat there thinking, he decided he needed to know a whole lot more about Forest Decker!

Before leaving the office for the day, he started a probe into the background of Forest Decker. Within a few days he would learn everything there was to know about that young man. He had gathered some information such as driver's license applications, real estate tax information and anything else that was available from county records.

He made a mental note to get a judge to grant a warrant to search his financial situation as well.

As he passed the dispatcher's desk, he saw Conway sitting alongside Irma and watching and listening to her as she did her job.

Beck stopped and said to Conway, "What are you still doing here Conway? You haven't been assigned a schedule yet. You haven't been here all day have you?"

Conway looked up at the Sheriff glaring at him and quickly got to his feet and almost coming to attention he said, "Well, yes sir I have been. I thought I'd stick around until Irma's shift ended. I think I've seen enough now though and I'm ready to handle it on my own."

Irma turned away from the board and glancing at the Sheriff said, "He seems to have a pretty good handle on it Sheriff. What do you think? Should we get him on schedule?"

The Sheriff thought about it for a minute or so, then said, "No, I don't think so. Not yet anyway. Conway your shift for the next few days will be from seven to seven. Irma, you move over and let him run things for a day or so. If everything goes okay, we'll set up a new schedule starting next week, Okay?"

Irma nodded and with a wave of her hand turned back to the microphone in front of her and acknowledged a call from one of the deputies on patrol. Conway had also turned back and sat down paying close attention to the conversation Irma was having.

Beck stood watching for a few more minutes, then turned and left the building. When he arrived home that evening, Lynda surprised him by greeting him with a drink in each hand.

"What's this?" he said, "Did I forget our anniversary again?" he joked as he took the drink from her hand.

"Nope," Lynda replied. "I know how much stress you've been under the past few days and I've decided you need to relax and forget about all this stuff that's going on, at least just for tonight anyway."

Beck took a sip of his drink and noticed the dining room table in the next room was set and candles were in place. Turning back to his wife he said, "Now I know why I married you in the first place. You know how to fix a great drink!"

"Oh come on now Cubby, I think you might have married me for a couple of other reasons besides just that," she laughed as they sat together on a large couch. "For instance, that night at the drive-in movie down in Rochester?" she said coyly.

"Hmmm," Beck said thoughtfully. "Oh yeah, I remember now, it was 'The Dirty Dozen' right?"

With that, Lynda poked her husband in the ribs almost spilling his drink. "Okay, okay," he said laughing. "I remember alright, matter of fact that's the night I asked you to marry me if memory serves me correctly."

"That was the night, but it was "An Affair To Remember," she corrected him.

The evening was indeed a very pleasant and relaxing interlude. Lynda had prepared his favorite meal with a bottle of chilled wine and a light desert. Much later, he lay awake listening to the even breathing of his wife and his mind involuntarily came back to the problems at hand. It took a real effort to clear his mind and finally drift off to sleep.

23

By the time Jeff pulled into Brenda's driveway, it was quarter to six. The discussions with Les and the hardware supplier had taken much more time than he had anticipated. It didn't help that the supplier had been twenty minutes late for his appointment. As he quickly walked toward the house, Jeff was trying to think how he was going to explain why he was so late. He decided that honesty was the best policy and let the chips fall where they may.

Brenda met him at the door, coolly looking him straight in the eyes saying, "Hello. Are you the gentleman I had the appointment with earlier. I'm sorry but being forty five minutes late is unacceptable and our meeting has been canceled!"

Jeff stood there, not knowing what to say. He wanted to take this beautiful creature in his arms and smother her with kisses but she was apparently in an extremely hostile mood.

Finally he said, "Brenda, I don't know what to say.

Our meeting ran long and ...." Brenda held up her hand to stop him.

"Oh shut up you big dodo! Mrs. Parsons called me and told me your salesman was late and you'd be late. Don't stand there with that hang dog look, come on in the house."

As she closed the door he turned and kissed her, saying, "You shouldn't do that to me. I'm very sensitive to your moods you know." Then drawing her close, kissed her again.

"Remind me to give Mrs. Parsons a raise. What would I ever do without her?" he smiled.

They went back to the 'Big Room' and Jeff fixed drinks for them. Standing behind the bar he starting talking about his day and Brenda sat on one of the bar stools in front of him.

Then he asked, "What is that smell? Or I should say 'aroma'? Whatever you're cooking out there is making my mouth water."

Brenda laughed and said, "Oh, it's nothing special. Just a beef roast. Really pretty easy to fix. One of these days I'll have to fix you a real gourmet meal. I love to cook, but other than dad, I don't get to show off my cooking to anyone."

A short time later they were in the small dinette nook off the kitchen enjoying the roast beef dinner she had prepared. Jeff was hungry and he thought the meal was delicious.

He said, "This definitely beats the Coffee Cup Cafe, which sometimes goes by the name of the 'Greasy Spoon'. I don't get very many home cooked meals like this and I'm not much of a cook. My cooking is limited to frying eggs or grilling hamburgers and that's about it."

Brenda laughed at this, saying, "You should spend more time with my dad. He's a good cook. I think he spends a lot of time watching those folks on TV that have those cooking programs. He's always trying something new."

"I was only there once for dinner," Jeff said "And your mom was still alive and I thought she had done the cooking that night."

"She might have," Brenda replied. "But he's done most of the cooking for as long as I can remember."

They each had a glass of wine and had moved back into the 'Big Room' now and Brenda switched on the stereo system. They sat talking and enjoying each other's company when Jeff happened to notice a picture album on the coffee table in front of them. Picking it up, he casually began leafing through it.

"That's a family album," Brenda said. "Dad used to have it at home and after mom died he'd stuffed it in a box full of old snapshots. So, I brought the album home and the box too. I didn't want some of those things lost."

Jeff was leafing through the album and stopping suddenly and looking at her, asked with a wicked grin, "There wouldn't be any of those bare bottom baby pictures of you in here would there?"

Brenda took a sip of her wine and said, "No, I made sure all of those were destroyed a long time ago. There are a lot of them in there of me though. Start at the beginning," she pointed at the book. "And it becomes pretty obvious that I was an only child and spoiled rotten too."

Jeff laughed at this and as he went through the album

she sat close and pointed out pictures of her and her parents at different stages of her life. There was Brenda with a number of children sitting around the table and all were wearing party hats and a cake in the middle of the table with the number seven displayed. Other pictures of her parents in different settings, vacation pictures Jeff guessed.

There was a picture of a teenage Brenda wearing what was apparently a 'Prom Dress' and standing with her was a tall very good looking young man dressed in formal attire. Brenda's date for the evening.

Looking closer, he asked, "Is that Bill? I had no idea you two went back to high school together."

Brenda said softly, "Oh yes, we knew each other for a long time before we were married. That was the first time I ever went out with him and I had finished college before we started going together for real."

Quickly moving on through the album he stopped at a picture of George and Lydia standing in front of a St. Bernard dog. A second picture on the same page showed Lydia petting the dog, but Lydia was sitting in a wheel chair with one leg raised in a cast.

Jeff was looking at these pictures and asked, "I don't remember that big dog. I was working here when your mom broke her leg though. Was that George's dog?"

"No, that's Bolivar. He belonged to a neighbor a couple doors away, but he was always hanging around mom's house because she was always sneaking him table scraps."

With a sad smile, "That damned big brute of a dog is the reason mom broke her leg in the first place."

Jeff was curious at this, "What do you mean. Did the dog attack her or something?"

"Oh no nothing like that. Bolivar's a real pussycat. It was wintertime and mom was getting out of the car and as she was walking to the house, here comes Bolivar just jumping for joy at seeing her. He slipped on the icy sidewalk and slid into mom. She fell over him and somehow twisted her leg under the two of them. Dad said he thought he'd heard the bone crack when she fell. Scared him half to death."

"Gol, I guess it would," Jeff said. "How long was she laid up like that anyway."?

"She was on crutches for a while, but by spring she was walking with a cane. I don't think she ever walked without it again. At least I don't remember her without it."

Smiling, "Dad used to say he wouldn't ever be able to take her an airplane again. She'd probably set off all those alarms and they'd want to strip search her."

Carefully, he asked, "What did he mean by that, why would she set off airport alarms."

"Well, because," Brenda said "It had been a compound fracture and they had to put her leg back together with screws and a metal rod of some kind."

Jeff thought the blood must have drained out of his head in an instant. Quickly he took a swallow of his wine, then finished it completely. He suddenly had total recall of his visit with Sheriff Beck that morning and the pictures he had looked at. In his mind, he could see them again, the screws and the rod.

"I see," Jeff said, "Do you mind if I have another drink?

148

I think I'd like a little of your dad's Famous Grouse."

Jeff had suddenly lost interest in the album and stood at the bar thoughtfully stirring his drink. He was thinking there couldn't possibly be any connection to those pictures he'd just seen. There was no way. Lydia had died almost a year ago now and he still remembered how stricken George had become at her loss. But the coincidence of that broken leg ....

Brenda said, "Well if you're going to stand there all night, you might as well fix me a drink too. My wine glass is empty if you hadn't noticed."

With a start Jeff said, "Oh, sure, sure. Let me have your glass. I was just wool gathering I guess."

As he poured the wine he couldn't stop thinking about what he had just learned about Brenda's mother. How she broke that leg and how it was repaired. And the pictures!

"No, no" he thought, "there can't be any connection. None at all." With that, he tried to clear his mind of the images in the photos and returned to sit by Brenda on the couch.

After a short time, Brenda opened a cabinet below the television and with a wave of her hand at the contents said, "There must be every movie ever made here," she joked. "Well, quite a few of them anyway. Do you have any favorites?"

Jeff knelt before the cabinet and tried to concentrate on the movie titles on the CDs in the cabinet, but the nearness of Brenda and the subtle essence of her made it difficult for him to concentrate.

Finally, he sat back and said, "I can't pick one, you've

got so many. Why don't you pick one of your favorites? I'm sure I'll like it too."

"Okay then, how about 'Sleepless in Seattle'? That's a nice mushy film." Seeing the look on Jeff's face, she giggled and said, "Oh all right. I suppose you want to see something more manly, like 'The Sands of Iwo Jima.'"

"Do you really have the 'Sands of Iwo Jima?" Jeff asked.

"No I don't, but from the look on your face just then, I'm sorry I don't," she laughed.

"Oh, let's just forget a movie for tonight. Let's just talk. Tell me more about yourself. You've told me some of it, about growing up in Wisconsin, what else? I want to know everything about you."

Taking his hand, leading him back to the couch, she turned and switched on the stereo again. The soft music playing and the subdued lighting in the room made for a very intimate setting.

Jeff said, "There really isn't much to tell that you don't already know. I have a feeling the best part of my life is just beginning."

They sat close and talked softly for the next couple of hours with neither aware of the passing time. Brenda suddenly heard the big mantle clock striking in the front room and glancing at her watch gently pushed Jeff away.

"Do you know that it's midnight and I have to go back to school in the morning. I think it's time you went home Jeff." Leaning forward she kissed him softly, which provoked an immediate response from Jeff.

"Why don't I just stay here for a while yet? I haven't even had a chance to tell you about my days in the paper mill yet."

He reached for her and kissing her again and again said, "I'm sure you'd find that very interesting," kissing her again.

Brenda pushed him away saying, "Paper mill my foot. I know what you've got in mind, but you're just going to have to wait Buster! And if it's any consolation, I'm getting pretty anxious myself!"

With a soft smile, she continued, "Will you have to work late again tomorrow night, or can we watch that movie we didn't get a chance to see tonight?"

Jeff, embarrassed said, "Brenda, honey, I've got a problem tomorrow night. I'm sorry but it's my turn to have the guys for poker. I forgot all about it until Dwight reminded me," careful not to tell her when Dwight had spoken to him.

Brenda was disappointed and said, "Are you sure it's poker and not another one of your old girl friends and you're just trying to give me the brush off?"

Seeing the shocked expression on Jeff's face, she leaned forward and kissed him saying, "Oh don't worry about it. I'll see you Thursday night, okay?"

With that she was standing and pulling Jeff to his feet. Standing on tiptoes, she kissed him and said, "Good night lover. Win a lot of money tomorrow night and you can treat me to a big meal at the Log Jam."

As Jeff drove away his mind was in turmoil. He knew now, that he was in love with Brenda. He had absolutely no doubts about that. At the same time the images in the photos the Sheriff had shown him and the snapshot of Lydia Gunderson in a wheel chair, kept intruding on his thoughts. Try as he might, he couldn't get the thought

24

The next morning, Red Waters was waiting for Jeff as he walked into the building. He stood up as Jeff walked in the door. "Good morning Red. You're here bright and early this morning. Did you get a chance to talk with Birdie last night about my proposition," Jeff asked?

With a smile Red answered, "Yes sir, we talked for a long time. What we decided was, that I'd like to take your offer."

With a concerned look he continued, "I would like to be able to keep my shop for a while though, if that would be all right. There's a lot of folks here in town that kind of depend on me when they need help. I wouldn't ever let it interfere with my job here, though. That I can guarantee," he finished.

Jeff stepped forward, holding out his hand he said, "Welcome aboard Red. Why don't you come in Monday morning and we'll get you with Mrs. Parsons and she'll give you some papers to fill out, then when she's through with you, we'll send you out in the shop with Bud. He'll be your direct supervisor from now on. Any problems, go to him with them. Anything he can't handle, he'll see to it that you get to the person that can help you. Okay?"

"Yes sir, that sounds great" Red said. "And about my shop..."

"That's no problem Red. I'll take your word for it, that it won't get in the way of your position here."

Jeff continued with a smile, "I hope this doesn't mean I'm going to lose Birdie in this deal. She's pretty important to me too you know."

"Oh, no sir. We talked about that too. She might cut down a little," Red hesitated, then, "You know, the baby and all. She does want to be able to spend more time with him at home."

"Okay Red, I was just kidding. Birdie's a great gal and I'm sure with you two as parents, your son will be a fine young man too."

Mumbling his thanks again, Red shook Jeff's hand once more and left.

The rest of Jeff's day was filled with the business of running a small company. It was almost five o'clock when Mrs. Parsons stepped to his door saying, "Phone for you Mr. Lawson. Line one."

Jeff picked up the phone and heard the voice of Phil Benson, one of his golfing/poker-playing friends. Phil was calling to let him know that he wasn't going to be able to make the poker game that night. His daughter had the flu or something, he said, and his wife was worn out trying to take care of her. So Phil wanted to stay home and help out with the situation.

As he was leaving, he passed by Les Noonan's office and stopped to see Les sitting at his desk and concentrating on a computer screen. "Come on Les," Jeff said. "Time to call it a day."

Looking up and seeing Jeff, Noonan said, "Yes sir, I'm just shutting this thing down. It takes a couple of minutes. I'll see you in the morning boss."

Jeff started for the front, then stopping, came back to Noonan's office. Les was standing and arranging some print outs on his desk. He looked up in surprise at seeing Jeff standing there in the door again.

"Say Les," Jeff said. "Do you suppose 'Short Round' would let you out of the house tonight for a night out with the boys?"

Before Les could answer, Jeff said, "One of my poker players can't make it tonight and we could use another player. We don't play real late, we usually quit at ten thirty or so."

"That sounds like fun," Les said. "I'm not much of a gambler though, what kind of stakes do you play for?"

"Oh it's just nickel, dime. Last time we played I don't think I won a pot all night and I only lost a little over ten bucks. So you won't go home broke, but your ears might be ringing some. After a few beers it gets pretty loud and highly profane," Jeff laughed.

Les was grinning and asked, "What time. I'll check with Myra when I get home and if she hasn't anything planned, I'll be there. If there's a problem I'll call you. Okay?"

"Okay, get out to my place by 6:30 or so. I've got some rolls of nickels if you don't have any so don't worry about that."

Later that night as the poker game was drawing to a close, Jerry Wainright happened to ask Jeff about the 'bones thing'. As a result, the poker game ended with Jeff relating how he had stumbled on the remains while hoping to get a picture of that big deer.

Everybody had questions or comments and when Jerry asked if Jeff would go back this season and sit by that stump, Jeff answered, "No I don't think so. I think I'll give up deer hunting altogether. I never have felt very good about shooting an animal as pretty as a deer, and besides that," he continued. "Even if I did shoot one, what the heck would I do with it? I don't even like venison!"

As they were leaving, Wainright said, "You know, there's something screwy about all that. Why would anyone just dump those bodies like that? If it were animals, like a dog or cat, I think I'd understand that. But a person, it just doesn't make any sense."

Jeff, looking confused, said, "What makes you think leaving a dog or cat in the woods would make a difference?"

Jerry said, "Well, you know, I see it all the time. People bring their animals to me and when they have to be put to sleep, they just leave them. If I wanted to, I could just take them out in the woods and dump them. I suspect a lot of folks would do the same thing if they had a pet die for some reason and they didn't want to go to the bother of burying it."

Jeff stared at Wainright for several seconds before saying, "I hadn't thought of it that way before. What do you do with a dog or cat when you have to put them to sleep?"

Wainright was the local Veterinarian and had a small clinic just outside the town limits. He said now, "Oh I've got a crematorium. That way, the ashes can just be sent to the local landfill. I sometimes have two or three at a time. Saves a little money that way. That thing can be expensive to operate."

Les was the last to leave and he stopped at the door saying with a grin, "Thanks for your hospitality Jeff. I really enjoyed myself, especially since I won a couple of dollars."

Jeff was so preoccupied with his conversation with Wainright that he hardly acknowledged Les. Mumbling that he'd "see him the morning", he turned and went back to the poker table and started picking up empty bottles and snack trays.

Later, he sat in front of the TV set for a long time before he realized he hadn't bothered to turn it on.

As he was getting ready for bed, his mind was in turmoil. Finally, he thought, "I've got to talk with the Sheriff again and the sooner the better. I think I'll take a run down there first thing in the morning!"

25

Sheriff Beck was interviewing a dispatcher prospect when a deputy stepped to the door saying, "Sir, Mr. Lawson is outside and would like a word with you when you get a minute."

Beck thought about that for a minute, then cutting his interview short, told the young woman across the desk from him, that someone would give her a call later in the day to make an appointment with the county personnel office. Walking her to his door, he told her she could probably start in a couple of days.

Jeff was sitting outside his office, along with several other young people. Beck motioned for Jeff to go into his office saying, "I'll be right there Jeff. I have to speak to one of my people first."

Stopping by Irma's dispatcher desk, he noted that young Conway was acting as dispatcher, while Irma sat to one side watching and listening. Beck motioned for Irma to join him outside the dispatcher area asking her, "How's Conway doing? Can you leave him for a couple of hours?"

Irma nodding her head said, "Oh sure, I think we can put him in the schedule with no problem."

"Good," Beck said. Handing her a file folder with applications he said, "There's three or four people outside waiting to be interviewed for the dispatcher's position. I've just hired one and I don't have time to talk to anymore of them today. So, you know the drill, use the empty office down the hall and you handle the interviews. Any problem with that?" he finished.

"I guess not Sheriff," she hesitated. "But I don't have any authority to judge these people. Do you want to reschedule interviews with you for the ones I like?"

"It's your job now Irma. You've just become our Dispatcher/Office Manager. We'll work out the details later, but for now, if you find someone you like, hire them! We need at least three more that can work the board or help with the secretarial work around here. Just give me a memo on what you've done. Okay?" the Sheriff asked.

Jeff was fidgeting in his chair when the Sheriff walked back into his office. Stepping behind his desk he said, "Good morning Jeff. Would you like a cup of coffee? You look like you could use one." Pressing a button on his phone it was answered immediately over the speakerphone. "Yes sir, Sheriff," a disembodied voice said.

"Bring us in a couple of mugs will you please Bill." Looking up at Jeff, asked "Sugar or cream?"

"Black thanks," Jeff said, thinking, "I probably do look like death warmed over after all that beer and then not sleeping all night."

The deputy was just leaving after bringing two mugs of coffee, when the Sheriff asked, "Say Bill, I didn't get a chance to ask you before, but you were first officer on the scene for Doc the other day weren't you?"

"Yes sir," the deputy replied. "Actually, I was the only officer there. I contacted the city but their units were all tied up at the time."

Seemingly as an after thought, the sheriff asked, "By the way Bill, did you happen to pick up a small note pad at the scene? About so big," the Sheriff gestured. "With a kinda spiral hinge affair."

The deputy thought for a few seconds then said, "No sir, I don't remember anything like that. We picked up around the car pretty good too. We really didn't find much of anything that seemed important."

"Okay," Beck said. "Good job." Waving the deputy out of the office he took a sip of his coffee and looked at Jeff saying, "Well, Mr. Lawson, what has brought you to my office this bright sunny day?"

The day outside was actually gray and heavily overcast and the temperature had dropped significantly during the night. "And looking like something the cat dragged in at that! Looking that bad, it must be something pretty important to take you away from your deathbed," he laughed.

"Yeah, well the coffee helps." Jeff looked at the Sheriff saying, "I had too much beer last night. Poker night," he explained. "But the main problem is that I don't think I slept all night. I had a few things on my mind."

The Sheriff, no longer laughing said, "What kind of things. Something to do with what we talked about yesterday?"

"Yeah, those pictures and some others. And a conversation I had with a Veterinary friend last night."

Jeff talked for nearly forty-five minutes. He told the Sheriff about the pictures in Brenda's photo album and the injury her mother had suffered a number of years ago. The coincidence of the same type injury in the pictures he had taken of the remains in the woods. He talked of the disturbing discussion he had had with Jerry Wainright the night before.

The Sheriff sat quietly listening carefully, without interrupting until Jeff seemed to have said everything that was bothering him.

Looking at the Sheriff now, Jeff asked, "What do you think Sheriff? Do you think those bones I saw could actually be those of Lydia Gunderson? It would kill George if that turned out to be the case."

Beck sat thinking for a few minutes, then asked, "Jeff, other than the injury to her leg, why would you think those remains could be Mrs. Gunderson?"

Jeff stared at the Sheriff saying, "Sheriff, didn't you hear me tell what Jerry said last night?"

Beck said, "I'm not sure I'm following you Jeff. What did that have to do with this?"

"Sheriff," Jeff replied patiently, "I was present at the funeral service of Lydia Gunderson. It was actually a memorial service. Lydia had been **cremated(!)** and the only thing present during the service and the burial was an urn, which supposedly held her ashes!"

The Sheriff finally understood what was bothering Jeff. He said "Jeff, do you remember what Funeral Home handled the service for Mrs. Gunderson?"

"Well, there isn't one in Lakeview, so George arranged for one here in town. I don't think I knew the name of it, but it's not to far from here. I'm sure if I heard the name I'd remember it."

"How about Decker? Does that ring a bell?" The Sheriff asked.

"That's it! I remember now. Young guy there handled everything. He seemed very competent. He helped George and Brenda a lot with all the details," Jeff recalled.

"But I just remembered something else that he said. He told George he'd have to take Lydia to another Funeral Home because he didn't have a crematorium. It had delayed the internment a couple of days."

"How old would you say Mrs. Gunderson was when she passed away?" the Sheriff asked?

"I don't know for sure, but George is in his seventies, so I assume she would have been seventy two or three." Jeff answered.

"You probably don't know this, but then again, it sounds like you were pretty close to the Gunderson's," the Sheriff said. Then, "Do you know if Mrs. Gunderson had false teeth?"

"No, I'm afraid not. As you know, I've worked for George a number of years, but we didn't socialize a whole lot together." Jeff sat thinking, "I'm trying to remember if George ever said anything like that. I can ask Brenda. I'm meeting her tonight. She'd know."

"No, No! Don't say anything to her about this," the Sheriff exclaimed. "As a matter of fact, don't discuss this with anyone at all. I'm pretty sure you've come up with some pieces that fit very neatly into this puzzle. And because of what you've told me, now I think I've got a pretty good idea the direction this investigation is going."

Beck and Jeff sat for a long time discussing various aspects of the information Jeff had produced. Finally as Jeff was leaving, the Sheriff glanced at his watch and said, "It's a little early, but how about some lunch on the county?"

Jeff stood up, saying, "I really should get back. I didn't even go into the office this morning, I was so anxious to get down here."

He paused for a second or two, then, "But, you know what," he said. "I'm the boss these days, so if I'm a little late, who's going to give me a hard time about that. Lunch sounds good. Where do you have in mind? I'll meet you there."

" It's just a little neighborhood bar down the street. It' called Duffy's. We can get a hamburger and a beer if you want one. I'll just have a coke," he laughed. "Like you I'm the big cheese around here, but I have to answer to the county commissioners, so it's not good for me to be seen guzzling beer when I'm supposed to be on duty."

Jeff laughed and replied, "Okay, I know the place. I'll see you there in a few minutes." With that he turned and left the office.

26

It was late afternoon before Jeff returned to his office in Lakeview. He and the Sheriff had spent much longer at Duffy's then either one of them had intended. Beck had talked softly while they ate a light lunch of sandwiches, coke and beer.

He told Jeff that in recent days, he had become suspicious of one Forest Decker and after listening to Jeff's thoughts, he was more convinced then ever, that Decker was deeply and criminally involved with the remains found in the woods. Now, he had to start building his case against the man.

He explained that he was already gathering information about Decker's background and financial dealings since moving into this area. But he needed much more. He told Jeff about seeing the missing note pad in Doc's pocket in the photos. He said that that was what the question had been about with his deputy as Jeff sat in the Sheriff's office earlier.

Jeff listened with interest, but couldn't understand why the Sheriff was giving him all the details of his investigation till now. He was thinking that what he was hearing, would normally be considered confidential and information that would not generally be shared with someone like him.

Finally, when the Sheriff stopped talking to take a swallow of his drink and finish eating his sandwich, Jeff asked, "Sheriff, why are you telling me all this? I'm not a law officer. I'm just an interested citizen. Are you sure I should be privy to all your thinking on this matter?"

"Oh you haven't heard the worst part yet," the Sheriff replied.

Then, "Why am I telling you all this? That's a very good question. I'm not sure I can give you a good answer but I'll try."

He hesitated, then picked up his Coke glass and drained it. Holding it up for the bartender's attention, he pointed at it saying, "One more Harry, then we've got to leave." Looking at Jeff, "Do you want another beer?" When Jeff nodded Beck turned and held up two fingers making a circular motion.

Jeff suddenly realized something. "How often do you come in here for lunch anyway? That bartender, Harry? Seems to know you pretty well."

Beck chuckled, but before he could answer, the bartender brought the drinks to the table.

Beck looking up said, "Thanks Harry." then as the bartender turned away said to Jeff, "I drink a lot of this stuff, I'm kind of a 'cokeaholic', I guess. But Harry here adds a little bit of Jack Daniels once in a while too. That way, if one of our 'temperance' commissioners happens to come in while I'm eating, all they see is, that I'm drinking a Coke"

Turning serious, Beck continued, "Okay, you asked

why am I telling you all this. Problem is, I've got some very good deputies and a couple of pretty good lieutenants too. But most of our work till now, has been involved in traffic accidents, minor criminal activities, a few drug busts here and there, a couple of burglaries and once in a while an assault and battery problem. I need objective thinking on this situation, and my people, as good as they are, do not have the skills I need to see the coincidence of a picture of a lady in a wheelchair and a picture of some old bones strewn around in the woods!"

Taking a sip of his Coke, looking Jeff in the eye, he said, "That's why I'm sharing this information with you. The last thing I need is for the State boys to come in here and take this case away from me. They were going to send up a forensics specialist this week to examine the remains, but he can't be here before next week now."

Jeff replied, "But Sheriff, I'm not any kind of 'investigator'. I just happened to be unlucky enough to stumble across .... you know. And as far as my seeing a coincidence in the two pictures of Lydia and those bones, there might not be any connection at all."

As an afterthought, "And I hope there isn't!"

"You're right Jeff, you're not a **trained** investigator, but you've got a clear, sharp mind, that sees possibilities that others miss altogether."

Beck was thinking about the screws and rod in the bones Jeff had found. Beck had looked at those pictures over and over and missed that most important clue. Yet, Jeff had spotted them within a few seconds of glancing at them.

"I'd appreciate it if we could meet once in a while in the next week or so to talk about a few things."

"Do you think it would take that long to pin this on Decker?" Jeff asked. "Seems like you've got enough now for a case."

"No, no not yet. Before you can pin something like this on anybody, you've got to find out 'why'. Why would he do something like this?"

Beck leaned forward in the booth and said just loud enough for Jeff to hear, "And I told you a few minutes ago, that wasn't the worst of it. I'm convinced that Son of a Bitch killed Doc Schmidt somehow. And before I'm done with Mr. Decker, I'm going to prove it and he's going to wish he never heard of Sheriff Tommy Beck!"

As Jeff pulled into his parking space, his mind was in turmoil over the conversation he had just had with Sheriff Beck.

On the one hand, he was flattered to think that the Sheriff put so much value on his thoughts and opinions, but he was also troubled by the fact that Beck didn't have the same confidence in the officers on his staff and department in general. Jeff was sure that some of those fellows had been through some pretty extensive training for situations such as this.

There were several 'call back' notes stuck to his phone as he sat at his desk. He noted that 'Mrs. Dexter' had called around three o'clock. Glancing at his watch, Jeff was surprised to see that it was nearly four already. Picking up the phone he punched in Brenda's phone number.

At the sound of her voice, Jeff's heart skipped a beat as she said, "Hello lover. What took you so long to get back to me and why didn't anyone know where you were all day? You're a big shot owner now, and people have to know what you're up to every minute, you know that!"

"And hello to you too," Jeff said with a smile. "How did you know I wasn't some vacuum cleaner salesman calling? He'd have had his batteries charged for the rest of the day."

"Caller I.D." Brenda replied. "And answer my question. Where've you been?"

Jeff didn't know what to say. He sure didn't want to tell her he'd just spent most of the day with the Sheriff because she'd immediately want to know what that was all about. So he lied.

"Just business over at the county seat. A couple of other papers to sign, that's all." He was uncomfortable with the lie and hoped it didn't sound as phony to Brenda as it did to him."

"All day?" she continued. "Shouldn't take you that long for a couple of signatures!"

"Hey, what is this anyway? You giving me the third degree here?" Jeff tried to sound indignant. "If you really must know, I ran into an old girl friend and we spent the afternoon in the Cozy Inn Motel! Anything else you need to know?"

There was dead silence, and then suddenly the line went dead with the sound of Brenda hanging up!

"Oh great!" Jeff mumbled as he reached to redial her number, but before he could do that his phone buzzed. It was Mrs. Parsons.

"I've got a gentleman who's been on hold for the last few minutes and he said it's important that he speak with you. He wouldn't give me his name, his voice is familiar but I can't place it."

Jeff punched the 'hold' button and said, "Hello, this is Jeff Lawson. Who am I speaking with?"

The voice was curiously familiar, but like Mrs. Parsons, Jeff couldn't quite recognize it. "It's not important for you to know who I am Mr. Lawson, it's just important for you to know what I've got to tell you."

The caller's voice was somewhat muffled, as though speaking through a handkerchief. Jeff said, "Okay, why don't you tell me what's on your mind?"

"I understand you've just hired that Indian kid, the one that killed that Raeford fella and crippled his brother! Just thought you'd better be aware of how dangerous that little shit can be!" With that, the phone went dead as his caller hung up. Jeff sat holding the phone to his ear, stunned at what he'd just heard.

Like everyone else in Lakeview, he'd heard all the stories about Red's father and the Raeford brothers. But he'd never heard anything about Red's involment in the death of the one Raeford brother and the injury of the other.

Jeff buzzed Mrs. Parsons, who answered immediately. "Helen, do you have that application that Red filled out the other day?" When she said she did, he said, "Bring it in to me would you, please."

As Mrs. Parsons laid the file folder on Jeff's desk she said, "I've got Mrs. Dexter holding for you on line two. Can you speak to her now?"

"Oh sure, sure," Jeff said reaching for the phone.

Before he had a chance to punch the button to speak to Brenda, Mrs. Parsons said, "You better be careful with that woman Mr. Lawson. I don't know what you said to her before, but she sounds mighty upset."

Mrs. Parsons was glaring at Jeff and continued, "You

should know how vulnerable she still is, even after all this time and be a little more gentle with her!"

With that, she turned and left Jeff staring in wonder at her as she left the office.

Punching a blinking button he said into the phone, "Hello honey, I'm sorry if I upset you. I was just trying to be funny."

The voice that answered wasn't Brenda. It was a man's voice that said, "Well, honey, I'm not really upset with you. And you probably are hilarious." It was George Gunderson.

"Oh Hell, how did this happen? Hold on a minute will you George. I'll be right back," Jeff said hurriedly as he punched another flashing button on his phone saying, "Hello, Brenda?"

"Oh Jeff, I'm sorry. I guess I was just worried about you that's all." Brenda sniffed. "That was childish of me to hang up on you like that. Forgive me?"

"Don't be silly, there's nothing to forgive. It's all my fault anyway. I guess I thought I was being funny."

"You're a dear." Brenda said, trying to sound cheerful. "When can you come by tonight?" she asked.

"Well, how about if I pick you up and we'll go over to the Log Jam for dinner. I did win a couple of bucks last night," he said, thankful that she didn't seem upset with him any longer.

"That sounds like a winner," she said. "Come in for a drink before we go, okay?"

"Okay," he answered. "I'll see you around five thirty."

Punching on the line for George, Jeff said, "Sorry about that George. I'm afraid I had your daughter upset with me. I think I'm back in her good graces again." He paused, then, "What's on your mind today old friend?"

George was laughing, saying, "She'll have you chasing your tail before you know it. And you won't even mind, is my guess."

Then seriously, "Say Jeff, I got a call this afternoon from somebody. Claimed that young Waters was involved in something pretty bad. Said he wanted to warn me before I hired him. When I told him I was out of the business and you were the man to talk to, he just hung up! Did you hear from him?"

"As a matter of fact, I just got a call a little while ago. Did you recognize that guy's voice?"

George answered, "Nope. And he wouldn't tell me when I asked him. I can't imagine who's got it in for Red so bad that they'd do this to him. What'd the guy say to you?"

Jeff related the conversation he'd had with the anonymous caller and George said he'd never heard anything like that before either. They decided it was somebody outside the company, or they would have known that Jeff was now the new owner.

"I don't know what to make of it" George said. "It sounds like a fairy tale to me, but it'd probably be a good idea to check it out. What do you think?"

Jeff said, "Other than his job Ap, I don't have any other way of getting information like that. I was just about to read through that when you called."

"Probably somebody that thinks they know something. I never paid much mind to folks that wouldn't give me their name or sign a letter. That's probably all this is too. Let me know what you find out, if anything, will you?"

"Sure, no problem," then with a sudden idea, said, "Hey George. Brenda and I are going to the Log Jam around six or a little after. How about meeting us there?"

George hesitated and said, "Oh, I don't know Jeff. I hate to intrude. You and Brenda are just really getting to know each other. I don't think she'd mind, but well .... Oh what the Hell, okay I'll stop in about six thirty, how's that?"

"Great," Jeff said. "See you then," and hanging up the phone, opened the file folder with Red Waters application in it.

There was the usual information such as date of birth, educational background, etc. Jeff was about to slide the application back in the folder when he saw a name that rang a bell. Taking back the document, he started reading the descriptions under the title 'Previous Work Experience.'

It showed a couple of minor jobs that Red held during high school, gas station attendant, janitorial work and a month or so with the local saw mill. But, another position, held for several months, was as a 'grounds keeper and general handy work' for Decker Funeral Home.

"Why in the world was he going way down there to mow grass for Forest Decker?" Jeff wondered. "A minor job like that would hardly cover his gas cost for driving back and forth. He decided he'd better have a little talk with Red on Monday morning. After his discussions with Sheriff Beck earlier in the day, Jeff was uneasy with this latest bit of information concerning the Decker Funeral Home.

27

"**W**haaat?" Brenda exclaimed. "We're going to meet my dad at the Log Jam? How in the world did that happen? I thought we were going to have a nice intimate dinner together and you've invited my dad to join us? I don't believe you!" she finished.

Jeff couldn't understand why Brenda was so upset. He said, "Brenda, honey. Please. I didn't think it would upset you this much."

He started to laugh and couldn't stop, even when Brenda, glaring at him said, "What's so funny? Am I a big joke to you or something?"

Jeff, still laughing, said, "I really don't think of the Log Jam as a place for, what did you call it, 'an intimate dinner'. We'd have more privacy in the middle of Times Square, than we'd have there!"

Brenda said, "Oh, you've been in the middle of Times Square have you?" Then trying not to, she started to smile. Then, "Oh all right," she conceded. "But some day you're going to have to prove that to me."

Now Jeff didn't understand. "What do you mean, prove what to you?"

"That we'd have more privacy in Times Square silly. Have you really been there?"

"Oh, I see," he said. "And yes, as a matter fact I have been there. Dwight and I took a weekend after basic and went to see the Big Apple. I don't care to go back. A city that size is pretty overwhelming to a small town boy like me." Then, "If you're all cooled down now, maybe we could have that drink you promised me."

They were walking back to the Big Room and Brenda turned to him and said "Oh sure. And Jeff, I'm so sorry I was so short with you this afternoon. I was so worried when nobody knew where you were. That's all. And I know it's really none of my business what you do or where you go, but I ....."

Jeff stopped her by putting a finger softly on her mouth, saying, "It's okay. It's okay. I've been on my own for so long that I didn't think that anyone would be worried about me."

Giving her a soft kiss he said, "I guess that's something I'm going to have to get used to too. Actually," he smiled. "Its kind of nice knowing there's somebody worrying about me. It's a new experience for me."

Jeff fixed their drinks and as he handed a glass of wine to Brenda she said "What's with dad meeting us for dinner anyway? And before you answer, it's okay. I was just so surprised when you told me that I overreacted."

Jeff told her about the phone calls that they had received, concerning Red Waters. He didn't mention the connection with the Decker Funeral Home. He explained that it was just a spur of the moment thing, asking George to dinner, while they were talking about the phone calls.

"You don't suppose there's anything to what that guy said do you," Brenda asked? "Why would someone do that? Do you think it's just because he's an Indian? There's a lot of folks in this area that just don't like Indians you know."

"I don't know," Jeff replied. "I've always known there's a pretty large Indian population in this area, Chippewas I think. But I've talked to a lot of folks recently about Red and without exception, everyone has had good things to say about him. I can't imagine who'd have it in for him."

It was about six fifteen when Jeff and Brenda entered the Log Jam. George was sitting in a back booth and waved at them when they walked in. Brenda stopped and gave him a kiss on the cheek, and then she and Jeff slid in across from him. George had a glass of beer in front of him and a small dish of peanuts.

"I didn't expect you for another ten or fifteen minutes," George grinned. "I thought I'd have a chance for another glass of beer before you got here."

Without thinking, Jeff said, "Well go ahead, but I'm developing a taste for Famous Grouse and that's what I plan on having."

Both Brenda and George looked at him in surprise, but before Brenda could say anything, George raised his hand and called the waitress to the table. When she stepped up he said, "Barbara, take this beer back and pour it down the sink. I think we're going to have a real drink. What'll you have Brenda, a glass of wine?"

Scowling at the two men, she responded, "Heck no. If I'm going to sit here with a couple of drunks, then I'm drinking whatever you're drinking! Scotch on the rocks please," she said to the waitress.

"Well blow me down," George exclaimed, looking at his daughter in surprise. Jeff was staring at her too.

"Oh don't act so shocked you two. I've been nipping at your bottle for a long time dad. Just once in a while though. So don't worry, it's okay" she laughed at the expressions on the two men.

Jeff didn't know what to say to this. But George said, "I guess it's true what they say, you do learn something new everyday." Then they were all laughing at once.

While waiting for the drinks, George asked, "You find anything in Red's application that changes your mind about him?"

"No, nothing of any consequence." Jeff replied. "But, on the other hand, if I were a murderer, I doubt I'd put that on a resume."

Later, after they had eaten a light dinner, George suddenly waved at a couple of older gentlemen across the bar. "There's Curly and Moe. Looks like they're looking for a rummy game. I think they're waiting for me."

Before Jeff could say anything, George said, "Don't ask. There's another old codger that's Larry, and that isn't me!"

As he got up to leave the table, he scooped up the tab saying, "You can leave the tip. I'll take care of this."

Jeff said, "Come on George, I asked you to dinner, not the other way around."

George said, "I know that. And I'm glad you did. And I've really enjoyed myself tonight. Thank you for inviting me. Now, I'm going over and sit with Curly and Moe" he paused then said, "and there's Larry now. You two go on and I'll see you in a day or so." With that, George turned and walked to the end of the bar where the cash register was.

Later, Jeff was sitting on the floor in front of the television in the Big Room at Brenda's. He was sorting through the DVDs in the cabinet below. He had found a couple that he hadn't seen before and had set them aside. He was just getting to his feet, when Brenda stepped into the room.

Jeff thought that his heart had stopped beating altogether. Brenda stood there in a very slinky, very 'see through', negligee! She saw the DVDs in his hand and said in a soft, husky voice "Do you really want to spend the rest of the evening watching old movies?"

With that she turned and casually walked out of the room. Later, Jeff couldn't remember if he laid the DVDs on the coffee table or just dropped them on the floor. What he did remember, was following that tantalizing negligee, that very 'see through' negligee, down a hallway and into a softly lit, bedroom.

28

Jeff was at his desk early. He was marveling at how soon he had settled into the idea of actually owning his own business. So far, there hadn't been any glitches that had spoiled the experience. Around eleven, he took another call from George.

"I forgot to tell you last night," he said. "I bought a new car a couple of days ago. Would you send someone out here to pick up my old one? It's titled to the company, so legally, that makes it yours."

Jeff said, "George, I told you before, we don't need a company car. We'll probably just send it over to the county car auction." Then with a smile, "After we hose it down of course. Any potential buyer should at least know what color it is."

"Ha, Ha. Very funny," George said. "But I'll have you know I've had it completely detailed. Cost me a hundred bucks, but that was still cheaper than sending it through a fifteen dollar car wash every week."

He continued, "And I wish you'd reconsider selling it. I think you should hang onto it for a little while anyway."

Then, "Why don't you give it to young Noonan? He doesn't have a very good car does he?"

Jeff said, "You know, that's not a bad idea. I might just do that." He paused for a moment, then, "George, how come I never knew that Les was Helen's nephew?"

"Hmmmm," George said thoughtfully. "I guess when I hired him I didn't think it was important enough to share with my Executive Vice President." Then he laughed. "Actually, I liked the young man and I'm glad you've moved him up. That was a very good move."

"Okay George" Jeff conceded. "Les gets the car. I'll have someone bring him out this morning to pick it up." After a pause, "So, what did you get this time? Another CTS?"

"Heck no. I'm planning on driving to Florida next month and I wanted something that could hold all my stuff! I got me an Escalade! Great big mother too. You'd love it." Finally, "I've gotta go. Send Les out anytime. Tell him the keys are under the floor mat. Okay."

As Jeff walked to Les Noonan's office he was laughing to himself. Old George in an Escalade! Those things were huge. George was no more than five nine in his stocking feet. How the heck much 'stuff' did he plan on taking with him when he went to Florida?

As usual, Les was tapping away on a keyboard with his eyes on the computer screen. He looked up as Jeff came in and sat down across the desk from him. He said, "Hi Jeff. I was just going to come over to see you for a minute. I've run across something here that I don't quite understand."

Jeff said with a smile, "Oh. What's that? Somebody running off with the payroll or something?"

Laughing, Les said, "Oh no, nothing like that. It's just

that in our asset holdings, I've run across a couple of things that I don't believe are on hand anymore. We've probably sold them, but I can't find where we received any money for them."

"Okay, what's missing?" Jeff asked.

"Well, there's a couple of lathes and a computer operated drill press that I can't account for. They were replaced, but I can't find what happened to them. It doesn't appear that we turned them in on the new ones."

Jeff said, "We've still got them. There's a big equipment auction down in St. Paul in a couple of months and we're going to send them down there, then and see if we can get something for them. Is that it, anything else?"

Les made a couple of notes on a pad, and then looking up he said, "That'll take care of that, but the other thing is, it looks like we bought a Cadillac a couple years ago for George. Was that part of the deal when you bought him out, that he could keep the Cadillac?"

"Actually," Jeff said. "I didn't know anything about that until just a few days ago. And no, it wasn't part of the deal. As it happens, I was just talking with George about that very thing. It turns out he wants us to come and get it, so I thought maybe you could have your Aunt Helen run you out there and pick it up during the lunch hour."

Les was startled at the mention of Mrs. Parsons as his 'Aunt Helen' and he didn't answer for a second or so. "Well, I guess," he stammered. "I guess I could do that, but I ..."

"No buts! Go get it. And if that tightwad hasn't filled it up with gas for you, stop and fill it up on your way back. And you better check and see if it needs an oil change too. George sometimes would let things like that slide too."

Les replied, "Okay, where do you want me to put it when I get back here? Are you going to take it? It's carried on the books as a 'company car.'"

Jeff said, very patiently, "Lester, I want you to drive it back here where you will continue your day and when the day is through, you will take it home, where you will pick up 'Short Round' and bring her back here to pick up 'Her' car, then you will drive 'Your' company car home and park it in 'Your' garage. Is that all clear?"

Les was grinning from ear to ear, "Yes sir," he said excitedly. "I sure do appreciate this Jeff. We were talking just the other day about getting a second car for Myra." Then grinning, 'For 'Short Round'. Now we won't have to do that. Thank you sir. This will sure mean a lot to us."

Laughing Jeff returned to his office, stopping at Mrs. Parson's desk as he went by to say, "Your nephew has a favor to ask you during your lunch hour. I told him you'd be glad to help him out." She looked up, and opening her mouth to speak, but no sound came out. Jeff laughed and went into his office.

He started sorting through the mail that was on his desk, mostly correspondence from vendors and invoices that required his signature approval. There was a plain envelope there too. Jeff wondered why Mrs. Parson hadn't opened it as she did most of the daily mail. Then he noticed the caption PERSONAL marked on the address. The address appeared to be a childish scrawl, written in pencil. The envelope was postmarked from St. Paul.

Curious, Jeff opened the envelope and pulled out a single sheet of plain typewriter paper. Spreading it out on his desk, he saw that the note was written in pencil with the same childish scrawl as the address.

remember you been warnd
that indion wil kauz a lot
of trubl for you. he is a
killer. I no cuz I seen him
do it.
a frend

Jeff read the note several times. Who could be trying to destroy this young man? And more importantly, WHY? This couldn't possibly be true. Or could it. He pulled the file forward containing Red's job ap. Again, he read through it and again, he was troubled by the connection with the Decker Funeral Home.

Should he call the Sheriff and let him handle it? Maybe he should just forget all about it. He sat for some time considering the alternatives. Finally, he decided he wouldn't do anything for the time being. He would think about it over the weekend and make a decision on Monday about what to do, if anything.

29

Like Jeff, the Sheriff was at his desk early. He had called in three deputies and a senior lieutenant, William (Wild Bill) Reynolds for an 'in office' conference. All three deputies were normally sent out on road patrol and their shift was just starting. They had assigned patrol cars and generally started their day as soon as they left their home. Today they had been pulled in just as they got started. 'Wild Bill' stepped up to the Sheriff's door and said, "They're all here Sheriff. They're waiting in the conference room."

Beck looked up and said, "Okay Bill, have someone send in a pot of coffee and cups will you? And make sure they've got note pads and pencils, too, please. I'll be along in just a minute."

He gathered up the files with the photos as well as Doc's lab book. He also stuck, what he had come to call Doc's 'lab papers' that Stony had given him at the funeral home, into the file as well. Like the lab book, the papers were filled with Doc's undecipherable handwritten notes.

In the conference room, the deputies were quietly

drinking their coffee and wondering what this was all about. They didn't rise from their chairs when the Sheriff walked in as he took his seat at the head of the conference table. He looked at each in turn and finally started to speak.

"What I'm about discuss with you this morning is strictly confidential. If any of you discuss this matter, in any manner, that is not pertinent to the assignments you are about to be given," Beck looked at every person at the table, "I'll have your badge and in addition, I'll have you locked up for interfering with a criminal investigation!" Then, "Now, if any of you think that you can't handle that, tell me now."

He sat waiting for a full minute. The deputies were uncomfortable under the Sheriff's probing glare. Finally, Lieutenant Reynolds said, "Tommy, I think these fellows understand. I know I sure as Hell do. We've seen that jail remember!"

With that the tension in the room was broken as the deputies laughed uneasily.

So the Sheriff began to speak. He covered all the details that he had come up with in the last few days. He told them about Jeff Lawson and the discovery that he had made looking at the photos. The photographs were spread out over the table as the deputies fingered through them.

He also confided the speculation that Lawson had made concerning Mrs. Lydia Gunderson and the remains shown in the photographs. He told of the missing notebook that had disappeared from Doc's pocket after he was found in his car at Walgreen's. Everything. He passed on everything he knew and everything he suspected.

Beck assigned one deputy to take a run over to

Waushawa and talk with the funeral home director that Decker had alluded to in his conversation before arrangements were made for Doc's funeral. He instructed him to get all the information he could about their dealings with Decker.

"Tell him if we have to, we'll get a warrant to seize his business records. I don't want to have to do that if we don't have to," Beck said. "And another thing, warn him against discussing your visit with anybody! We've got to be sure we've got something before this gets out. It could be very damaging to Decker if I'm wrong about this!"

"Also," the Sheriff continued grimly "Try and get some idea of the costs involved in a cremation. Find out everything you can about the process too. Get over there today and get back to me in the morning."

At this the deputy said, "Sheriff, if I get the information today, and I can get back here before you leave, could I talk with you then. Tomorrow's my day off."

Beck thought about that for a few seconds, then, "Okay, but I want a detailed written report on everything you get. And I want it by tomorrow morning. You're authorized overtime to be sure that gets done. I suggest you take a tape recorder with you, so you won't forget any details. We'll get somebody around here to transcribe them for you, but that probably won't get done till Monday."

The Sheriff turned to the other two deputies and said, "I want you two to get over to the library and go through all the local newspapers going back a couple of years. I want obituaries and names of all the funerals handled by Mr. Decker." He continued "And as I just said. Do it quickly, but be thorough. If you can determine if there were cremations, even better. Get it done today. Put everything together and get it to me today if possible, tomorrow morning for sure."

"You guys get going. Any problems call me. I'll be available all day, unless of course something else comes up. Irma knows how to get in touch with me. Do you have any questions?" He looked at the three deputies shaking their heads and then said, "Okay, get out of here."

Turning to the Lieutenant, he said, "Okay Bill, what do you think you could dig up on Decker? What kind of background can we run on him so he wouldn't know it's being done?"

The young Lieutenant took a sip of his coffee, made a face when he realized it had grown cold, and then, placing the cup on the table, said, "Well, I'll tell you Sheriff. Give me the rest of the day and I think I can give you a pretty complete background on our man. The Internet has a river of information on just about anything, or anybody you ever heard of. If I can get his social security number, I'll trace his life back to when he was still wearing diapers."

The Sheriff smiled and said, "Good, good. Get right on it then." As 'Wild Bill' got up to leave, Beck said, "And Bill, why don't you get a fresh cup of coffee. I think yours has grown cold!"

Laughing, Bill hurried out of the room. Beck sat back and thought, "I'm gonna get you, you son of bitch. I'm gonna get you. And when I do ..." He got up without finishing the thought, and gathering up the scattered files, returned to his office.

30

"**I** think we should probably watch a movie tonight, don't you?" Brenda said softly. Jeff was lying on his back looking up at the white canopy over her bed.

He turned and kissing her gently said, "That might be a good idea, but later on maybe. You're never going to believe this, but I'm hungry!"

Sitting up suddenly, the sheet that had covered her slipping down to her waist, she said "Hungry!" Then with a twinkle in her eyes she said, "Well, I guess I can understand that. After all the calories we've burned up in the last hour or so, I think I'm hungry too."

Looking at her sitting there like that he said "Well, looking at you right now, maybe I could wait a little while before...." At that Brenda swung her legs over the edge of the bed and ran toward the bathroom.

"Oh no you don't" she called back to him. "You're hungry, remember? I'll just jump in the shower and when I'm done, you can use it. I'll find something for us to eat while you're in here." Jeff sat there keeping the vision of her hurrying away alive in his mind. Soon he heard the shower running and he swung around and got out of bed.

He looked around the room and saw picture frames on a chest of drawers. Looking at them he saw a very young George and Lydia smiling at the camera. Beside that was another picture of them standing behind a table with a large cake on it. The numbers 'twenty five' were visible on the top of the cake. And there was a picture of Bill in his National Guard uniform and Brenda on their wedding day. She had been a beautiful bride Jeff thought. There were other pictures too. He stood admiring them for some time. He was thinking what being a part of a family like that must have been like.

He suddenly realized that the shower had stopped and turning found Brenda standing at the bathroom door looking at him. She had on a neat housecoat and Jeff seeing this, realized he was standing there stark naked. She was looking very directly at him when she said softly "You have a beautiful body." With that she walked quickly out of the room.

After leaving the shower and toweling dry, Jeff found his clothes hanging neatly over a bedside chair. Dressing quickly, he hurried to the kitchen where, much to his surprise, he found Brenda, completely dressed and busily chopping vegetables beside the stove. Looking up, she said, "How do you feel about an omelet? I'm sorry, but I don't have much of anything else on hand."

Jeff said, "An omelet will be fine. Do you need any help?"

"Sure, you can set the table and make some toast. How many eggs do you want in your omelet? Two or three?

"Three please," he replied. "Do you want a drink before you start cooking? I'll go fix them if you do."

"Nope," she said. "If you look in the fridge you'll see a bottle of champagne. I've had it for ages and I'd like to get rid of it. Look around in the cupboard and you should find a couple of champagne glasses. You can set those out when you set the table."

"Whooaa!" he exclaimed, "Champagne? We should save that for a really special occasion, don't you think?"

Brenda looked thoughtfully at Jeff and said, "Tonight *is* a special occasion my darling. I've decided that what I've been feeling for you is much more than lust. I think I've fallen in love with you!"

Then blushing slightly, "It hasn't happened to me for a long, long time and I think what I'm feeling lately is pretty special. So I'd like champagne tonight, okay?"

Jeff stepped across the kitchen and embraced her. She dropped a knife on the floor with a clang that made them both jump. Then laughing, they embraced again, Jeff saying, "I don't know what to say. But I think I've felt the same way about you for some time. I only know, I've never felt this way about anybody, or anything in my life."

Giving her a kiss, he stepped back and said, "Okay, Champagne it is!"

The next morning, it was becoming obvious that the weather was definitely starting to change. Jeff had been planning to play golf with a couple of friends, but both called and canceled because of the weather. He had hoped to get one more round in before the season would end, but it was overcast and getting colder. Temperatures had dropped well down into the low forties and the sky was leaden gray overcast. It looked like it was going to be one of those dreary late fall days.

It had been late when he came in the night before. Jeff had wanted to spend the night with her, but she would have none of it. After their dinner of omelets and champagne, they sat closely together on the big couch watching a Tom Hanks movie about a young impersonator who passed himself off as an airline pilot.

Afterwards, the two sat and talked softly together for hours. Brenda had again turned on the stereo system and when they weren't talking, they just sat quietly and let the soft music envelope them.

He spent the day dividing his time between televised football games and working on his computer. He was deeply troubled with the situation that seemed to be developing with Red Waters and in addition to that, he wasn't sure he'd done the right thing by confiding with the Sheriff about Brenda's mother. It was growing dark when the phone rang. Answering on the second ring, he was happy to hear Brenda's voice on the line.

"Hi," she said. "What's going on out there? You didn't play golf in this weather did you?"

"No, I didn't. It's just too cold. I've got the furnace running out here. How about you? Got a log in the old fireplace?"

"Nope, just sitting here thinking of you. How about if I come pick you up and we'll go get a burger at the 'Jam'?"

"Sounds like a winner to me. You sure you want to drive? I'd be happy to come and get you."

"No, I just got back from the grocery store and my car's all warmed up. I'll be there in ten minutes." The line went dead as she hung up.

When they entered the Log Jam, they saw George sitting at a table near the back of the room with 'Larry, Curly and Moe'. They were engrossed in a game of cards when Brenda walked up and gave her dad a kiss on the cheek. She said, "It looks like you guys are spending a lot of time in a bar these days. I'm not sure I approve."

George looked up with a smile "I'd have them at the house, except if we play here" he said, waving his hand at the bar area, "There's somebody here to wait on us, I don't have to buy the beer and I don't have to clean up after these birds when we're done."

Jeff and Brenda sat in a side booth and ate their sandwiches, Jeff a BLT, Brenda a chicken salad. Brenda said, "He's been coming here pretty regularly lately" nodding her head towards her dad. "I'm glad he's found somebody to spend his time with. Those other three are all widowers too. They all seem pretty good for each other."

Jeff smiled and said, "Maybe that's why he bought such a big car. He might be planning on taking them to Florida with him next month."

"Big car!" Brenda asked. "What big car? Did he buy another car? I didn't know anything about that."

Jeff told her about the new Cadillac Escalade and the suggestion George had made concerning the disposition of the CTS. Laughing, he told her what George had said about how he needed such a big car for his 'stuff'. Brenda looked across the room at George and she began to laugh.

"I'll be surprised if he actually takes that trip he's been talking about. He started out for Chicago a couple of years ago and he got about half way there and turned around and came back! Mom was with him then and she said he couldn't handle driving in traffic."

"I remember that" Jeff said. "They were going down to a retailers expo at McCormick Place. I was surprised when he turned up at the office the next day. He told me the reason he came back was because your mom's leg started bothering her and she was getting pretty uncomfortable with all that riding."

Unbidden, the picture of Lydia sitting in that wheel chair and the photos of the bones, flashed into Jeff's mind. "There just couldn't be a connection between the two," he thought, but the coincidence was just too overwhelming to ignore. He was looking at George across the bar laughing with his three friends and he couldn't imagine the emotional turmoil this revelation, if true, would cause. Not only with George, but Brenda too. The family album, the pictures on her bureau and the happiness that these family pictures represented, went through his mind.

"What's wrong? Why are you looking like that?" Brenda was touching his hand and looking at him with concerned eyes. "You looked so sad and," she paused. "Well, kind of scared too! What're you thinking about?"

Jolting his thoughts back to the present, "What, what did you say? Oh," he stumbled. "I don't know what I was thinking about. Just wool gathering I guess." He finished lamely.

Brenda wasn't convinced, but she didn't question him further. She was sliding out of the seat saying, "Well you sure had a funny look on your face." Then, with a smile, "Come on. Go pay for this incredibly 'intimate dinner' and I'll take you home."

As she turned in the driveway to Jeff's cabin, they were surprised to see a pick up truck parked in front of the garage. Jeff said, "That's Dwight's truck. I wonder what he's up to." Turning to Brenda, he said, "Come on in, Donna's probably with him."

Walking toward the cabin, Brenda exclaimed, "You didn't lock your doors again? What's wrong with you? Anybody could just walk in any time."

As Jeff opened the door, he answered, "Well that sure is the truth. Look at these burglars, excuse me, I should have said 'Bunglers.'"

Dwight and Donna were sitting on the oversized couch watching television. Dwight had a drink in his hand and Donna was just placing a beer can on an end table. She looked up with a guilty expression on her face as Jeff and Brenda entered.

"This was all Dwight's idea," she said quickly. "He said he needed a drink and you had the only good scotch in town."

Dwight gave a listless wave of his hand, saying, "Oh sure, blame it all on me. The only reason you came in the first place was to see if we could catch these two in bed!"

Jeff laughed as Donna fumed, "That's not true Jeff. I wouldn't ever...."

"Oh never mind," Jeff said. "How'd you find my scotch? I thought I had it hidden and out of sight."

"Out of sight my aunt Nellie," Dwight replied. "It was sitting right there on the kitchen counter. I did have a helluva time trying to find a clean glass though."

Brenda stood gaping at this exchange and finally found her voice and said, "My gosh, did you two just walk in? I told Jeff he should keep his door locked. He's so darn trusting."

Dwight guffawed at this, saying, "Out in this neck of the woods, nobody bothers to lock their doors. What are you saying Brenda? You don't think we should come over and enjoy the comforts of my friend's hospitality?"

"No, No. I don't mean that at all. I just ...." red-faced she stumbled on. "It's just that....well you know ..... with all those murders and all ...."

"Oh dear, you're right, I didn't even think about that," Donna said. "We're just so used to walking right in that ...." she didn't finish.

Jeff said, "Now, now Donna. You know you're always welcome here. But next time, leave the old man at home will you? How'd you get away from the 'crumb crunchers' anyway? You get a baby sitter?"

Dwight answered, "As a matter of fact we did. We had dinner down at Duffy's at the county seat tonight. And we were on our way home, and realizing that it was still early, we decided we should stop and see my old army buddy."

"I see," Jeff said. "But I only see one drink there. Where's ours? We both drink that stuff too you know."

Dwight jumped up from the couch, gave a smart bow and proceeded over to the kitchen area. Getting ice from the fridge he was about to pour a second drink, when he looked up at Brenda and said, "Did I miss something. Is he serious? I thought you didn't indulge in the higher octane spirits."

Jeff said, "Yes, she's decided if she's going to be around the likes of you and your young bride, that alcohol will be necessary to tolerate this friendship. And bring Donna another beer too while you're at it."

Dwight brought the drinks and then went back to sit beside his wife. Jeff and Brenda were sitting cozily side by side in an oversized love seat. After taking a sip of his drink, Jeff said, "Ah yes. You do mix a good drink for a naive young farm lad." He took another swallow and asked, "What were you doing down at the county seat anyway? I didn't think there'd be anyone there on a Saturday."

Dwight and Donna were grinning conspiratorially at each other as Dwight answered, "Well, actually there isn't, but the Registrar of Deeds is an old friend of mine. I couldn't get down there yesterday, so I'd called and asked if he and his wife would meet us for dinner. I asked him to bring some stuff with him."

He was fumbling with a large envelope that lay beside them on the couch, finally pulling out a sheaf of papers and reaching across to hand them to Jeff.

He said, "I thought it would be kind of fun to give you the deed and the mortgage agreement marked 'Paid In Full' in person, rather than just sending it to you in the mail."

With a grin, "That just seemed so inappropriate somehow."

Jeff was stunned! "Whaaat! I didn't have any idea I was this close to paying off my mortgage! I've just had the bank make the monthly payments out of my account!" He turned and saw Brenda smiling and looking at the Sutherlands.

Dwight said, "What you've obviously forgotten about old buddy, is that nice bonus George gave you a couple of years ago and how you used it to pay down a big chunk of the principle."

Jeff was looking at Brenda and suddenly realized what was going on, "You knew about this! You're part of this insidious scheme! Now I know why," he paused." ..... ya know, I wondered why you folks had just walked in like that. Not that I mind, but I swear I had locked that door when I left."

"You did," Dwight said. "But as usual, you forgot all about the sliding door in back. Matter of fact, I was pretty put out to think you didn't trust your neighbors any more than that."

Jeff stood up and said, "Well, whatdaya know. I actually own something! I think we'd better have several more drinks to celebrate." Stopping for a moment, he had a sudden thought, "I know!" he said excitedly, "I'll have a mortgage burning party! Next weekend. Saturday night. Maybe I'll even have it catered."

"Whooaa there cowboy" Dwight said. "You know better than that. If you have food, Donna and Brenda will handle that. You can supply the booze, but no caterers. Right ladies?"

"That's right" Donna said looking at Brenda who was nodding in agreement "We'll handle everything. You just decide who you want to come and we'll take care of the rest."

Much later, after several more drinks and excited conversation, the Sutherlands were leaving when Dwight said "I'm fraid we're goinna havta spen tha night here ole buddy." He slurred.

"Oh and why is that ole fren" Jeff replied.

"There's a strange car sittin there behin my truck an I doan think I can get aroun it!

Jeff said, "I'll get it moved, but are you okay to drive? I wouldn't want you to get picked up for drinking, driving. I mean driving, drink, driving drunk," he finally finished.

He heard Brenda say, "The keys are in it Jeff. Would you move it for me please?"

"We'll be okay," Dwight said. "We'll take it easy. Might even take the shortcut through the back pasture and stop and do a little neckin on the way." This last while leering drunkenly at Donna.

Jeff laughed at this and followed them out to the driveway.

When he returned, Brenda was just coming in from the hallway. He heard the toilet refilling down the hall and laughed out loud. Brenda looked at him blearily and asked, "What's so funny?"

"Donna," he replied. "I'll bet she drank six or eight cans of beer tonight and she never went down the hall once!" For some reason Jeff found this hilarious and couldn't stop laughing. "And you only had a few little glasses of 'high octane' as Dwight called it and that's the first time you had to go!"

Brenda said very seriously, "Well, when ya gotta go, ya gotta go!" Then, "Come on lover. We'll clean this up in the morning."

With that she lay down on the couch and was instantly asleep. Jeff stood looking down at her for a moment and finally, picked her up and stumbling down the hall, carried her back to the bedroom. Pulling off her shoes he laid her in the bed and pulled the covers over her.

Then he went back to the main room and lay down on the couch and was immediately asleep.

31

Sheriff Beck spent most of the day behind the closed door of his office. He was going over the reports that his deputies had come up with the day before. He hadn't heard anything from 'Wild Bill' Reynolds yet, but he had seen him in his office talking on the phone when he walked by. Glancing up, Reynolds gave an absent minded wave and returned to his conversation.

The newspapers had come up with twenty-two obituaries in the last three years. Beck thought, "That can't be all there is? That doesn't seem like very many over a three year period."

There had been twelve older women and six older gentlemen. The remaining four were all younger people that died from injuries sustained in automobile accidents. Two teenagers, girls, a forty seven year old man and his forty four year old wife.

The Sheriff sat back in his chair thinking. That man and wife, there was something about that accident that he was trying to remember. He logged on to his computer and started reviewing accidents in the county for the last year or so.

The two teenage girls had been killed when a semi tractor-trailer stopped suddenly in front of them. The girls had been driving too fast, without seat belts and couldn't stop before crashing into the trailer. They had both been dead at the scene.

The middle-aged couple died when they lost control of their car on an icy stretch of county road and went off the road, crashing into a tree. The man had been thrown forward into the windshield and was dead at the scene. The woman had lived in a coma for over a week but died from internal injuries.

There was nothing in the Sheriff's records or the newspapers that indicated if any of these victims had been cremated. But one fact had shown through in all cases.... All the victims were eventually taken to the Decker Funeral Home.

Beck had the small recorder on his desk that the deputy had taken with him to interview one Joe Davidson, director of the Memorial Gardens Funeral Home in Waushawa. He had been surprisingly cooperative and had answered all the deputy's questions without hesitation. It was apparent to Beck, that this guy didn't like Forest Decker one little bit! It seemed that a couple of years earlier, Decker had run up unusually large charges and had leaned on professional courtesy to delay making any apparent effort to pay.

The situation had gotten so bad that Davidson threatened to refuse acceptance of any further bodies for cremation until his account was paid up. After several months of 'dribs and drabs' of payments, he had finally brought his account current. And it had remained pretty much up to date since. Davidson commented, that there had been a four or five month period a year or so ago, that he had not received any requests whatsoever from Decker. Davidson assumed that he had transported any remains to a crematory in the twin cities during that period.

The Sheriff stopped the tape. He was nearly in a state of shock when he realized what the implications of this information meant. Forest Decker had not had those bodies cremated in the twin cities or anywhere else! He had merely taken them out in the woods and dumped them! He had made an effort to get them as far off the nearest county road as he could.

The fire trail that Jeff Lawson had driven down was ideal for just such an unholy activity. With the wildlife in the area, it was unlikely that any of the remains would ever be found. It was a miracle that they had been able to recover as much of them as they did!

Now Beck realized that Jeff Lawson's suspicions were apparently right on the money. He'd bet a month's pay that the remains that Jeff had found would turn out to be those of Lydia Gunderson! And then he thought of something else. The younger man with the terrible skull trauma that Stony had told him about. Beck was now convinced that he was the accident victim whose obituary he had just read. Looking at the accident report, he read again, how 'the man had been thrown against the windshield' and was dead at the scene. He'd find out for sure when he was able to probe Decker's files, but Beck was sure he would learn that this victim was supposed to have been cremated too.

Beck was filled with disgust at the pictures flashing through his mind at that moment. Those bodies had literally just been 'thrown away' with the full expectation that the wild foragers of the forest would destroy any evidence of their ever having been there!

"I wonder what those ashes were in the funeral urns," Beck thought.

Lieutenant Reynolds knocked on his door and Beck motioned for him to come in. Reynolds came in and was waved into a chair across the desk from the Sheriff. He had a yellow legal pad with several pages of handwritten notes.

Beck said "Well, Bill. What have you come up with so far? I saw you on the phone when I came in. Was that anything to do with this?" Indicating the 'Bones' files on his desk.

"Yes sir, it was." Reynolds replied. "It's the only thing I've been working on since our meeting yesterday morning."

He was sorting through several pages of his notes when he looked up at the Sheriff with a confident look.

"I think I can tell you anything that you want to know about Mr. Decker, including the fact that he's apparently gay!"

"Well, I'll be!" The Sheriff said as he gaped at Reynolds. "I thought a lot of things about that bird, but that sure as Hell wasn't anything I even suspected! He doesn't act it or anything that would make you think it. He acts more like a frustrated athlete with all his body building and running, and all." Beck was shaking his head in disbelief.

"That was one of the interesting things that I found out," Reynolds said. "It appears that he didn't get into this physical fitness thing until he was eighteen or so. What happened was, he made an unwelcome proposal to another young man, who reacted by beating him to a pulp.

Not only that, when this kid told a bunch of his friends, they got a hold of him one night and after half beating him to death, stripped him naked and tied him to a telephone pole and just left him there."

"He was there overnight before he was discovered and to make matters worse, there was a foot of snow on the ground!"

"My God," the Sheriff exclaimed. "Did they catch the guys that did this to him?"

"No sir, they didn't. Decker wouldn't file charges so the whole thing was dropped."

Reynolds continued. "Everyone thought they knew who the hoodlums were, but nothing was ever done about it. The really interesting thing is, that was when Decker started this body building thing and a few years later, all five of the suspects in the case had died under suspicious circumstances."

"Great Scott!" the Sheriff said, "Are you saying that those guys might have been murdered by Decker? Was he ever accused of that?"

"No sir, no connection was ever made. By the time those guys started dying off, Decker had been out of the state for a long time. That was about the time he had entered into Mortuary Science studies out in Pennsylvania somewhere."

Reynolds continued, "Another thing I discovered," Reynolds continued. "Before he went to this Mortuary School, he had been in his third year of med school and was asked to leave. Seems he was doing some unauthorized research with certain non prescription drugs!"

"What do you mean?" the Sheriff asked. "He was

a drug user? A dedicated body builder like him? That doesn't sound like what someone like him would be doing to himself."

"No sir, he wasn't a user. It was like I said. He was trying to come up with some kind of legal euthanasia substance." Reynolds referred to his notes and continued, "He apparently was, I should say, is, really quite a brilliant fellow. Almost a genius one of his cohorts told me."

"Euthanasia?" The Sheriff exclaimed. "Why would he be fooling around with something like that? There's already a ton of medications out there that can be used to quietly let a person die! It's done all the time!"

"I don't know about that sir, but he apparently had come up with some kind of powder, made from castor beans of all things, that would kill instantly! He was caught killing research animals with this stuff."

The Sheriff leaned back in his chair and to cover his confusion, turned to the small fridge and pulled out a Coke.

Turning he held it up to Reynolds, who said "Sure, I'm driern a bone. I think the heat's come on and it's drying out the air or something."

Beck picked another can from the fridge, pulling the tab he turned back to face Reynolds. "Did you find out what this powder was? Was it just castor beans ground up or something?"

Reynolds shook his head, taking a swallow of coke he said, "Nope, nobody could find out what it was. They just knew that castor beans were somehow involved. And," he paused, taking another swallow, "they couldn't find any of his notes on his, so called, 'experiments.' When he wouldn't turn them over, or tell them what was involved, they booted his ass out of school!"

"So," the Sheriff said. "What it appears we've got, not only involves the remains found out in the woods here, but also, maybe, the willful murder of five other human beings!"

Suddenly, the Sheriff leaned forward and exclaimed, "Forget euthanasia! This bird wanted that poison he invented for only one reason. That was to kill those guys that had done that terrible thing to him so many years before. He must've had nothing but revenge on his mind for years! And he finally made his dreams come true with that powder he invented!"

Reynolds replied, "That's just about the scenario I've come up with Sheriff. There's more in his file, but this information seems to be the most important so far. I've got a few more leads to follow up, but it'll have to wait until Monday. Can't seem to get in touch with anybody because of the weekend."

"That's okay Bill," the Sheriff said thoughtfully "We're closing in on that murdering son of a bitch now. From here on out, it's just a matter of nailing his coffin shut, so to speak." Then, "Come to think of it, that's pretty ironic isn't it? We're going to close down the lid on that rotten undertaker!"

32

Jeff woke a little after eight with a dull pain behind his eyes. At first he couldn't understand why he had been sleeping on the couch. Then he remembered the night before, the drinks of celebration and Brenda seemingly passing out and his putting her in his bed.

As he sat up, he saw the mortgage papers and deed that Dwight and Donna had brought to him. He picked them up and fingered through them for a minute and finally with a smile, tossed them on an end table and walked to the kitchen.

He started the Mr. Coffee on the kitchen counter and then took eggs and bacon from the refrigerator. He was wondering how many eggs Brenda would eat, when the phone rang. He was surprised to hear Brenda's voice on the line.

"Good morning lover," she said brightly. "And how do you feel this fine morning?"

"How did you get out of here without waking me up?" Jeff exclaimed. "And when did you leave? I was just about to go wake you up and ask how many eggs you wanted. And I feel awful," he finished!

"I woke up around six," then, "Actually, I think I 'came to' rather than woke up. You were sleeping so soundly, I didn't want to disturb you. Besides, I had to get ready for church and so I just came home to change into my Sunday best," she said lightly.

"Am I going to see you today?" Jeff asked. "How about coming out for lunch or something."

"Nope, no can do," she explained. "I promised Myra Noonan that I'd go down to Edina with her today and go antiquing. We probably won't be back till later in the day. If we get back early enough, I'll call you, Okay?"

"Oh," Jeff said, disappointed. "Well have a good time then. And say hello to 'Short Round' for me."

"Short Round," Brenda exclaimed. "What's that all about?"

"Well, maybe you should ask her about that. It's kind of a pet name Les's dad came up with, for her."

"Okay love," she said. "I'll give you a call when we get back. Bye, bye." And with that, the line went dead.

Jeff spent the rest of the day between a Vikings game and his computer. After the football game ended, he slipped on a heavy jacket and walked down to his gazebo and sat looking at the lake. The day was darkening and the clouds lay gray and heavy in the sky. There were even a few snowflakes drifting down. Jeff hardly saw them. His mind was in turmoil.

No matter how hard he tried, he couldn't get the memory of those bones and the picture of Brenda's mother out of his mind. He was filled with thoughts of Brenda too. He was in love with her, he was sure of that now. And amazingly, she had said that she was in love with him too.

If his assumption about the fate of her mother turned out to be true, he didn't know how she would ever be able to accept the horror of that situation. And he was concerned what that information would do to George.

Unbidden, he was visualizing what must have happened. A body, stripped of all identification, no jewelry, no clothing, nothing! Somebody had carried that body deep into the woods and carefully hidden it by a fallen log. It might have been there forever, undiscovered and unknown, if Jeff hadn't just happened on it that day.

Then came the animals, sniffing the air and scenting the putrefying remains of that poor human being. Jeff couldn't stop the horrifying images that were racing through his mind.

"Oh God," he thought. "Why me? Oh God, I wish I hadn't gone anywhere near the forest that day. What if that really was Lydia Gunderson?" Sickened by his thoughts he finally got slowly to his feet and started back to the cabin.

As he was stumbling along, head down, he failed to see a person standing on his rear deck waiting for him. Looking up, he was surprised to see his friend Dwight standing there.

He smiled and gave a slight wave of his hand as he walked up and said, "Hi there. What brings you back to the scene of the crime? Just checking to see if there's any scotch left?"

Dwight laughed and said, "Don't worry, I've sworn off scotch or anything else for a couple of days. I think I may have overindulged just a bit last night!"

"Well that's too bad, cuz I was just about to fix myself one. I've been out here in this cold air and it's put me in the mood."

"Hmmmm," Dwight replied, "I guess if I'm careful, I could handle a taste or two. But don't tell Donna, she'll never believe it. I don't know how she does it. She's no biggern a minute and she can drink beer till it's coming out her ears, then ask for another!"

Jeff laughed at this as they entered the cabin, slipping off his coat, he hung it in a closet and then headed toward the kitchen area where Dwight was already fixing the drinks. Jeff noted that the bottle seemed to have quite a lot left in it and he didn't understand for a second, then realized that this was the bottle that he had taken to Dwight's cook out a week ago.

"What's this? You feeling guilty for drinking up all my booze last night and now you're bringing me your private stock?" Jeff was reaching for his glass as Dwight laughing picked it up and handed it to him.

"Are you kidding? Between you and that lady friend of yours, that scotch bottle was right down to the fumes by the time we left here last night." Smiling, he picked up his drink and reached out and put his hand on Jeff's shoulder and said, "That's a fine lady you've got there my friend. Donna and I really like her. Cheers," he said as he raised his glass and took a drink.

They sat on stools at the counter and sipped at their drinks. Jeff finally said, "How does it happen you are out here on your own tonight. Where's your better half anyway?"

"Aw, she's off to some kind of ladies church meeting," Dwight said. "After watching the Vikes get beat today, I felt like getting out of the house for a while, so I called Debbie to come over and watch the kids for a couple of hours."

"Have you had anything to eat? I was just going to fix myself a sandwich. Do you want one?"

"Sure, that sounds okay. I can always eat" Dwight answered.

Jeff pulled a small canned ham from the refrigerator. He had it out of the tin and was slicing thin slabs for their sandwiches. He fussed over them for a few minutes and finally putting some potato chips on each plate, sat them on the counter in front of Dwight and started around the counter to sit down.

Dwight pointed at the refrigerator and said, "Grab some mustard before you sit down will you please."

As Jeff placed the mustard beside the plates, Dwight said, "These look good. You're going to make some lucky girl a good husband some day."

"Yeah, yeah. Let's not go there shall we," Jeff said. Then, "You know Dwight, I've been a bachelor for a long time now. I'm crazy about Brenda and I think we'd be great together. But we've both been alone for a long time. I guess I'm getting a little scared of where this is going. What do you think?"

"What do I think?" Dwight said as he took a bite of his sandwich. "What do I think, well I'll tell you what I think. I think you'd be nuts if you let this one get away. She's beautiful, she's rich and it's pretty obvious that she's in love with you, you big dummy!"

Before Jeff could respond, Dwight asked, "You got any beer left. This is good scotch but I hate to use this just to wash down this dried out sandwich!"

"Hell no there isn't any beer left. That's the only way I was finally able to get rid of you last night, was to tell Donna that we were out of beer." Laughing Jeff said, "And that reminds me. Doesn't your bride ever have the need to use the ladies room? If I drank that much beer I'd be running every ten minutes! And she never had to go once."

"Yeah, ain't she somethin?" Dwight said? But you weren't with us when we got home. Man, it sounded like Niagara Falls in there!"

Popping a potato chip in his mouth he said "So what's the big deal about you being a bachelor for a few years? You think that makes any difference to Brenda?"

"No, probably not," Jeff replied. "But there's some other problems involved with this relationship that could really complicate things."

"Oh, what kind of things?" Dwight asked.

"I'm sorry Dwight, I just can't talk about it. As I said, it's complicated and it involves George too. And you know how I feel about George," Jeff said.

Before Dwight could say anything Jeff continued, "You know, they were a pretty close knit family and since Lydia died last year, Brenda and her father have grown even closer. That's something new for me. I've never been part of a family before and until Brenda came along, you and Donna were just about the closest thing to a family I think I've ever known."

Dwight was somewhat taken aback by this and said, "Gee Jeff, I would think that should be a real plus for you, being a part of their family and all. I told you before, you better grab that gal. She's too good for you, but I think she might be what you've been looking for all your life."

Just then the phone rang. The phone was located on the wall next to Dwight. Grabbing the phone he answered it "Jeffery Lawson's Cathouse and Massage Parlor!" Pause, then "No mam, no mam, no un uh. We're not looking for any part time help just now."

Jeff was grabbing for the phone, but Dwight wasn't giving up easily. "Yes mam, Mr. Lawson is here, but he's interviewing prospective massage therapists at the moment. If you will give me your name and number, I'll be glad to tell him you called."

Jeff finally wrestled the phone away from Dwight. As he started to speak, he heard Brenda laughing on the line. "Sorry about that," Jeff said. "You just can't hire decent help anymore."

"Well, if you're going to be involved in a business of such questionable morals as that, you deserve what you get." She was giggling. "We just got back and Les was waiting here with his new company car. He wants to come out and say hello, would that be okay?"

"Sure, come on out. What'shisname here and I just had a sandwich. Will you want something to eat?"

"Nope, we'll be there in ten minutes." The line went dead.

Jeff looked at Dwight, holding the receiver in his hand and said, "You know, she never says goodbye. She just hangs up! I'm going to have to speak to her about that."

"Yeah, I'll bet you will. Well, there goes my night out with the boys. I'll shove off so you and your lady fair can be alone." Dwight was standing and finishing the rest of his drink.

"Don't worry about it," Jeff said. "She's bringing Les Noonan and his wife with her. Or rather, they're bringing her. They're just coming out for a little while and you won't be in the way. You remember Les from the poker game the other night?

"Oh yeah, nice guy. He won all the money as I recall.

Well, if you insist," Dwight said, reaching for the large bottle of Famous Grouse. "Actually, I'd kind of like the opportunity to rest my eyes on the lovely young blonde lady that you seem so infatuated with. I'm trying to figure out what she sees in you."

"Gad," Jeff said, "I sure hope Les doesn't drink beer!"

33

Sheriff Beck often complained that Sundays were nothing more than an interruption of his workweek. He did not have particularly strong religious beliefs and was uncomfortable with the trappings and rites that he forced himself to sit through every Sunday. When involved in his work, as he was now, he much preferred to be in his office taking care of the county's business. But, Lynda Beck had deep and fundamental beliefs that sometimes made him feel guilty because she worried about his lack of faith.

As he sat with head bowed this Sunday morning, his thoughts were far from the incantations of the minister. He was so close! He was so close! All the revelations of the past few days were running through his mind. In addition, he thought of Irma who had told him the day before that she would be sitting in a couple of times today, with two of the new dispatchers.

Beck knew that she had come in during the night shifts as well. He was going to have to get her a good salary increase, he thought, along with an appropriate title. She was doing a better job than he had anticipated.

Which gave him pause, was he wrong telling Lawson that his staff was not capable or intelligent enough to deal with the 'bones' case? Wild Bill sure had come up with more detailed background information concerning Forest Decker than he had hoped for. And the deputies had done good work too. That interview of the undertaker in Waushawa had been done very professionally.

He had studied Doc's lab notebook, as well as the lab notes into the very early hours of this morning. He just couldn't make heads nor tails of them. He was able to understand only one of every ten entries. He finally realized that a portion of the scribbling was written in German. He just couldn't figure out what the other words were.

Aside from the terrible handwriting, the language Doc had used was almost indecipherable. He and Lynda were going to be with Sharon Schmidt for Sunday dinner this afternoon. If the opportunity presented itself, he'd try and have Sharon take a look at them. Maybe she could read Doc's handwriting.

He'd have to put everything together in an airtight package before he could take it to the county District Attorney for arrest warrants. The present D.A. was a young aggressive attorney who was hoping for bigger things in his future. He would go after a case like this with everything he had, but, before committing himself, he wanted to be assured he'd not be embarrassed with a failure to stain his, so far, unblemished record of convictions.

The devil is in the details! How many times had he heard politicians of all stripes make that comment? And in this case, the details had to be pulled together and presented in a fashion that would insure the young D.A., that he had an airtight case. Sheriff Beck was determined that he would do just that. All he needed now was a little more time!

Young Jack Schmidt and his wife had stopped by earlier in the day and Sharon had convinced them to stay for dinner. When Beck and his wife arrived, Jack was in the kitchen with his mother, mashing potatoes for her. He gave a friendly wave when he saw the Sheriff and Lynda, saying, "Hi Sheriff. I'll be done with this in just a second. How about a drink before we eat. I know my dad always had a bottle of Jack Daniels in the cupboard just for you. How about it?"

"That's sounds okay with me. I know where the fixins are, you want me to do the honors?" Beck answered.

"Nope, I'm done now, so I'll do it. And what will your lovely bride have?" Jack said turning to Lynda.

"Oh, I don't think I'll have anything right now," Lynda replied with a smile.

"Go ahead," Sharon Schmidt, said stepping into the family room to give each of the Becks a hug. She continued "I'm even having a little of George's bourbon! I have to have a lot of Seven Up with it, but it tastes pretty good on a cold day like this."

She laughed, saying "I thought I was going to freeze walking to church this morning. I didn't realize the weather had changed so quickly and I didn't wear a very heavy coat."

Jack's wife, Emily came out of the kitchen and welcomed the Becks. She was carrying a glass with ice and what appeared to be tomato juice. "Bloody Mary," she said, holding up the glass. "Would you like something like that Mrs. Beck? I'd be glad to fix you one."

"Oh, Emily," Lynda said, "To tell you the truth, that does sound pretty good. And Emily dear, please call me Lynda. We're almost family you know."

As they sat in the big family room, Lynda asked Sharon, "Why in the world did you walk to church this morning? That's quite a walk isn't it?"

"No, not really," Sharon answered. "It's only a little over a mile. It wasn't raining or anything and George always encouraged me to walk a mile a day. He always said," her voice breaking slightly, "he always said that walking was good for the heart."

With a tear running down her cheek, she finished, "Isn't that ironic. As much walking as he did and then die of a heart attack!"

The group grew quiet for a few minutes, sharing in silence the grief of their mother and friend. Then Jack spoke up, trying to lighten the situation said, "Hey, you know what, I think the Vikings are playing about now. How about it mom, is it okay if I turn on the TV?"

"Sure, go ahead," Sharon said finishing her drink. "It'll be a little while before the meat is done. You folks stay here and watch the game. I've got to set the table yet."

Emily and Lynda spoke together, "We'll do that. You stay in here and watch the game with the men."

Sharon responded, "Oh no. I don't care anything about football. If you want to help, I can find something for you to do in the kitchen."

Jack fixed another drink for the Sheriff and they sat watching the TV without comment. Beck couldn't concentrate on the game, although Jack became quite animated over several of the official rulings and carried on a running commentary about the quality of play. When half time rolled around, Jack asked if he'd like another drink, and when he declined the conversation turned to the investigation that the Sheriff was involved with.

"Anything new on the skeletons that were found a couple of weeks ago," Jack asked.

"Oh, things are moving along. I can't really say anything more than that," Beck replied.

"Any idea who those people were? It must be pretty hard to develop any identity in situations like that," Jack continued. "I'll bet that's got everyone in the area locking their doors at night," he laughed.

"Well, I think we've got a pretty good idea at this point who most of them were." Before he could continue, Sharon Schmidt called from the dining room, "Come on everybody, everything's ready. Come and get it."

The dinner was over and the women were in the kitchen cleaning up and Beck found himself in the Family Room with Jack again. The Sheriff saw a lot of his father in Jack. He was quick witted and smart.

Because of that, Beck was careful how to ask, "Jack, we've got some of your dad's notes on that 'bones' case, as we call it, but we can hardly read any of them. It looks like he used some kind of shorthand and on top of that, he had such terrible handwriting we can't read half of what he's written. Over the years were you ever able to translate his handwriting?"

Jack laughed, saying, "I know what you mean, but I'm sorry to say I was never able to read anything he wrote either. He was always mixing his English with German and Latin on most things he wrote."

Beck was stunned, "Latin? Why Latin?" he asked. Then, "Of course. Doctors have written prescriptions in Latin for years. I should have thought of that!"

Jack laughed again and said, "I don't know if that'll help you or not. He had a typical doctor's handwriting. I used to kid him about it. Told him that none of them ever seemed to be able to learn basic penmanship."

But the Sheriff now had an idea how to get those notes interpreted. A handwriting analyst could probably do it, even if he didn't have knowledge of Latin. He could always find someone to interpret the Latin and someone else to interpret the German.

Latin!! Why hadn't he realized that till now? He thought, "Maybe I am getting too old for this job. I'm too young to retire, but I'm vested in my retirement program. I could retire tomorrow and start drawing a pension."

Then mentally kicking himself he thought, "Who am I kidding, I'm not going to retire now or anytime soon. Quit feeling sorry for yourself Tommy Beck and get the job done!"

It was dark by the time the Becks returned home. It was getting colder with flakes of snow in the air here and there. Tommy went directly to his den, where he sat and pulled out the lab notebook and with the latest information, tried his best to interpret Doc's notes.

After two hours, he gave up and was surprised to find that Lynda had already gone to bed. Fixing a nightcap of Jack Daniels and Coke, he went back to the den where he sat sipping his drink and staring at the lab notebook, wondering again what secrets it contained.

34

Monday morning dawned with a light covering of snow on the ground. Temperatures had dropped during the night into the mid thirties. Jeff had showered and dressed for the day when Birdie Waters knocked on the door.

Jeff wondered why she was knocking; she usually just walked in with her cleaning supplies. Then he remembered Brenda telling him to 'lock up' when she left with the Noonans the night before. Jumping up from the counter he ran to unlock the door for Birdie. She stood in the door wearing a hooded winter jacket and a large plastic pail with a number of cleaning paraphernalia.

"Good morning Birdie," Jeff said. "Sorry about the door being locked. I guess I'm going to have to get you a key. I'm being instructed to keep my doors locked these days and I'm just not used to doing that. Maybe I can just hide a key out here on the porch somewhere."

Birdie smiling entered the cabin and said, "No problem Mr. Lawson. I'd rather not have a key, but if you hide one out here somewhere, that would be okay." She slipped out of her jacket and laid it on the couch, then went to the entry closet and pulled out a vacuum cleaner.

"I've got the Mr. Coffee maker working this morning Birdie, would you like a cup before you get started?"

"I sure would," Birdie said. "This cold weather seems to go right through me. I remember when I was little, I couldn't wait for the first snowfall. These days though, I can't wait for spring."

"Well, I'm afraid you're in for a long wait now. Winter isn't even here for a few more weeks and spring's a long way off yet," Jeff laughed.

He poured her coffee into a mug and refilling his own, they sat at the counter sipping it. Jeff asked, "I suppose by this time, Red's already gone in to his new job hasn't he?"

With a smile, Birdie replied, "Yes sir, I don't think he slept all weekend, he's so excited about it. He sure thinks the world of you Mr. Lawson. This job will sure mean a lot to us and help us make ends meet."

"Been pretty tough going for you two hasn't it?" Jeff asked. "How's that little guy doing these days? I'll bet he's growing like a weed already isn't he? By the way, who looks after him when you're out cleaning houses around town?"

"My mother takes care of Wesley while I'm out," Birdie said.

"Wesley? Is that the baby's name? I hadn't heard that. Wesley Waters," Jeff said. "I like it. When he gets older we'll just call him W W!"

Birdie laughed at that and said, "Red didn't want to give him a tribal name. He's never liked his own name and he said he didn't want his son to feel that way, as he grew older. I never thought much about it until Red and I were married. He can be pretty hardheaded when it comes to that sort of thing."

A sudden thought popped into Jeff's mind and he said, "Say Birdie, I was curious about something. I glanced over Red's job application Friday and saw that he had worked for Decker Funeral Home for a while. How'd he happen to take a job like that so far away?"

The coffee mug slipped out of Birdie's hand and shattered on the counter. Both Jeff and Birdie jumped back to avoid the splashing coffee. Birdie quickly ran around the counter and grabbing a towel started mopping up the coffee. Her hands were trembling as she was picking up broken shards and placing them in a wastebasket by the refrigerator.

"Oh Mr. Lawson, I'm so sorry," Birdie exclaimed, "I don't know how that happened. I'll clean this up right away and I'll pay for the cup. I'm so clumsy sometimes."

Jeff replied, "Oh for heavens sake, don't worry about that. It was just an old coffee mug. I've had them for years and I've still got two or three in the cupboard. Grab another mug and finish your coffee. I've got to get going anyway. I'll leave your money on the dresser."

Birdie was still mopping up the spilled coffee when Jeff, shrugging on a heavy jacket was headed out the door. Turning back he said, "Will you be back on Thursday? I'll see to it that you get a key for the front door before then."

With a slight wave of his hand, he went out the door to the attached garage. Birdie heard the garage door opening and the Blazer backing out to the driveway. As Jeff drove away, she hurried to the telephone and with shaking hands, tried to dial a number. Her hands were shaking so badly that she misdialed the first time. Finally she had it right and she waited for the call to be answered, but as she waited, the phone at the other end just rang and rang and rang.

As Jeff drove carefully along the county road to the main highway into Lakeview, his thoughts returned to the previous evening. Brenda and the Noonan's were stomping the snow off their shoes as they entered the front door, Dwight was slipping on his jacket preparing to leave.

Brenda seeing this said, "Hi Dwight, are we the reason you're leaving? Please don't go on our account. If I thought we're driving you away, we wouldn't have barged in like this."

Seeing the scotch bottle on the counter said, "Oh, oh. What have you two been up to? Didn't you guys get enough of that stuff last night?"

Laughing at this, she said, "Oh come on Dwight, stay for a little while anyway. We're not going to be here very long. And I want you to meet these folks."

Dwight said "I know Les already, he was out here for our poker game the other night." Shaking his hand he said with a grin, "Have you been enjoying my money this week?"

Les, smiling replied, "Oh I didn't win much. I was a little ahead I guess, but not that much." Then turning slightly he caught his wife's hand saying, "I'd like you to meet my wife, Myra." Motioning with his free hand, he continued, "This is Jeff's friend, Dwight Sutherland."

Brenda spoke up at that, saying, "No he's not! Not anymore." Dwight was gaping at her, as she continued, "He and his wife are OUR friends not just Jeff's."

With that she stepped forward and gave Dwight a kiss on the cheek. Stepping back she said, "And where is

Donna by the way? How come she lets you out alone at night?"

Les didn't want anything to drink but Coke and Myra just sipped at a glass of ice water. Brenda found the wine bottle in the refrigerator and poured a small amount into a wine glass. Then, seated in the main room area, they sat and chatted for the next hour or so.

Finally, as they stood and started putting on their coats and jackets, Brenda, standing on tiptoes gave Jeff a soft kiss, whispering in his ear, "Sorry about the Noonan's. Myra wanted to see your cabin. Call me tomorrow. Night, Night."

Stepping out the door Dwight turned and said to Les, "Holy mackerel, how much did I lose the other night anyway?" Then, "Here I am driving an old beat up truck and this guy is driving a Cadillac! What's wrong with this picture?"

As he was driving to his office the next morning, Jeff was smiling at the memory of the evening and remembering that soft kiss of Brenda's. Then, suddenly, without warning, all the concerns he'd been worrying about for the past several days descended like a dark cloud on his mind. He felt consumed by a feeling of impending disaster!

Les met him in his office and they were discussing a problem with a vendor's late deliveries, when Mrs. Parsons stepped inside. She said, "Excuse me Mr. Lawson, but I'm about to send for Bud to come up front and take Red out to the plant. Did you want to talk with him before I do that?"

Jeff glanced at his watch and shook his head, "No I guess not Helen. I don't have time today. I'll see him sometime later in the week. Just make sure he has a hard hat and safety glasses. Okay"

As he left the office for lunch, the memory of Birdie dropping the cup of coffee that morning intruded on his thoughts. The more he thought about it, the more he became convinced that she had dropped the cup because of what Jeff had asked her about Red and Decker Funeral Home! Why had that gotten her so upset, he wondered? Remembering that he had wanted to ask Red directly about it, he now regretted not having had the time to talk to Red that morning. If he could find the time, he'd take a walk through the plant a little later this afternoon.

As he entered the cafe, he saw Les Noonan and Helen Parsons sitting together at a table together. Les saw Jeff and waved for him to join them. Looking around, Jeff realized that the little restaurant was crowded with noonday patrons. Sitting down at the table with the two, he said, "Thanks, it looks like they've got a full house in here today. What's the special today?"

Helen replied, "Potato soup and sandwich. I had the chicken salad and Lester had tuna. I recommend the soup, I can't say the same for the sandwich!"

A waitress placed a glass of water on the table in front of Jeff and looked at him inquiringly. Jeff said, "Okay, guess I'll have the potato soup and an egg salad sandwich."

As the waitress left to place his order, Helen spoke, "You know Mr. Lawson, we didn't really mean to mislead anyone. About Lester being my nephew I mean. When I spoke to Mr. Gunderson, I don't think he was thinking about selling the company at that time. We just thought it would be a good idea not to let anyone know that Lester and I were related. I hope it doesn't make a difference to you."

"Listen Helen, think about it! Do you think I'd have given him George's Cadillac if I thought it was a problem?" Jeff was motioning for the waitress, "And I don't think you should ever be ashamed to admit he's your nephew just because he isn't as good looking as you are."

Les said, "I told her it probably wouldn't make any difference to you, but she's a worry wart" he finished smiling at her fondly.

Embarrassed, Helen said quickly, "Well, if you'll excuse me, I have to stop at the drugstore before going back to the office. I'll see the two of you there. Thank you for the lunch Lester." And with that, she got quickly to her feet and hurried out of the cafe.

35

Sheriff Beck spent the morning reviewing his notes and the reports submitted by his deputies and Lieutenant Reynolds. By the time he was through he had a very thick file that laid out all the details of his investigation into the 'bones' case, as well as suspicions of additional criminal activity on the part of Forest Decker. Until he could obtain search warrants to search the funeral home facilities and files, all the information he had developed so far was circumstantial at best.

He called to make an appointment with the county District Attorney after lunch but learned he was going to be in court all afternoon, so he made the appointment for eight o'clock the next morning.

He had just hung up from that call, when he received a call from the State's forensic lab. They informed him that they were finally able to send up a forensic team to analyze the remains in the county morgue. A team? How many people were they sending the sheriff wondered? The caller advised that the 'team' would be there Wednesday morning and would he arrange to have someone there to open the building for them?

Beck asked Irma to come to his office. When she came in, Beck noticed that she appeared tired and in need of rest.

"Irma, love, what are you doing to yourself? As soon as we get through here, I want you to go home and get some sleep. This place can get along without you for a few hours. I didn't give you this new job to have you working twenty hours a day!"

"I think we've got things running pretty smoothly now. I don't think the new folks need such close supervision anymore." she replied tiredly. "And you're right, I'm worn out! I've been in and out of this place a hundred times since last week. I appreciate your noticing."

The Sheriff leaned back in his chair, reaching to his refrigerator; he retrieved a Coke and offered it to Irma. She shook her head and said, "No thanks Sheriff, that stuff just makes me hyper."

Beck laughed at this and said, "Okay, let's talk about your new people. How are they working out? Any problems with any of them so far?"

Irma hesitated, and then said, "Well, I do have a little problem with officer Conway."

Beck groaned, "Oh no, what's the problem with Deputy Fife now?"

Irma laughed at that and said, "It isn't anything real important, but he's just trying to impress the rest of the dispatchers that he's just doing this to help you out. And he's trying real hard to look like the 'old hand' at this job."

She paused, and then said, "As I said, it isn't anything

real important, but the other dispatchers are getting a little tired of his superior attitude."

Beck thought about it for a minute. "Do you want me to call him in on the carpet?"

"Oh no. I'll handle it. If he causes any real problems, I might send him to you for 'counseling,'" she said.

Beck liked that. She wasn't trying to slough her problems off on somebody else. "Okay" he said. "What's your pay grade these days Irma? You're a four aren't you?"

He had already talked to the county human relations officer earlier in the morning and was told her pay grade.

"Yes sir. I've been a Grade four a year or so now."

"Well, I've got some news for you. You are now a pay grade six! You get one grade increase on merit, and the second pay grade is for your new managerial position. I hope this makes up for all the B.S. you've had to take from me for the last year or so."

Beck was laughing at the expression on Irma's face. Her jaw had dropped and she was looking agog at him.

"My God Tommy," realizing what she had just said. "I mean Sheriff, that's like a ten thousand dollar a year raise!" She was fumbling in a pocket for a hanky as a tear started to roll down her cheek. "I can't believe it. Are you sure? Will the commissioners have to approve this?"

"Nope. It's all covered in my annual budget." Standing he walked around the desk and gave Irma a hand as she stood up. "Congratulations old girl. You've earned every penny of it. Now go on home and get some sleep and we'll see you in here bright and early tomorrow morning."

"I don't know how to thank you Tommy," she said. "This is a wonderful surprise. I can hardly wait to tell my old man," she finished with a grin.

"Go on. Get out of here," Beck responded with a smile. "I'll see you tomorrow."

Moving back to his desk, he had just opened the can of Coke when 'Wild Bill' knocked on the doorframe. "Did you want to see me Sheriff?" Beck waved him to a chair in front of his desk.

"Bill," the Sheriff explained, "I've got an appointment with the D.A. at eight o'clock tomorrow morning. I'd like you to go with me. I'm going to give him a lot of information and some of it is stuff you've developed so far. If he starts asking questions I can't answer, I need you there for back up."

Reynolds leaned forward excitedly saying "Does this mean we've got enough to go after him? Are you going to get some search warrants too?"

Sheriff Beck replied, "It means I'm going to ask for everything I can think of. Search warrants are only the beginning. If I get everything I'm asking for, by this time Friday, Mr. Decker will be a guest in our nice new jail!"

"I don't know if I'll need the information Doc had in these now or not," Beck said, holding the lab book and Doc's lab notes, "But I need a handwriting analyst to try and decipher these things. I'd like you to run these down to Edina this morning and turn them over to a Jillian White, in the Forensics Lab there. She knows you're coming."

As Reynolds was about to leave Beck said, "Oh, and one more thing. Tell her that these notes seem to be written in three different languages. We think they're a combination of German, English and Latin."

Reynolds laughed at this and said, "Sounds like we're going to need an altar boy to interpret the Latin and deputy Heiss to interpret the German."

Beck said "Heis? Does he speak the language? I could probably get a priest to interpret the Latin, but I never thought about Heis."

Reynolds said, "Oh he speaks it alright. He's second generation. His granddad was a P.O.W. here after the war and was allowed to apply for citizenship instead of going back. Seems he was from the part of Germany that had fallen under the Russians and he didn't want to go back after that."

"Well," the Sheriff said, "We'll give Deputy Heiss a shot at this thing when we get it back."

After a moments thought he said, "Before you go Bill, how about running off copies of the lab notes there and letting Heiss take a crack at them this afternoon. I don't think he'll be able to read Doc's handwriting, but until we get it back from Jillian, it might be worth a try.

Sheriff Beck was hungry and he decided he'd leave a little early and go down to Duffy's for a quick sandwich. As he was leaving his phone rang and he stepped back to answer it. Rhonda was on the board and it was her voice he heard saying, "Sheriff, we've got a little problem up in Lakeview again."

"Lakeview," the Sheriff said. "What's happening up there now?"

Rhonda said, trying not to laugh, "Well, it seems that Marshal Quint Mason has just wrecked that patrol cruiser we loaned him a couple of days ago!"

"What? Are you serious?" the Sheriff exclaimed. "How did that happen? Do we have a car up there?"

"I'm not sure how it happened Sheriff, but it seems that Marshal Mason drove through a front window of a store on Main Street! Deputy Tuttle is up there right now and," she paused, then said, "he believes Marshal Mason to be drunker'n a hoot owl!"

"Oh no. It isn't even noon yet and he's drunk? You've got to be kidding!"

"Afraid not Sheriff," Rhonda was laughing. "And it appears that Marshal Mason is taking umbrage with officer Tuttle because he's out of his jurisdiction. Claims that everything inside the town limits are his responsibility!"

"Oh for crying out loud. Sit still, I'll be right out. I want to talk to Tuttle."

Hanging up the phone he ran out the door and hurried out to the dispatcher's board. Rhonda was talking into the headset microphone, saying, "Stand by, here's the Sheriff now." Turning she indicated another headset on the desk beside her. "You can use that one Sheriff."

Sitting down and slipping the headset on he pressed the transmit button and said, "Tuttle. Was anyone injured there? Do you need an ambulance?"

"No sir. As luck would have it, there wasn't anybody near the front of the store at the time. Sir, this guy is smashed out of his mind." Tuttle sounded disgusted. "What do you want me to do with him? I've got him in the cruiser right now and he's being pretty uncooperative, to say the least!"

"He's got a holding cell in that office of his there on Main Street. Take him over there and lock him up! And if he gives you any problem, shoot the son of bitch!"

Beck paused for a moment, then said "Well, I guess you better not do that, but get him over there to that holding cell and start pouring coffee into him. I'll be up there in a half hour or so."

Tuttle answered "Yessir. I'll get him in there right now. His office is just a couple doors up the street from here."

He paused, and then the Sheriff heard him ask, "Sheriff, you sure I can't shoot him? It would be my pleasure."

Rhonda had been making a serious attempt not to laugh at this conversation, but now she couldn't hold it back any longer and burst out laughing. Beck glared at her, then he laughed out loud too.

"No, don't do that," he said to Tuttle. "Just get him out of sight until I can get there. Have you got a wrecker coming after the car?"

"No sir. I just took a couple of pictures of it and got in and started it up and just backed it out of the store. Got a broken head light and a little damage to the hood and that's about it. It had a 'cow catcher' that protected the grill and front end of the car pretty much," he finished.

"Okay. Get him out of sight. Don't let anyone in his office. I'll be there as quick as I can." As an afterthought he said, "Try to get him to blow into a Breathalyzer. That might help us when he gets sobered up."

It was almost exactly a half hour later that Beck pulled up to the Marshall's office in Lakeview. He saw the patrol car parked in front of the Marshall's office and Tuttle's car parked beside it. He walked around the damaged car, noting, as Tuttle had reported the broken headlight and damaged hood. He also saw a cobweb breakage in the windshield. Beck turned and walked into the office. Deputy Tuttle was seated casually behind the Marshall's desk and he came to his feet when the Sheriff walked in.

Tuttle pointed to a door at the back of the office and Beck stepped through. The holding cell was a ten by ten foot arrangement at the back of the room. There were two bunk beds on either side of the room and the typical fixtures of a jail cell. A toilet, with no seat and a sink with a single faucet. Mason was lying on the bottom bunk, his back to the cell area and from all appearances was asleep, or, Beck thought, passed out.

The Sheriff stepped up to the cell door and called, "Quint, wake up. Wake up and sit up there."

There was no response from the sleeping Marshall. Tuttle was about to unlock the cell door when Beck held up his hand saying, "Never mind. Let him sleep for an hour or so. I haven't had lunch and I'm hungry."

At that a soft snoring sound came from the bunk bed.

36

As the Sheriff walked into the Main Street Cafe, it seemed that every table was taken and he was about to turn and leave when he saw someone wave to him. It was Jeff Lawson, sitting near the back of the room. Jeff was motioning for him to join him and as he got closer he realized there was another young man sitting across the table from him. As he stepped to the table Jeff said "Have a seat Sheriff. I just ordered a sandwich and Les here is headed back to the office. And I don't like eating alone."

As he sat down, Jeff made the introductions to Les Noonan, the young man sitting with Jeff. Before the Sheriff had a chance to say much more than hello, the waitress was placing a glass of water in front of him and asking what he wanted to order.

"Well, I'll have whatever the special is." Looking up at the blackboard behind the counter and said "I'll have the potato soup and a ham and cheese on rye. Diet Coke to drink please."

Jeff said with a grin, "Good choice Sheriff, but I don't

think you'll like the Coke here as well as what you get at Duffy's."

"I'm sure you're right about that," Beck laughed.

Les was looking at them in confusion and was pushing back from the table saying "Well, I've got to get back. Nice meeting you Sheriff. I'll see you back at the office Jeff." Leaving a couple of bills on the table he hurried to the cashier and was soon out the door.

"What brings you to our fair city Sheriff? Does it have anything to do with that hubbub I saw down the street a while ago? Was that one of your cars involved in that mess?"

"Unfortunately," Beck replied "It was a loaner we'd given Mason until he could get a replacement for his."

"I heard something about that, what was that all about anyway," Jeff asked?

"It was a little 'get together' with Marshall Mason and one of my deputies" Beck said.

Jeff looked at the Sheriff with a questioning look and Beck went on to explain what had happened and why he was in Lakeview today. Jeff laughed at the idea of Quint Marshall driving into the storefront, and then with a sober look asked "Was anybody hurt? That had to be quite a surprise to anyone in the store!"

"No, luckily, there wasn't anyone near the front of the store at the time. I just came from Quint's office and he's stretched out in a holding cell snoring like a pig! This might be the end of his career as a law officer. I have to make a report to the town council and they're about fed up with Quint as it is!"

Jeff was suddenly very still as something flashed through his mind. "Sheriff, I think I got a call from

Marshall Mason the other day, but I didn't recognize his voice at the time. He was trying to disguise it, but now that I think about it, I'm pretty sure it was him."

Beck said, "What do you mean, he was trying to disguise his voice? What was the call about anyway?"

Before Jeff could answer, the waitress returned to the table with their orders. She carefully placed a large bowl of soup before each of them and a sandwich on the side. The Sheriff, looking up said, "Don't forget my Coke, please, Miss." The waitress hurried away and quickly returned with the Sheriff's drink.

They were sipping the soup before resuming their conversation and the Sheriff said, "Boy, this is good soup. What did you mean, Mason was trying to disguise his voice? Why would he do that?"

Jeff related the calls he and George had received concerning Red Waters and then told of the letter he received the next day. He said, "What do you think Sheriff. Why would he have it in for Red do you think?"

The Sheriff sat not answering and continued thoughtfully sipping at his soup. Finally he asked, "Did you keep that letter? I'd like to see it if you did." Then, "I have no idea why he'd do something like that. Are you absolutely sure it was him?"

Jeff replied, "No, not 'absolutely sure' but let's say I'm ninety percent sure! I've still got the letter in my office if you'd like to see it. When we're through here, why don't you stop by and I'll give it to you."

The Sheriff said, "I'll do that. I wanted a chance to talk with you anyway. I'm afraid I have some very bad news for you." Jeff looked up with concern at this and Beck continued, "We're pretty sure those remains you found are those of Mrs. Gunderson. Your speculation about that appears to be right on the money."

"Oh no, no, I knew it. Oh no, how will I ever be able to tell George .... and Brenda?" Jeff laid his spoon on the table looking at Beck and said, "There's no doubt? You're sure? My God Sheriff, this is awful. It'll kill George when he finds this out!"

"As you said a few minutes ago, I believe we're ninety percent sure. We're going after arrest and search warrants in the morning and by tomorrow afternoon we'll have Decker's files and records." Beck was looking at Jeff closely and continued, "I'm sorry Jeff, but the relatives of these victims will have to be informed. I don't see any way around it. I'm very sorry."

Jeff suddenly felt nauseous as the vision of Lydia Gunderson and the bones he'd found flashed through his mind. He sat with head bowed seeing images of the years he'd worked with George and the fondness, even love, he had developed for this man that had been the closest thing to a father Jeff had ever known.

He was heartsick and didn't know if he was going to be able to face Brenda again. He said as much to Beck.

The Sheriff leaned across the table and touched Jeff on the arm, saying, "Take it easy Jeff. I'm depending on you to soften the blow, so to speak. I want you to talk to Brenda and prepare her for this. It's going to be rough alright, but you can handle it."

"We'll probably have to get some kind of grief counselor's for this situation. We'll get help for you, believe me," the Sheriff said. "We won't leave you out there by yourself. And remember, there's four other families that are going to be affected by this. They're going to have to get through it too."

Jeff stood up, saying, "I've got to get out of here before I throw up. Come by the office Sheriff, when you're through here." Tossing a bill on the table he stumbled out the door and out of sight. Beck watched him go, hoping he hadn't made a mistake by taking him into his confidence.

37

Jeff sat in his car for several minutes before realizing that he was sitting in the parking space in front of his office. As he opened the door, he was thinking, "What a mess. Why me? These are people I love more than anything in my miserable life until now."

As he walked into the building, he was aware of Mrs. Parson's saying that there were call notes on his desk.

He sat as if he were in a fog for some time, until Mrs. Parsons stepped to the door and asked, "Mr. Lawson, are you okay? You don't look well. Would you like a cup of coffee or," she paused awkwardly, "or something? Do you need an aspirin maybe? You really look terrible!"

"What, What did you say?" Jeff said. "Oh, no, no Helen. I'm okay. I just need to use the men's room for a minute I guess."

With that he got up and walked down the hall to the Men's room. He tossed cold water on his face and looked at himself in the mirror. The color had drained from his face leaving him with a pasty and drawn appearance. Sweat was forming on his forehead even after tossing the cold water on his face. He leaned against the wall trying to think, but was overcome with images of Lydia and George and Brenda.

Brenda! How would he ever be able to tell her this terrible news? Yet, as the Sheriff had said, he was going to have to do it! He and Brenda together, were somehow going to have to prepare George for this unbelievable situation. Tossing more water on his face, he finally grabbed a towel and dried himself. He glanced in the mirror again and saw the color returning to his face. As he returned to his office, the Sheriff was standing by Mrs. Parson's desk talking softly with her. As Jeff approached he pointed to his office and motioned the Sheriff through the door.

As the Sheriff sat down, he said, "What do you think Sheriff? Should I tell Brenda right away, or should I wait until you are one hundred per cent sure that we're talking about her mom? It sounds like you're pretty darned sure right now."

Beck said with conviction, "Jeff, I wish I could tell you that I have doubts. But I'm sorry to say, I'm convinced that further investigation will confirm our suspicions in this matter. I'm very sorry."

"Why? Why Sheriff? Why would he do this terrible thing?" Jeff was becoming distraught. "Why would anybody do something like this? It's too unbelievable to be real!"

Beck shook his head sadly and said, "Why? There's always a reason and I think the reason in this case is simply the fact that Decker needed money. And he needed money badly. He was deep in debt, still is for that matter. And a year or so ago he had to rely on another funeral home to perform cremations when they were needed."

The Sheriff continued, "But we now know that he owed so much money for past services to this other funeral home, that they wouldn't handle any more service until his debt was paid in full   So, if they didn't perform any such service, there was no cost to Decker. But his clients didn't know that and he was able to charge for a service that they never received! So, it just boils down to money! The root of all evil!"

Beck paused a moment, then continued, "God only knows what other 'services' he charged for and never performed. State law requires all bodies to be embalmed, even if later cremated. It's my guess that in these cases in particular, that procedure was intentionally omitted."

Jeff sat silently for several moments, absorbing what Beck had just said. Finally, he said, "It's hard to believe isn't it? That an individual could be that callous to simply throw a human being away! That's what it looks like he did isn't it? He didn't need them for anything, so he just 'threw them away' like they were no more than a sack of trash!"

The Sheriff looked at Jeff saying, "You've seen terrible things before this. I have too. Not only in my job, but also when I was in Viet Nam. We've both seen some things, and maybe even done some things, that we'd like to forget, but the difference between then and now is, that was war. This is just a cold-blooded criminal act for nothing more than money.

Jeff was looking at the Sheriff and said, "Yessir, I have seen some terrible things and it was a war. But how do you know that about me?"

"Sorry, don't take offense, but I had to run a check

on you shortly after you found those remains. Nobody seemed to know much about you before you came to Lakeview."

The Sheriff smiled and said, "Among other things I learned, was that your friend Dwight Sutherland probably wouldn't be with us today if you had not 'acted in the best traditions of the service above and beyond' etc. etc."

Now Jeff was embarrassed. He said, "Oh that, it really wasn't that big a deal." Then looking up he said, "Sheriff, I'd consider it a real favor if that story didn't get around too much."

"No problem, but it was an impressive commendation. It's sure nothing to be ashamed of, or feel you've got to hide about."

The Sheriff was about to stand and then sat back down saying, "Dang, almost forgot what I came for. I'd like to see that letter you got. I'm going to have a little talk with Quint this afternoon and maybe I can get him to tell me what this is all about."

Jeff ran a copy of the letter and gave the original to Beck. After a few more words, the Sheriff turned and left, leaving Jeff staring after him. Returning to his office, he tried to concentrate on the 'call back messages' that were stuck to his phone. But his mind was not on business and he couldn't focus on the messages. Finally, he swung his chair around and stared out the window behind his desk. It was snowing again, but Jeff was not aware of it at all.

38

Marshal Mason was still passed out in his holding cell when Beck returned to the City Marshall's office. Deputy Tuttle was waiting for him and said, "We've got another car coming up to pick up the Marshall's car. Did you want to leave another one for him? You didn't say before you left."

"Hell no!" Beck stormed. "He's not going to wreck another one. He's already responsible for the loss of three cars already!" Shaking his head he continued, "I'm going to have to report this to the Commissioners and if I know them, they'll be after Quint's head! I expect the town council here will probably let him go after this latest little escapade."

Then, "Did you get a breathalyzer on him before he passed out?"

"Yes sir, he blew point one six. And I had him blow three times and it was the same every time." Tuttle said.

"My God," Beck said. "It's a wonder he didn't kill somebody. Well, when that other car gets here, wake him up and bring him back down to our jail. I can't tie up any more people taking care of this dummy. Lock the place up and get back on the road as soon as you can." With that, the Sheriff turned and left.

As he hurried back to his office, the Sheriff was surprised to hear Conway's voice on the radio. He listened carefully as Conway talked with the various patrolmen and decided that Conway had found his nitch. But Beck wondered why Conway was on the board already. Rhonda had been on when he left just before lunch. Looking at his watch, he was surprised to see it was after four o'clock already.

Picking up his mike he asked Conway if there were any messages for him.

"I'll switch you over to Irma sir. I think she's got something for you."

A minute or so later, Irma came on saying, "Well, I tried to call you on your cell phone again and as usual it started ringing in your office. I thought we talked about that before."

The Sheriff frowned, "We did. I'm sorry about that, but I thought I had asked you to go home and get some rest this morning. What are you doing back there again?"

"I just came back for a few minutes. I forgot something this morning and as long as I was here, I stuck around long enough for the shift change." Irma continued, "I'm just on the way out the door, but I'm glad you finally checked in. The D.A.'s office said that he wanted to set your appointment back a couple of hours in the morning. Said to make it ten o'clock."

The Sheriff laughed at the emphasis she had placed on 'finally checked in' and said, "Okay, thanks Irma. Get out of there. And I'll try and remember that damned cell phone in the morning."

When Conway came back on the Sheriff said, "Conway, I'll be back in the office in a little while. Anything else comes up, I'll be in the car."

"Ten four Sheriff. No other calls that I'm aware of. See you in a little bit."

As Beck was driving he thought back to his discussion with young Lawson. It was going to be a difficult conversation when he saw his girl in a little while. Thinking back to his last conversation with George Gunderson, Beck was thinking that if George's daughter was anything like him, Lawson might be surprised how strong she might be!

39

Jeff was about to leave the office when Mrs. Parson's buzzed him. Picking up the phone, he heard her say, "Line one Mr. Lawson. It's Mrs. Dexter."

"Thank you Helen," he said as he hesitated before punching the flashing button. "Hi there, I was just thinking about you. Are you home?"

"Yes I am, as a matter of fact. I've got a PTA meeting tonight, so we won't be able to see each other, darn it," she finished.

"Oh, What time will your meetings be over? I need to see you tonight. Are you sure you have to go?" Jeff was sweating. "Would they miss you if you didn't show up."

"Jeff, what's wrong with you," she laughed? "As a matter of fact I don't have any actual parent conferences scheduled tonight, but these things are part of my job you know." Then, "What's so important, and don't tell me it's what I think it is," she laughed again?

"Brenda, honey," Jeff paused, then, "It really is important that I see you. I have some very upsetting information that we must talk about. If there is anyway you can cancel your meeting tonight, I wish you would."

Brenda didn't answer for a minute and Jeff thought that she had hung up. Finally she said, "Is this really important Jeff? I know PTA meetings are probably not high on your list of activities, but they are very important to me and to the parents of those kids in my classes." Jeff was surprised at her apparent anger.

"Please Brenda," he said. "Would you come out to the cabin when your meetings are over? I don't want to talk about this on the phone. Please, no matter what time it is, please come out, I'll be waiting for you."

Silence. Finally Brenda said, "Okay, I should be through by nine or nine thirty. I'll see you then."

Jeff stopped at the Log Jam and had a cheeseburger and Coke on his way home. He hadn't finished his lunch earlier in the day and even though filled with dread of his meeting with Brenda later, he discovered he was hungry.

But after a few bites he found he couldn't swallow and the food felt like it was hanging in clumps in his throat. He swallowed the Coke in an attempt to clear the choking sensation and then paying his tab he quickly left.

As he walked in the door, he realized that Birdie must not have locked it this morning when she left. That was okay, probably just an oversight. She wasn't used to locking doors either. He stepped through the door and was taking off his heavy jacket when he was struck, hard, on the back of the head. As he was falling, he was conscious of being struck again and even though he didn't feel it, struck again after he fell to the floor.

40

Snow was blowing through the open door as he was starting to come to. Brenda was kneeling over him and crying his name over and over as he came more awake.

His head was filled with pain and it hurt to open his eyes. He tried to sit up, but he suddenly felt he was going to pass out. He groaned as he turned his head to Brenda and blearily looking at her asked, "Wha, what happened?"

"Lie still Jeff, I've called for an ambulance. They'll be here any minute. Who did this to you?"

Brenda couldn't stop the tears, "Oh my darling, you've lost so much blood. It's all my fault. If only I'd," she was interrupted as a couple of men stepped through the door. A patch on their blue jackets identified them as paramedics. There was also a Sheriff's Deputy standing in the doorway.

The medics politely, but firmly moved Brenda out of their way and knelt over Jeff. One shined a small flashlight into his eyes and moved from one eye to the other several times. The other was carefully cleaning the blood from his face and head.

Finally looking up at Brenda, he said, "A head wound will almost always look a lot worse than it really is. He seems to have a couple of cuts here that are bleeding quite a bit, but we can take care of them okay. It's possible he has a concussion though, so we're going to take him down to the county hospital. He's going to need x-rays. Are you his wife?"

Jeff heard all of this in a fog. He was surprised to hear Brenda answer, "Wife? No. No. Not yet anyway."

"Okay, well we're going to load him up and get him to the hospital. Sorry but there isn't room for you in the ambulance, but if you want to follow us down there he'll probably be in the ER there for a while. At least until they can get him a room. Okay?"

The Sheriff's Deputy was asking Brenda if she could tell if anything was missing in the cabin. Jeff heard her answer, "No, no. At least I don't think so. Let me look around a little."

At this Jeff closed his eyes and was going to sleep when one of the Medics shook him slightly saying, "Stay awake there fella. Can you tell me your name?"

"Yaass." Jeff answered.

The Medic said, "Okay, come on, tell me your name. Do you remember your name?"

Jeff thought, "This guy must think I'm deaf or something. Why is he shouting?" With a supreme effort he replied "Jeff Laawwssonn."

His head was pounding and all he wanted was to sleep, but the Medic kept him awake. They started an I.V. and finally loaded him in an ambulance. After that, Jeff was probably awake, but he couldn't remember anything until he came awake in a hospital bed.

With a groan he tried to sit up and there was Brenda. "Don't try and sit up yet. I can raise the bed if you want," she said. "You've got a concussion. The doctor said you'd be here a few days, but that you're going to be alright."

"Who did this Jeff? When I saw you lying there and all that blood, I thought my heart was going to stop. Who did this?" she repeated.

"Who did what? Right now, all I know is, that I've got the worst hangover in the history of the world!"

He was feeling the bandages on his head and asked, "What happened anyway? Last thing I remember was starting to take off my coat."

Before she could answer, a young nurse came in the room and seeing Jeff awake said, "How are you feeling today Mr. Lawson. Do you have a lot of pain?"

"My head feels like it's been used as a baseball, but other than that I think I'm okay," Jeff said.

"We don't want you to feel you have to grit your teeth and bear it, Mr. Lawson. If you're in pain we can relieve it. You're going to be with us a day or so, and we want you to be comfortable."

"Oh no, I can't be here for two days! I've got a business to run. I can't stay around here just because I have a headache. Which reminds, me, where's my cell phone? I've got to call my office."

Trying to sit up, Jeff was overcome with dizziness and lay back on the pillow. "Well, maybe I can stay a little longer," he said.

Brenda said, "Oh my darling, I'm so sorry I didn't have you come over that night. This might not have happened.

Jeff, you've been here since Monday night. It's almost noon Wednesday now! The doctor decided to keep you unconscious until now. You've been asleep for the past forty hours."

That brought Jeff fully awake. Forty hours! It seemed just a few minutes ago he was slipping off his jacket and trying to think how he was going to tell Brenda .....

"Oh God" he said. Remembering why he had wanted to see Brenda so badly.

Fumbling with the controls on the side of the bed he found the control to raise the head. Brenda was standing by his bed, watching him with concern in her eyes.

Jeff started, "Brenda, I have something terrible to tell you. It's been driving me crazy and that's why I insisted on seeing you las... Monday night. I think you'd better sit down. This is going to..."

"Jeff," she said softly, "I know. The Sheriff told me yesterday! Dad knows too. The Sheriff arrested that undertaker yesterday. He's in the county jail and goes in front of a judge Friday for a trial date. Sheriff Beck doesn't think he'll be able to raise bail, so he'll have to wait in jail until his trial."

"You know? How's George? Is he okay? I'm so sorry Brenda. I wanted to be with you when George was told. I can't imagine how you two must feel." Jeff was reaching for her and she came into his arms. "I'm so very sorry," he said again.

"Well, it looks like our friend has finally decided to return to the land of the living," a voice at the door said. "And as usual, the first thing he does is grab his nurse" Jeff looked up to see Dwight and Donna coming in the room. Donna was carrying a small bouquet of flowers and Dwight had a rolled up copy of Playboy in his hand.

"Did I ever tell you about that nurse he had in Saudi Arabia. She couldn't keep her hands off him either."

"Saudi Arabia? Nurse? Were you in the hospital in Saudi Arabia?" Brenda asked looking at Jeff.

"Yeah, I had a bad case of athlete's foot," Jeff said, glaring at Dwight.

"Well anyway," Dwight said, "The doc tells us you're going to be okay. Who the hell did you get mad enough to waylay you like this?" pointing at Jeff's bandaged head.

"I don't have any idea," Jeff said. "Must have been a burglar." Turning to Brenda he asked, "What all did he get anyway?"

"Actually," she replied "I couldn't tell if anything was missing or not. Everything looked the same as the last time I saw it."

"Even the bedroom?" Dwight asked, leering at her, Donna jabbed him in the ribs and laughing he continued, "Well I hope our supply of Famous Grouse wasn't taken. I figure on stopping in there on our way home and have a shooter or two," he finished with a grin.

Donna said, "Oh don't listen to him Jeff. He about went crazy when he heard about this. You know there's a closer bond between you two than just friendship."

Before Jeff could say anything, Brenda said, "Okay! Now what's that all about? I want to know! You two have been beating that thing around the bush ever since I've met you," she was looking at Dwight.

"Sorry love, but I can't tell you. It's a state secret and if I tell you then I'd have to kill Jeff," Dwight said.

"Oh stop it," Donna exclaimed. Turning to Brenda

she said, "Jeff saved Dwight's life in Iraq during that first invasion over there. And almost got himself killed doing it," she finished.

Looking at the two of them with tears in her eyes she said, "There's a bond between these two guys that's stronger than any love one brother has for another. And look at them," she waved a hand at the two men. "They're embarrassed to even talk about it."

She stepped over to the bed and kissed Jeff on the forehead and Jeff said, "Don't you think you ought to find a vase or something for those flowers. They're liable to wilt without water."

"See what I mean," Donna sniffed as she stepped back. "But this is a very good man here Brenda and you better snatch him up while he's ripe!"

"Ripe!" Dwight exclaimed. "Danged if that doesn't sound like you're about to fall off the tree. Either that or you're ready to be picked!"

With a grin he left the Playboy on the bedside table and said, "Come on big mouth, let the young man get back to being 'picked.'"

Donna placed the flowers, already in a vase, on the side table as well. Before leaving she leaned over and kissed Jeff again and with a wave of their hands, they left the room.

41

Jeff had the TV on and was watching a M*A*S*H rerun. He still had a sharp throbbing pain behind his eyes, but it wasn't the blinding pain he remembered when he first came to on the floor of the cabin. He remembered Brenda telling him that he had bled all over the place, so there would probably be stains in his rug when he got home. Oh well, he'd give Birdie a couple extra bucks and see if she could get them out with some kind of heavy duty cleaner.

Brenda had gone home earlier, saying she would be back that evening. Jeff had finally been able to sit up and swing his legs off the side of the bed, without feeling like he was going to faint. He sat there for several minutes and then lay back down on his pillow. His head was pounding and he found the call button for the nurse. She came in the room a few seconds later and Jeff asked her for an aspirin or Tylenol. "Anything," he said, "That will get rid of this killer headache."

"Oh, I think we can do a little better than an aspirin," the nurse said. "I'll be right back."

A few minutes later she returned with a hypodermic needle and injected the contents into his I.V. "This will make you a little groggy for a while, but it should dull the pain. The doctor will be back to see you in an hour or so."

Jeff felt the effects of the injection immediately. He tried to ask the nurse something, but his tongue was too difficult to control, so he lay back and closed his eyes.

"She's right," he thought. "I don't feel a thing. I wonder what that stuff was." He drifted in and out of sleep for the next couple of hours.

"I wondered if I'd have to wake you up," Sheriff Beck said. "I've been standing here for five minutes as it is! Now that you're awake, do you think you can answer a few questions?"

"Hi Sheriff," Jeff said. "I don't know what that was that the nurse gave me, but it must be powerful stuff. My headache is almost gone." Then, "Brenda told me that you talked with her yesterday, or was it the day before, I'm not tracking too well right now."

"Yeah, it was yesterday. George too. I spoke to both of them, right here in your room."

The Sheriff paused and said, "You know Jeff, that girl's got a lot of grit! George too, for that matter. After the initial shock wore off yesterday, they both sat here and wanted to know all the details."

The Sheriff paused and glanced at the door, then continued, "I answered their questions as best I could, without getting into a lot of the bad details, and you know, the animal thing. I just said the remains decayed naturally. I'm sure they both realize what must have happened out there in the woods, but they don't want to accept that yet."

"Well, it sure has given me nightmares, that's for sure," Jeff said. "Did you say George was here too? This morning is the first time I've been aware of anything for a couple of days I guess. Brenda told me you arrested Decker too. Sounds like you're going to be able to wrap things up pretty quickly now."

"I wish! This is just the beginning," Beck said. "The D.A. feels he can get a solid conviction on the remains found in the woods, but we've still got a lot of loose ends to tie up. I'm convinced he murdered Doc somehow, but we haven't been able to come up with anything solid yet. And on top of that, we think he's responsible for the deaths of at least five other people a few years ago."

Beck told Jeff what they had discovered about Decker's background and the suspicious circumstances surrounding the sudden deaths of the men who had degraded him years earlier. He told of his pre-med studies and how he had been expelled for practicing unusual experiments. How it appeared that he had tried to develop a killing substance using 'castor beans' of all things.

Castor beans! What did Jeff remember about castor beans? He searched his memory but couldn't think where he had read about them. He remembered, because they were used to make Castor Oil and the woman that had more or less raised him, would always make him take a tablespoon of the awful stuff whenever he was sick.

The Sheriff had pulled out a small hand held tape recorder. Jeff recognized it as the same type that Beck had used when he first met him in the woods that day. The Sheriff was fiddling with it, trying to find the record button. Finally, he held it up to his mouth and gave his name, the date and place saying this was an interview with the victim of an assault!

He then said, "Mr. Lawson, what can you tell me about the attack you experienced on Monday evening of this week?"

Jeff said, "I really can't tell you much Sheriff. I had just walked in the door and was taking off my coat when somebody hit me from behind. I never saw him or heard anything. Brenda tells me that nothing seems to be missing, so I have no idea why he was there. I must have come home before he could get away with anything."

The Sheriff asked, "Do you know of anybody that would have it in for you for some reason?"

"I don't think so Sheriff. I can't think of anybody that I've crossed. I can't believe it was somebody laying for me. It had to be a thief and when I came in, he must have panicked and clubbed me before I'd see him."

Jeff paused and then asked, "What'd he hit me with anyway? A ball bat?"

Beck replied, "That's just it Jeff. We don't know what he hit you with. And it might even have been a ball bat for all we know! My men walked all over the area, and they couldn't find anything that could have been used as a weapon."

The Sheriff was looking at Jeff and said, "We think the intruder brought the weapon with him and was waiting for you. In other words, it appears to be a premeditated assault with the intent to do great bodily harm. He was trying to kill you!"

"What? Why? I can't think of any reason for anything like that," Jeff said.

"Off hand, I can't either," Beck replied. "But things like this just don't happen without a reason. I can't imagine why, but I have this feeling that it's tied in somehow, with this Decker thing we've got going here."

"Sheriff, that's crazy! Other than finding those bones, I haven't been mixed up in that thing at all." Jeff sat trying to think.

"What does Decker have to say anyway? Has he told you anything that will help?"

The Sheriff exclaimed, "Nothing! As soon as we arrested him he started screaming for a lawyer and refuses to answer any of our questions. We got all his files since he's been in business though. We've been able to determine that our suspicions were correct and it was common practice for him to charge folks for a lot of services that were never provided, including cremations!"

"And Jeff," he continued softly. "We have been able to confirm that those bones you found, were definitely those of Lydia Gunderson. We got the x-rays from the doctor that fixed her leg."

He paused and then said, "We also have been able to have a pretty good understanding of what Doc's notes were and what he thought he'd found. Mrs. Gunderson had been embalmed! There was evidence of this in the remains that he had examined. He apparently was going to check it out himself before talking to me about it. According to his notes he wanted to be sure he was right."

Looking at Jeff, his eyes had watered slightly and he said, "George Gunderson confirmed that Mrs. Gunderson had been embalmed because the family had requested a 'viewing' before she was cremated. George said he didn't receive the urn until several days after the actual funeral."

"My gosh," Jeff exclaimed! "That's right. I remember now. George said that she had suffered so much before she died, but she looked so peaceful in the casket."

Jeff shaking his head, "I didn't go to the funeral itself, I just went to the memorial service when he had interned her ashes."

"Well, I guess that's enough for now," Beck said standing. "Just be careful when you get out of here and keep your doors locked. Might not be a bad idea to leave a light on too. They tell me you're going to be out of here tomorrow. If you think of anything else, give me a call."

Jeff was troubled by the Sheriff's inference that whoever attacked him, did so with the intent to kill him! Who did he know that would hate him that much?

He was still trying to think it through when Dwight Sutherland stuck his head in the door and said, "No nurses this time? Are your winning ways and simple charms not working anymore? That always bugged me about you, how you were like a light bulb attracting bugs into your clutches. You feeling any better?"

"Yeah, I think I'm going to live now. I didn't know for a while there though," Jeff said.

"I just saw the Sheriff down in the parking lot," Dwight said. "He told me he'd just been up to see you. Has he got any ideas about this," motioning at Jeff's bandaged head.

"Not really, except he thinks it was an intentional attack. He doesn't think it was a thief who'd been in there to steal stuff. He thinks that whoever it was, had waited for me to come in and then put my lights out!"

Feeling the bandages on his head he said, "And he did a pretty good job too. I've got lumps on my head the size of ostrich eggs!"

Dwight laughed and said, "You've had worse. That couple of weeks in 'tent city' still gives me nightmares that I'll probably have forever. This is much nicer," waving at the hospital room. "At least there isn't any dust blowing across your bed here."

"Yeah, and what was that business about me'n nurses in Saudia Arabia? The only nurses I saw over there were Medics and they were all male!"

Jeff was laughing. Then asked "What are you doing back here anyway? I thought you went home two or three hours ago."

"Oh no. When we come to the Big City, I can't get Donna out of town until she's seen all the latest doo dads, touched them and then usually ends up saving the money for groceries. I'm going to meet her down at Duffy's in a little while."

Then with a grin he said, "Maybe I can talk that lady friend of yours into coming along with us. She obviously isn't going to get any satisfaction from you tonight!"

Jeff grinned, but before he could answer, Dwight continued, "Jeff, that gal is a real winner. She told us about her talk with the Sheriff, about the thing with her mother's bones. She said the Sheriff tried to put the best slant on it he could, but she knew how terrible it must have been and you know what? She was more concerned about how bad you must have felt about it because the Sheriff told her you'd known about it for quite a while. How did that happen anyway?"

Jeff told Dwight about the photos he'd taken, the repaired bones, the picture in Brenda's photo album and the conclusion that he'd come to as a result and all the discussions he'd had with the Sheriff. As he told his friend all the doubts he'd had and the pain he knew this would cause Brenda, and George.

He said, "That's what I was talking about the other night when I told you there were 'complications' with our relationship."

Dwight leaned forward, gripping his friend on the shoulder saying, "Well, I think you can relax now my friend. She knows, and she's dealing with it. As I said, that's one great gal you've got there. Don't let this one get away."

The nurse came in a little later and asked Jeff if he needed anything for pain and left when he said he didn't.

Dwight stayed for a while longer and then looking at his watch said, "Well, I guess I'd better get down there and meet the old ball and chain at Duffy's. She'll probably be waiting for me with a beer in one hand and fighting off all those old retirees in the place with the other."

Jeff laughed and said, "Thanks Dwight. Tell Donna thanks for the flowers too. I should be out of here and back home by tomorrow. I feel pretty good, so I'm hoping the doctor will let me out of here. This I.V. makes it too difficult to use the bathroom."

Dwight laughed at this and giving a mock left handed salute, turned and walked out of the room.

Jeff was still grinning from his friend's visit, when Lester & Myra Noonan stepped into the room. Myra was carrying a card and a small package that Jeff assumed was a small box of candy.

Jeff said, "Well Hi there folks. Who's running the store Les?" With a grin, Jeff said, "I leave you in charge for just two days and here you are taking time off in the middle of the day!"

"Middle of the day," Les snorted. "You better get a clock in here. It's almost six o'clock."

"What!" Jeff said. "And they haven't even brought me anything to eat. No wonder I'm feeling empty."

Myra stepped up to the bedside and said, "Oh Mr. Lawson, are you okay? We've been so worried about you."

"Short Round, if you call me Mr. Lawson again, Les is fired!"

Myra gaped at him and Jeff pulled her close and gave her a hug saying, "Oh I'm just kidding. Can't fire a man who drives the only Cadillac the company owns. But you'd better not call me Mister again and I mean it."

Jeff lay back smiling at the two of them.

"Are they taking good care of you boss?" Les asked. "Is there anything you need? Anything we can do for you?"

Les was carrying a leather letter case and as he sat down by the bed, he was opening it. Myra sat on the other side of the bed watching Jeff.

"Oh I'm sure they're taking care of me, except for this dinner thing. I thought they fed us 'sickies' a lot earlier in the day than this."

Pressing the call button by his bed, he said, "Excuse me just a minute Les, I'm going to ask the nurse about that."

Seconds later the nurse stepped in the room saying, "Do you need pain medication sir?" Then seeing the visitors she stopped and waited for Jeff to answer.

"No, nothing like that. As a matter of fact I feel pretty good. I was just wondering if I could get something to eat.

I don't think I've had anything, but whatever is in this I.V. all day."

Then as an after thought, "And incidentally, will I be seeing a doctor yet today? And, who is my doctor by the way. I don't even know his name!"

The nurse said, "Oh, yes sir. That's Dr. Sing. He'll be making his rounds a little later tonight. And I'll get you a sandwich and some juice right away. Are you sure you're feeling better, no pain at all?"

"Oh, I wouldn't say there's no pain. But it's more like a very dull ache. Nothing like I had this morning," Jeff said. "Doctor Sing you said. What nationality is he anyway?"

"I believe he's from India. He's been here, at this hospital for several years now. He's a real nice man," the nurse answered.

With that she turned and left. Les was handing Jeff some print outs and said, "I brought these along in case you wanted to see the daily production and shipping figures."

Jeff glanced at the papers and said, "Are you having any problems, everything running smoothly?"

Les said, "Yes sir, everything is humming right along. Matter of fact, our sales figures went up a couple of points this week. Business is good right now." Jeff was handing the papers back to Les.

"I'll look at these when I get back to the office. If you should have any problems, you handle them!"

Jeff turned to Myra and continued, "I think it's only fair for him to run the operation when I'm gone, don't you? Unless, of course, you don't think he can handle it!"

"Les can do anything," Myra responded loyally. "He won't let you down Mr. La ... Jeff."

Jeff laughed at this and said, "I'm sure he won't. He has my total confidence. But don't let him tell you he has to work late at the office. If he isn't home by five thirty, call the cops!"

Suddenly, this made Jeff think of the situation with Quint Mason. And he asked Les "Have you heard anything about the mess that Marshal Mason has gotten himself into?"

Les laughed out loud, saying, "Yeah, he drove a 'borrowed' sheriff's car into Jamison's hardware a couple of days ago. The story is, that he was polluted and the Sheriff locked him up in his own jail, and then transferred him down to the county jail. As far as I know, he's still there!"

Just then the nurse returned with a tray and Les motioned to Myra saying, "We'll let you eat your dinner Jeff. Hurry back to work, but don't overdo it. We want you back, but we want you healthy too." With a slight wave they left the room.

Jeff was looking at a sandwich with some unidentifiable filling, a small bag of potato chips and a small carton of orange juice.

He looked up at the nurse in distaste saying "Egads maam. Is that the best you could do? What kind of filling is that anyway? They don't serve horsemeat here do they?"

42

It was nearly nine o'clock before Doctor Sing made an appearance. He was a short bespectacled individual of indeterminate age. He was dressed in a suit with a stethoscope hanging over his shoulder. He smiled at Jeff as he introduced himself and lifted his arm taking Jeff's pulse.

Finally, taking out a small flashlight from his pocket, he asked, "Well, Mr. Lawson, they tell me you're feeling a lot better than the last time I saw you."

Jeff replied, "I have no idea when that might have been Doctor, but if you're asking me how I feel, I'm feeling good enough that I want to get out of this place!"

Doctor Sing gave a short laugh, saying, "I don't think I have a patient in the building that doesn't tell me exactly the same thing."

He was shining the flashlight from one eye to the other. Putting the stethoscope to his ears, he listened to Jeff's heartbeat, then, asking Jeff to lean forward, placed the instrument on his back telling Jeff to take a couple of deep breaths.

Straightening up and taking the stethoscope from his ears he said, "Are you having much pain? Do you have a headache at all?"

Jeff said, "Oh yes I do, a little, but it's not bad at all. The bandages are starting to bother me more than anything else. I feel like a mummy with all these things wrapped around my head."

Doctor Sing smiled and replied, "Do they itch?"

As Jeff nodded, he said, "Well, we'll take a look and see how the lacerations are coming. Would you mind pressing the call button for a nurse and we'll change them for something that might be a little more comfortable."

As they were waiting for the nurse, Doctor Sing explained, "When they brought you in the other night, I was afraid you had a fractured skull. You must have a very hard skull Mr. Lawson. You didn't have a fracture, but you had been struck with such force that the skin separated, leaving a couple of really serious wounds. One in the back of your head and the other on the frontal area over your forehead. Took a lot of stitches to sew them back together. But, other than a couple of interesting scars, you shouldn't have any further complications from this adventure."

Before Jeff could respond, "Actually, the scars will all be covered by your hair, once it grows back in."

"Once it grows back in," Jeff exclaimed? "Just how much hair did you have to remove anyway?" He thought about what he had just asked then said, "Never mind Doc, I'm just glad you were here when they brought me in. You've done a good job and I appreciate it."

"Thank you," Doctor Sing replied. "I'm a little curious about a couple of other injuries I see that you've experienced sometime ago."

He was looking at Jeff curiously and when Jeff didn't respond, "You have a number of scars on your lower back and a large scar on one of your legs. Can you tell me about them?" he asked.

Reluctantly, Jeff said, "Shrapnel from a mortar round in the back and rifle round though the leg. Is it important?" he asked shortly. "I got them all on the same day a few years ago. As far as I'm concerned they're ancient history," he said.

"Hmmmm, I thought so," Sing said. "I saw a lot of those kind of wounds in Viet Nam. I was a Navy corpsman in those years. Whoever worked on you, knew what they were doing," he finished.

As he turned, the nurse came in and together they removed the bandages from Jeff's head. Doctor Sing had the nurse sponge the cuts and nodding his head said, "Well, these look good. I think we'll let you go home tomorrow morning Mr. Lawson. I'd like you back here Saturday morning and we'll remove these stitches. In the meantime, if you have any sudden serious pain or nausea, or anything else that feels unusual, get back here immediately. Okay?"

Jeff was grinning and said, "You bet Doc. But I hope I never have to come back here again. They have the worst chicken salad sandwich I've ever eaten."

43

When Sheriff Beck returned to his office, he gave the recorder with Jeff's interview to Irma and asked her to find somebody to transcribe it. He was just settled at his desk when Lieutenant Reynolds tapped on his doorframe before entering. Beck motioned him in to take a chair across the desk.

"What's up Bill?" the Sheriff asked?

"Well, I've been trying to find out why Castor Beans held so much interest for Decker," he said.

"Oh, what have you found out?" the Sheriff asked with sudden interest.

Reynolds had several pages printed information and was referring to them as he said, "Well sir, aside from being used to make Castor Oil, the bean has the characteristics for the development of an extremely deadly poisonous substance called 'Ricin'! It is a protein toxin extracted from the castor bean!"

"Ricin!" The Sheriff exclaimed. "Isn't that the stuff the government thinks could be used as a terrorist poison of some sort?"

"That's it." Reynolds referred to his notes and said "Ricin is part of the waste 'mash' produced when castor oil is made. Back in the 1940s, the government experimented with Ricin as a possible warfare agent. There is some suspicion, that Hussein used this stuff on his own people in the eighties. It can be delivered as a powder, a mist or a pellet."

The Sheriff sat back trying to comprehend what he had just been told. Then he asked, "If it is inhaled or swallowed, does it kill immediately, or what?"

"No sir. As far as I can find out, Ricin by itself, takes anywhere from eight to twelve hours to actually kill a human being."

Reynolds referring to his notes again, continued "And from what I've been able to learn so far, an individual exposed to Ricin would go through Hell before they died. Vomiting, Diarrhea, seizures and any number of other unpleasant conditions."

"That fits with those fellows that he apparently murdered a few years ago." The Sheriff was opening a file folder and leafing through the pages, "Here it is," he said. "All five of those fellas died in unusual circumstances. All went through a period of intense sickness before dying. All died within ten hours or so after getting sick."

"But, that's not what happened with Doc," the Sheriff continued. "He apparently died instantly, and there was no indication that he had been sick before he died. According to Stony, Doc looked like he had just dozed off and went to sleep."

Looking up at Reynolds, he said, "Keep digging Bill. I think we're on the right track here, but, this guy is smart, maybe even a genius. We've got him cold on the 'bones' case, but the D.A. won't pursue the earlier deaths or that of Doc until ..... We have to find the answers before we can charge him! Stick with it, okay?"

"Yes sir. If I come up with anything I'll let you know right away!" With that he got up and hurried out of the office.

Beck was leafing through his file again when Irma entered his office. "Sheriff, what are you going to do about Marshal Mason," she asked? "He's been here all week and you haven't charged him." She was looking at him curiously.

"I don't know what I'm going to do with that jerk yet." Then with a sigh, "Oh Hell, why don't you have him brought down here. I guess it's time to talk to him."

A short time later a deputy escorted Mason into Beck's office. The Sheriff continued to be preoccupied with the file on his desk and was leafing through page after page. Finally he looked up at Mason, who was standing across the desk from him.

The deputy was standing by the door and Beck motioned for him to leave. He stared at Mason for a few more moments, at last saying, "Sit down Quint. I guess it's time you and I have a little talk."

Before Beck could say anything further, Mason said, "Sheriff, I know what you're going to say and you're right! I shouldn't have been driving that patrol car. It was a mistake and I'm sorry as I can be about it."

The Sheriff said, "Sit down Quint. You're in a peck of trouble and I don't think I'm going to be able to help you this time."

Mason still standing was about to say something

when Beck said, "Quint, I'm not going to tell you again, sit down!"

Mason quickly took his seat, and then said, "Tommy, you've got to do this for me one more time. I promise it's the last time I'll ever ask you to help me. I don't know what I'll do if the council fires me!"

Beck was disgusted and said, "Quint, you're supposed to be an officer of the law. And you go running all over the country getting drunk and chasing hookers. I warned you the other day about that, but you didn't want to hear it. Well, this time it looks like your chickens have come home to roost!"

"Listen Sheriff, if you'll get me off the hook this last time, I think I can give you some information that might make a big difference in that case you've got against Whathisname Decker. I saw him down in the cells and know you've arrested him for disposing of the bodies of some of his customers!" Mason was sitting forward on the edge of his chair waiting for Beck to answer.

The Sheriff decided to take a shot in the dark "Oh, are you talking about that thing with Red Waters? We know all about that! And we know you're the one that sent that letter to young Lawson and made those, so called, anonymous calls." Beck was watching Mason closely and saw his face pale at this information.

Mason was in shock. "But, but, if you know, why haven't you done something about it?"

Then suddenly, a sly look came across Mason's face. He said, "Oh ho! I see! All you know about is the thing with the undertaker. Well, I've got eye witness evidence that Red was a killer before he ever got involved with Decker!"

Now it was Beck's turn to be in shock. What in the world was Mason talking about? 'Involved with Decker'! What was Red Waters mixed up in here? Beck had to know.

The Sheriff decided to bluff, "Yeah, well we know there were rumors to that affect. But how do you know about the thing with Decker?"

"Humpf" Mason snorted. "When I heard what old Chet Beasley was telling folks, about what he'd seen Red do, I picked him up and brought him in for questioning" he said self-importantly.

"Chet told me that Red was working for this Decker fella down here. When I asked him about it, he said I might better ask Red about that." Mason was sniffing into a handkerchief.

"Well" Beck said! "Is that all you have?

"No, no it sure isn't," Mason said. "I took old Beasley out to the lake, where he said he saw Red Waters push Thad Raeford out of his boat with a canoe paddle and just let him drown. He said every time Raeford came up for air, Red ran over him with his canoe. He wasn't but hundred, hundred fifty feet off shore."

Mason paused and wiped his nose and continued, "Beasley told me he stood there in the trees and watched the whole thing. Said that Red just came up and bumped his canoe into Thad's boat and old Thad stood up and was cussing Red when Red just reached over with his paddle and pushed him into the lake."

"How come you never followed up on that?" Beck asked? "If you had an eye witness like you say, why didn't you go arrest that young Indian boy?"

"Because Beasley hated the Raefords as much as Red

Waters did! Maybe more. Those bastards were always pickin on old Chet and beating him up out of just plain meanness! He told me if I ever got him to court he'd swear he never saw nothin!"

Mason shrugged and said, "So, without Beasley, I had nothing! But, as sure as I'm sitting here, he did it, and he tried to kill the other brother too!"

"What makes you think that," Beck said. "Didn't you tell me that the other brother got hurt working at the sawmill?"

"Sure, but Red Waters was working in that saw mill at the same time! I heard a story about how Jeremy would find a bottle of whiskey in his locker every now and then and he didn't know where they were coming from. But he didn't care and just drank it up every time".

Mason paused and said, "There were those that claimed that it was Red that was supplying Raeford with the whiskey. And then one day, when there wasn't anybody close by to see it happen, Raeford 'accidentally' fell against that big saw. He was drunk all right, but he claimed someone had pushed him, but he never saw who it was. A week or so later, Red quit and started repairing lawnmowers full time!"

Beck sat staring at Mason and said, "Okay, so you figure this all happened because of what Red thought those guys had done to his father. You told me he fell under a train or something didn't you?"

Mason was nodding in agreement and the Sheriff said, "But what has any of that got to do with the Decker case? We've got all of his records, including payroll history and there isn't any record of Red working for Decker at all."

"I don't know, maybe he paid him in cash, or, maybe

he didn't pay him at all. He had buried Red's father and I think he was making Red work off the cost of the burial."

Mason was looking at his feet, then looking up said, "When those bones turned up, I remembered something else that Beasley had told me. He said that when Red was working down here, he saw him driving a hearse up on County Route twelve one day. He thought it was funny, because there's no cemetary or anything out that way. Where Beasley saw him, was only a few miles from where those bones were discovered."

Looking at the Sheriff, Mason said, "I think he was taking one of those bodies out to dump in the woods!"

44

Jeff had been dressed and waiting for Dwight to pick him up for the past hour. He was resting in an easy chair, which was normally available for visitors. He had called Dwight after Doctor Sing had left the night before and asked if he'd mind coming down and picking him up this morning.

Before Brenda had left, she had made an offhand comment that she was going to have to go to school today and try and get caught up for the past two days that she'd missed. Because of that, he hadn't called her, but knew if he asked, Dwight wouldn't mind assuming he wasn't tied up with some farm business

Which made him think of Brenda's visit last evening. She had come in a little after six thirty and seeing what was left of the sandwich on Jeff's tray, she said she'd be right back and left for nearly thirty minutes. When she returned, she was carrying a sack from McDonalds.

She said, "I hope I don't get you in trouble for this, but from the looks of that tray, you didn't think much of their sandwich, so, I brought us a couple of 'Big Macs.'" She was grinning at him and said, "French fries too. A double order, I haven't had anything to eat yet either."

"Now I know why I've fallen in love with you. It's definitely your cooking," he said! At the look she gave him he continued, "Among other things!"

Jeff had sat on the edge of the bed with his feet dangling over the side, with Brenda sitting beside him. They were using the serving table and enjoying the hamburgers when the nurse came in to get his tray.

She stopped and looked at the two of them sitting there and didn't say a word, but picked up the tray and left. While she had been looking at them, both Brenda and Jeff had stopped chewing waiting for her to comment, but when she didn't, they continued eating and laughed.

Jeff was laughing and said, "Maybe we should have asked her to bring us something to drink." He was reaching for a french fry when the nurse returned carrying two cartons of juice.

She was smiling and said, "Boy those look good. I'm sometimes surprised at the quality of the food we serve here!" As Brenda and Jeff laughed, she turned and left the room.

"That was awfully nice of her," Brenda said. "She must think you're something really special." She daintily dabbed her mouth and reached for the last fry.

"Of course I'm special. I'm probably the only patient she's got on this floor that she has to help pee!"

Brenda dropped the French fry on her lap and Jeff quickly snatched it up. Before she could stop him, he popped it in his mouth and said "Hmmmmm! The last one is always the best, isn't it?"

"You rat," She said. "If somebody hadn't already tried to 'brain' you, I might seriously consider it!"

"Careful how you talk there, sweetheart," Jeff stopped grinning. "If the Sheriff hears you say something like that, he's liable to be giving you the third degree, rubber hoses and all!"

Brenda laughed out loud, "Oh my, I'm so scared!" She said, "Why would the Sheriff ever do something like that to little ole me?"

Now serious, Jeff said, "Well, he's convinced that this didn't happen because I walked in on a robber. He thinks somebody was laying in wait and clobbered me, trying to kill me!"

Brenda was staring at him in astonishment. "Whaaat? Who in the world would want to do something like that? Do you have somebody out there that hates you that much?"

Then squinting her eyes she said, "Okay. Who is it? What's her name? It had to be a jealous woman! Somebody is that mad at you because of me!" She paused thinking, "Or maybe it's somebody who's got it in for me!"

Jeff was looking at her in wonder. "Where in the world did you come up with something like that? A jealous woman, for crying out loud! I haven't had anything other than a casual date with anybody for a year!" Jeff started laughing and Brenda was glaring at him.

He leaned over and kissed her tenderly and said, "I'm sorry my dear, I don't mean to laugh at you, but think about it. A woman! She'd have to be an Amazon to hit me as hard as this guy did!" As he said this, he was rubbing his head over the bandages.

Brenda had only been gone a few minutes when Doctor Sing had made his visit.

As he sat waiting for his friend, he had turned on the TV to a local news program and was soon engrossed in the lead story concerning the arrest of Forest Decker. He was appearing before a judge this morning for a pretrial hearing. The young District Attorney had been interviewed and was quoted as referring to the case as 'this reprehensible crime' and 'despicable conduct' on the part of Decker.

The news people had gone to some lengths to cover Decker's background and activities before purchasing this local funeral home. Interestingly, they somehow had the information concerning his financial difficulties. Jeff smiled at that thinking, that information had to have come straight from one of the Sheriff's 'off the record' comments.

"Morning sport," Dwight said as he walked in. "You ready to go? I had a little problem getting here. There was a wreck on the main road and I had to go around the long way."

"Oh boy, am I ready! I sure feel sorry for those folks that have to spend a couple of weeks in this place," Jeff replied. "This has got to be the greatest 'fat farm' in the state. I think I've lost seven or eight pounds in just a couple of days!"

Dwight laughed and said, "It's good for you. You big shot executives do too much sitting around and have a tendency to get a fat ass and a big gut!"

Jeff laughed at this saying, "Maybe you're right, but you should have seen the breakfast they served this morning. Rubber eggs, instant coffee and dried toast, without butter. The orange juice was okay, but that's about it."

Dwight said mockingly, "Oh my, you poor man. I guess they should have kept you on that I.V. so you could get proper nutrients!" Then he said, "Well grab your coat and let's go. Maybe we can get an early lunch at Duffy's."

Jeff nodded agreement, but then said, "That sounds like a good idea, but I don't have any money. I sent my billfold home with Brenda last night."

Dwight sighed and said, "Well I guess I can cover lunch for you this once. Come on get going," then as Jeff got to his feet, "are you alright, you look a little unsteady there." He was stepping forward to help him.

"Yeah, I'm okay," Jeff said. "I just get a little light headed if I stand up too quick!" He felt his head where the smaller bandages were now in place and said, "At least they took all those mummy wraps off my noggin!"

"Well, if you think that makes you look any better, you're mistaken," Dwight laughed. "You look like you've been worked on by a barber just released from an insane asylum!"

"Oh thanks a lot pal," Jeff replied. "The Doc told me it would all grow back and cover up all the sewing that he seemed so proud of. Give me another week and I'll look just like my old handsome self again."

As they walked out of the room, an older nurse was waiting for them. She was standing behind a wheel chair. Shaking a finger at Jeff she said, "I thought you'd try and sneak out of here without getting your mandatory ride in one of our wheel chairs." Then without fanfare she pointed at the chair and said, "Get in and enjoy the ride!"

Dwight was laughing out loud and Jeff with a hangdog expression sat down in the wheel chair and was trying to

45

The pretrial lasted only twenty minutes. Decker sat silently at the defense table dressed in the orange coveralls of a county prisoner. A mortician's association that Decker was a member of had supplied his attorney. The young attorney had not argued against any of the evidence presented except to describe it as highly circumstantial, but couldn't refute any of it.

He had asked that Decker be released on his own recognizance, but the D.A. quickly argued that there was reason to believe that the defendant might be a flight risk and recommended that bail be set at a million dollars! After a moments thought the judge had set the bail at half a million and said the trial date would be set for a month later.

After a few congratulatory words with the D.A., Beck headed for his office. He was thinking about the conversation he'd had with Quint Mason. Shaking his head, he didn't know why he had let him go. He had decided at the time, that it was possible that he was onto something that could be helpful in his case against Decker.

And Mason had been such a pathetic figure. Beck knew even as he released him, that the Lakeview City Council would undoubtly fire him at their next meeting, which was next Monday evening.

Beck had told Mason, that as a personal favor, if anybody ever asked about the circumstances of the release, that he would say it was simply because of a lack of evidence. He told Quint that he doubted if anybody would ever question his decision, unless of course, he continued with his abuse of alcohol and questionable activities when he went out of town on 'business'.

As a final gesture, he had handed Mason the card of a local AA group and suggested he contact them right away. With that he had told the Deputy, that had been waiting outside his office door, that Marshal Mason was free to go and to give him any assistance he might require to expedite his release from custody.

Back in his office he decided to call the hospital and see if Jeff Lawson was being released today. When he learned that he had just left the hospital, Beck sat back in his chair and was about to reach for a Coke from his refrigerator, when he suddenly decided to go down the street to Duffy's and have one of his 'special' cokes. He hadn't had breakfast this morning and he was hungry. Maybe he'd have a sandwich too.

There were only a few patrons in Duffy's when the Sheriff walked in. As he looked around the room he saw Dwight Sutherland sitting in a booth and over the back of the booth he could see the top of a bandaged head.

As he walked towards them, Dwight put up his hands and said, "Don't shoot Sheriff, this character that looks like the mummy, really isn't dangerous," motioning at Jeff.

Ignoring Dwight's comment, Beck said to Jeff, "Hi there friend. How are you feeling? I called the hospital for a report on you and they told me they let you go."

"And knowing Jeff as we all do," Dwight said. "You figured he'd probably head for the nearest bar, right?"

"Shut up Dwight," Jeff said good-humouredly, "Sit down Sheriff, we were just about to order a sandwich. Are you hungry?"

"I guess I am. Didn't get a chance to have anything other than a cup of coffee before I left the house this morning." He paused and continued, "I was over at the courthouse early for Decker's hearing. Thought maybe I'd have to testify, but it went off smooth as silk."

The bartender in his white apron approached and took their orders and returned to the bar. Dwight said, "Yeah I heard he was going to a pretrial this morning. How'd it go?"

Beck told them briefly about the hearing, and then turning to Jeff, he said, "I let Marshal Mason go yesterday. I don't know if I made the right decision or not, but he gave me some information that might prove helpful."

Then glancing at Dwight, he hesitated then with a shrug said, "He did have some interesting information on your young Indian up there. I'd like to come up and talk with him tomorrow if you're going to be in your office."

Dwight said somewhat protectively, "Hey Sheriff, give him a break. He's still recovering from getting whacked the other night! He shouldn't even be thinking about going back to work until next week."

Jeff grinned and said, "Listen to the old mother hen here. You'd think I was at death's door to hear him tell it."

With a small laugh "I think I'll go in for a half day or

so. So if you want to come up in the morning, I should be there until noon anyway Sheriff."

Curious, Jeff asked, "What did Quint tell you anyway? I hope he isn't getting Red in trouble of some kind. Should I have our attorney there when you talk to him?"

"No, I hope it doesn't come to that, but Quint made some pretty damning statements. I'd rather not go into them right now, but for the most part, everything he told me could be considered 'hearsay' anyway."

Continuing he said, "I'm not really interested in anything he's ever been accused of, except Quint made some comments about an association that Red may have had with Decker a year or so ago."

"What, with Decker?" Jeff exclaimed. "I intended to ask him about that after I got that so called anonymous phone call from Quint. Red had shown on his application that he had worked for Decker for three or four months. I thought it was funny because he'd have to drive way down here for minimal wage kind of work."

"Now that is interesting," the Sheriff said. "According to Decker's payroll information, Red Waters never worked for him! He's got very accurate records on the other part time folks that work for him from time to time. But nothing on Red Waters!"

The bartender arrived with their drinks and said that the sandwiches would be a few more minutes.

Jeff took a swallow of the Coke he had ordered and said, "Sheriff, I can't believe he could have been mixed up in this mess."

Shaking his head, he asked, "Why would he get involved in all this and not get paid unless ...." Jeff paused.

Beck said quickly, "Unless what?"

"What, oh," Jeff said slowly "I was thinking maybe he was getting paid under the table, or something. Is that what you're thinking Sheriff?"

"Until I talk with him, I really don't know what to think," Beck said. "I'll take a run up there in the morning and maybe we can talk to him in your office, if that'd be okay?"

"Yes sir that would be fine. I want to get this cleared up right away." Jeff said. "I've got plans for that kid. I sure hope what your suggesting turns out to be a waste of our time."

46

renda was waiting for them when they turned in Jeff's driveway. She was standing in the doorway with her hands on her hips watching Jeff struggle to get out of Dwight' pick up truck.

It was a four-wheel drive Ford 250 and it felt like it was three feet off the ground. As hard as it was getting out from that height, it was easy compared to the distortions Jeff had gone through to climb into the thing!

As Dwight came around the front of the truck, Jeff snarled, "Why in the Hell didn't you bring the Jeep station wagon for crying out loud. I feel like a circus monkey trying to get in and out of this thing."

Seeing Brenda, he broke into a smile and started toward her. It had been snowing and there was a slight accumulation on the ground. He slipped slightly as he stepped onto the porch and before Dwight could step forward to help him, Brenda grabbed his arm and pulled him onto the drier part of the porch.

"Thanks," Jeff mumbled trying to take her in his arms.

She pushed him away and turned and walked into the cabin.

"What's that all about?" Jeff said looking at Dwight who shrugged.

"Ah, maybe I should run along" Dwight said. "I've got a lot of work to do at home."

"Oh no you don't. Not until we find out what this is all about." Then somewhat self righteously, he said, "I don't get it. I didn't even have a drink either!"

As they walked in, Brenda had seated herself on the couch in front of the TV. She had not said a word to Jeff yet, but she turned and said sweetly to Dwight, "Thank you Dwight, for bringing this idiot home with you. Did you have a nice lunch at the Log Jam?"

Dwight started to answer, but Jeff, angered at Brenda's attitude, spoke, saying, "I think before this goes any further, you'd better tell me what this all about. What's got your jaws all tight anyway? And maybe you better start by telling us why you think we've been at the Log Jam!"

Brenda glared at him and said, "Because when I got here a little while ago, the front door was unlocked again! And you weren't here! When I called the hospital, they told me you had been released this morning. So, where else would you be, if not the Log Jam?"

"Are you saying that you think we were here earlier and left?" Jeff asked?

"Yes I am 'darling'. I was the last person out of here the other night, remember? And I locked the door when I left. But, it was unlocked again when I got here an hour ago. You were supposed to call me as soon as you got here, remember?"

She couldn't stop now, "My gosh Jeff, look at you!

Can't you remember a simple little thing like locking your door when you leave? What if that guy had been waiting in here again when I walked in the door?"

Jeff said, "Brenda, you're mistaken. You're all upset over nothing. There's got to be an explanation for the door being unlocked."

"I think I've pretty well told you why it was unlocked," Brenda sniffed. "And you didn't answer me, why didn't you call me before going in to the Log Jam?"

Jeff was angry and hurt. Brenda's lack of trust was unnerving. Finally he said quietly, "Brenda, I think you'd better go on home for a while. When you're ready to listen, we'll talk again, but for now I think you'd better leave before this goes too far!"

"Oh Jeff, No! I can't do that. I can't believe you'd do this to me. Not after what you've just been through. This whole thing is driving me crazy ...." She was crying.

Dwight stepped forward and was about to say something and Jeff with a look in his eyes that Dwight recognized as pure anger, motioned for him to step back and stay out of this dispute.

"Ahh, yeah, I guess I'll be running along Jeff. Don't forget, Wednesday night at my place for poker." With that he turned and left.

Jeff watched as Brenda stood up and, looking at Jeff, said, "Okay Jeff, I'll go home. But if I leave here without an explanation, I won't be back!"

Jeff exploded, "Okay, have it your way. I don't want you to come back either! A relationship has to include mutual trust. I don't want to give you an explanation! You don't deserve it! I told you that you were mistaken, but you had made up your mind about some silly reason you imagined why I hadn't called you. I guess I was wrong about where this was going. I'm sorry, good night Brenda."

He turned and walked away, down the hallway toward his bathroom. He had to take a couple of aspirin. His head had started to pound during the confrontation with Brenda. He heard the front door open and close and felt sick at the exchange of such bitterness. He swallowed three extra strength Bufferin and walked back into the main room. It was quiet and suddenly seemed so empty to Jeff that the thought brought tears to his eyes.

Walking to the kitchen counter he pulled down the bottle of Famous Grouse from the cupboard and poured the drink into a glass of ice. He stood there for several minutes thoughtfully sipping the drink and then, went back and picked up his coat that he'd taken off as he'd entered earlier. Slipping it on and grabbing a hat, he started out the back sliding door. Stopping he came back and refilled his glass and carrying it, walked out through the falling snow toward his gazebo by the lake.

Much later when he started back to the cabin, his feet were freezing and his ears felt like they were frozen. The temperature had fallen dramatically in the past hour. As he walked into the cozy warmth of his little cabin, he went to the counter and poured himself another drink.

Suddenly, Brenda said, "I guess you'd better pour one of those for me too. That is, if you can forgive a stupid fool like me."

"Jeff," she said walking toward him, "I'm so crazy about you I just can't stand it. And after you were attacked," motioning toward the bandages under his hat. "I guess I went a little nuts this afternoon. I saw Dwight out in the driveway and he told me in no uncertain terms what an idiot I am."

Shaking her head, "Boy, did he ever! I wish I had a friend like that."

Jeff stood looking at her as she came near. He didn't know what to say. He started to say something and she interrupted him "Just pour me a drink will you please."

Then, "I'm going to try real hard my darling, not to be a clinging vine type. I'm going to try and trust you implicitly from now on. If I try real hard, will you forgive me?"

"Will you marry me?" Jeff blurted. "I can't think of anybody in this world that I'd rather have 'clinging' to me." He paused, "Well, will you? Marry me?"

Brenda was staring at him and said, "Sweetheart" like speaking to a child, "That's a foregone conclusion. There was never any doubt that I was going to marry you!"

"I can't believe I said that!" Jeff said. "I've been wondering for days how to say that. I love you, but I was afraid you'd say no. I've been stumbling along here trying to ......"

Brenda stopped his rambling. She stepped forward and kissed him passionately and drew back looking at him, then stepped forward and kissed him again. His head was spinning with excitement.

She tenderly removed his hat and touching the bandages on his head asked, "Are they bothering you. You look so crazy with your hair shaved off here and there."

"No not really. They're sore is all. As soon as he takes the bandages off on Saturday, I think I'll go to a barber and have it all cut off. Then it can all grow back together."

Her laugh was light and happy. She said, "I'm looking

forward to seeing that." Then, "Pour my drink darling and let's talk. I feel like such a fool."

They were sitting on the couch talking softly when the phone rang. Jeff got up and answered it.

"Jeff, are you alright. Dwight just told me that you kicked Brenda out of the house! Are you crazy? She just misunderstood that's all. Are you nuts?" It was Donna Sutherland. "Please tell me you called her back and apologized. Please don't let her get away." Then, "There's no doubt she's too good for you, but that's neither here nor there. She's ....."

Before Donna could go on Jeff said, "I'd like you to be the first to know. I've asked Brenda to marry me and she's said yes! Now what have you got to say?"

Silence on the line. Jeff could hear Donna whispering something to Dwight. Then "Okay, We'll be right over!" The line went dead and Jeff was looking at the phone, thinking, did she say 'they'd be right over'?

Jeff returned to the couch saying, "Guess what? We're about to have company. That was Donna and she was afraid I'd shot you or something I guess. Anyway, they're coming over and should be here in a few minutes."

Brenda laughed and said, "Oh brother, I don't know if I can face Dwight after the tongue lashing he gave me. He didn't spare the rod, he let me have it full blast!"

Jeff was thinking, "You know, there's something I guess I better tell you before they get here. You deserve to know that anyway."

Brenda had a concerned look on her face, "I guess now I'll have to find out you were married to an Arab or something!"

"No, no, nothing quite that shocking, but I think you

should know why the door was unlocked. Today is the day Birdie comes to clean and she apparently forgot to lock it when she left this morning!"

Laughing out loud, he said, "And what do you think about that kiddo?"

47

Jeff groaned when the alarm went off. He had just about decided to stay in bed when he remembered he was supposed to meet Sheriff Beck at his office this morning.

As he rolled over, he suddenly remembered something else .... "Good morning darling," Brenda said sleepily.

She was lying there next to him wearing one of his tee shirts. She said she couldn't sleep without something on, so she'd gotten up and rummaged through his drawers and come up with this undershirt.

He leaned down and kissed her and then lay down again beside her. "Mmmmm," he said. "If this is what being married to you is going to be like, I'm going to like marriage."

"I'm going to be a good wife to you Jeff," she was snuggling into his arms. "I feel like an idiot about that scene I made last night. I won't embarrass either one of us like that again."

Jeff held her close and said, "Stop worrying about

last night. As it turned out, it was a pretty good night, all things considered."

He was softly running his hand back and forth across her back and suddenly realized that his soft caresses were actually working the undershirt up higher and higher until his fingers touched the warm flesh of her back.

"Oh dear, you better stop that. I've got to go home and get ready for school." She was squirming in his arms. "Oh boy, that feels good. I'm glad my first class isn't until ten this morning, otherwise I think I'd probably be late for sure!"

Saying this she ducked her head forward as Jeff eased the tee shirt over her head and tossed it on the floor.

As Jeff stepped out of the bathroom, he was tying the belt around his robe and hurried from the bedroom to the main room, just in time to catch Brenda before she left. She had slipped on a hooded coat and was just about to walk out the door when Jeff stopped her.

He kissed her softly, then a little more passionately and said," Give me a call when you get out of school today will you? I should be here this afternoon, but I'll have my cell phone with me anyway."

"Okay lover. But this was a one night stand," she said coyly. "I don't want to make a habit of this. People will talk."

"People will talk!" Jeff exclaimed. "What people? I don't have a neighbor within three miles!"

"You don't have to have neighbors. Word will get around without having neighbors." She lifted up on tiptoes and gave him a kiss and said, "Go back to the bedroom. You're all wet and when I open this door there's going to be a cold draft. I don't want you getting pneumonia on top of everything else that's happened."

She gave him a gentle shove and he stepped back and left her standing there waiting for him to get to the hallway.

He was wearing a bright orange John Deere stocking cap when he walked into the office an hour later. As he was taking off his coat, Mrs. Parsons looked up from her desk and commented, "The hat goes well with your tie this morning."

Jeff looked down to see he had put on a paisley tie with mostly purple colors running through it.

Mrs. Parsons came around her desk and walked to Jeff and gave him a hug. Stepping back she asked, "Are you supposed to be back to work so soon? Are you sure you feel good enough to be in here today?"

"I'm afraid I look a lot worse than I feel. I'm only going to be here for a few hours, then I'm going home and get some sleep." Jeff was walking toward his office, while Mrs. Parsons was taking his coat to a small closet on the side of the room.

Turning back to her, Jeff said, "By the way, Sheriff Beck is going to stop by sometime this morning. Will you let me know as soon as he gets here please?" Then he stepped into his office and gently closed the door.

As soon as this business with Red Waters and the Sheriff was over, Jeff was going to leave the office all right, but he wasn't going home to sleep. He wanted to see George Gunderson and see how he was taking the terrible revelation about Lydia. He sat at his desk and picked up the phone and punched George's number. The phone rang several times but there was no answer.

His phone chirped and he punched a button and he heard Mrs. Parsons saying that the Sheriff was coming in the lobby. Jeff moved quickly and was standing in his office doorway when the Sheriff came in. Jeff motioned for him to come in his office.

"Morning Sheriff, you're here bright and early. Would you like a cup of coffee? I was just about to have Mrs. Parsons bring one to me," Jeff said, nodding at Mrs. Parsons.

"Sounds good to me. It's cold out there this morning," then to Mrs. Parsons, "Black please."

When Mrs. Parsons brought the coffee, Jeff asked her to call Bud Lyndaman and ask him to send Red Waters to his office. He asked the Sheriff if he had developed anything further on his investigation concerning the death of Doc Schmidt.

"Well we found out what Decker's interest in castor beans was all about" the Sheriff said. He went on to tell about the information that Lieutenant Reynolds had come up with. "We think that was the method he used to kill those five men a few years ago. But it doesn't square with what we know about Doc's death."

"Ricin!" Jeff exclaimed. "I knew I had heard something about that castor bean thing! When I was in the army, we had a whole lot of indoctrination in chemical and biological warfare. That was one of the poisons that they talked about."

Before they could continue, the desk phone chirped and Mrs. Parsons said that Red was outside. Jeff said, "Send him in Helen, and close the door when he comes in would you please?"

Red Waters was smiling when he came in, but the smile

quickly faded when he saw the Sheriff sitting waiting for him. He glanced at Jeff with a questioning frown and Jeff quickly motioned to a chair facing the Sheriff.

"Sit down Red. The Sheriff needs some information and he thinks you can help him."

As Red took his seat, the Sheriff was watching him closely. Red's smile had been replaced by a stoic expression that was like a shade drawn over his face.

"Red, I'm Sheriff Beck. I don't think I've ever met you until today and I'm glad to finally meet you. I've heard a lot of good things about you. Including from Mr. Lawson here." Beck was smiling and nodded at Jeff.

"Red, your name has cropped up in one of our investigations and I'd like to ask you a few questions about your work for Decker Funeral Home a year or so ago."

The young Indian paled noticeably and glancing at Jeff, he said, "I knew I shouldn't have put that down on my job application!"

"Take it easy Red," the Sheriff said "Just relax and tell me about it. Your job Ap shows you worked for Decker two or three months, but there is no record of him ever paying you. Let's start with that, Okay? Why did you work all that time for him without pay?"

"I don't want to talk about this Mr. Lawson," Red said to Jeff. "It was a bad time for me."

"Why was it bad Red," Beck asked softly. "

"My father," he began. "My father had been killed and it was just a bad time for me."

"I remember," Beck continued, "Did Decker handle your father's funeral?"

"Funeral!" Red snorted. "Yeah, he put my father's body parts in a body bag and threw him away! Funeral!"

Red said again. "Birdie and I went to the funeral home to pay our respects and pray over him and that son of a bitch said he'd already had my father's body 'interred'. Which of course meant that he'd had him buried somewhere in the county cemetery. We don't even know where his grave is! So I wouldn't be surprised if he didn't take my father out in the woods just like he did those others!"

Beck glanced at Jeff and then asked, "Red, what can you tell us about them? As near as we can tell, you were working for Decker about the time those bodies were dumped in the woods."

Red hung his head and stifled a moan, then said, "Okay, I guess I should tell you. It's been a nightmare ever since you started finding all those bones. I can't sleep at night, I feel like I'm walking around in a daze all the time with this hanging over my head. I even went to our tribal shaman asking him to drive away the evil spirits that had invaded my soul!"

Looking up at the Sheriff he said, "Funny isn't it. The young redskin going back to his savage roots!"

Jeff started to say something, but the Sheriff held up his hand, motioning Jeff to silence. They sat there while Red collected himself and he finally began to speak.

48

The Sheriff was deep in thought as he was driving back to his office. Finally, he picked up his microphone and checked in with the dispatcher. It happened to be one of the new ones and she didn't recognize his voice.

She asked him to identify himself and when he did she said, "Oh yes sir, sorry sir. Mrs. Benson wants you to call her. She said if you had your cell phone with you, otherwise she'd come out here to the board."

"Okay, thank you. I'll give her a call," Beck replied. Unhooking his phone from his belt he punched in Irma's office number.

"Are you on your way back Sheriff?" Irma asked. "Lieutenant Reynolds says he has come up with some further information that might be what you're looking for."

"That's good news, tell him I should be there in twenty minutes. Also, will you please call that young District Attorney and ask him if I can see him this afternoon. Just tell him, I have some new information that will clinch the case on Mr. Decker."

"Oh, that's the other thing. I'm supposed to tell you that he made bail. He was released this morning."

"What, where'd he get enough money to post bail? He's only got a couple of thousand dollars in the bank!"

Irma said, "That morticians association put up the money. Anyway, he was released an hour or so ago."

"Oh for crying out .... Okay, get an unmarked car over there right now and sit on him! And keep one there around the clock. He's going to run just as sure as shootin. And I want to catch him when he does!"

As he walked past Wild Bill Reynolds office, the Sheriff motioned for Reynolds to come over to his office. The Lieutenant was on the phone and waved an acknowledgement and held up two fingers and pointed at the phone.

When Beck entered his office, Irma came in right behind him.

"Tommy," she said "Are you sure about this 'round the clock' thing for Decker? We'll have to pull in at least one patrol every shift to do it. I've got a car over there right now, but it's going to be tough to keep up an around the clock schedule."

"Irma," the sheriff replied. "I've never been more sure of anything in my life. That bird is about to sprout wings and I don't want him to fly away when he does. And have those guys report in every forty five minutes or so. I want them to watch his every move!"

"Okay, but it's going to make us shorthanded and the weekend is coming up. I sure hope we don't need these guys somewhere else for the next few days."

Reynolds was tapping on the door and Beck motioned for him to come in. As Irma was about to leave, the Sheriff said to her, "Irma, I'll make a little bet with you. I'll bet that we won't need anyone for this duty by this time tomorrow. He's going to run! And by this time tomorrow, he'll be back here in his cell! Wanna take that bet?"

"Nope," Irma said. "When you're this sure of anything, you know something the rest of us don't. So, no thanks, no bet!"

Motioning Reynolds to a seat, Beck sat down behind his desk. "Okay" he said. "What have you come up with?"

Lieutenant Reynolds replied, "I think I've figured out how he did it. Remember I said he'd done a lot of experimenting with his ideas on euthanasia?"

Beck nodded. "Well, I called one of his associates at the time, who is now a anesthesiologist down in Chicago. Anyway, he told me that Decker was always experimenting with ways to knock out the lab animals. He would use a mixture of two or three chemicals that would instantly render a lab monkey unconscious."

Beck said, "Would it kill instantly too?"

"Nope, but this is what finally got him tossed out. He had this stuff in a rubber squeeze ball, and when squeezed the stuff came out in a vapor. The monkey was knocked out instantly."

Reynolds paused looking at the Sheriff, "Then he would use an empty hypodermic needle and insert it into a vein. It produced a bubble that would travel to the victims heart within minutes and produce a killing heart attack!"

"Do we know what the formula was for the stuff that he used as a knockout potion?"

"Not totally, but this guy said it wasn't hard to produce. He said that Decker called it his 'love potion' because he said he was going to use it on one of his lovers that was being uncooperative!"

Reynolds was shaking his head and said, "The guy I spoke with, was definitely not one of Decker's buddies! He said that Decker would make the rounds of the homo bars in the area pretty regularly."

Beck was thinking and finally said, "Maybe we could wrench a confession out of the guy if we made him think we know what the 'love potion' is and we tell him we're going to exhume Doc's body."

Then he said, "Maybe we can even find that rubber squeeze ball or whatever he used there in his 'preparation' room. We didn't know what we were looking for the first time, but I think we do now. And another thing," the Sheriff said excitedly, "I can get that prescription and the nitro glycerin tablets from Sharon Schmidt! I'd asked her not to throw them away for a while."

Beck leaned back and looked at Reynolds, "I think we've got him."

Before Reynolds could leave, Irma came in and said, "Well, I guess you were right Sheriff, but you didn't have to wait till tomorrow! Deputy Carstairs just stopped Mr. Decker, as he was about to cross out of the county! He had several packed bags in his car and he had stopped at the bank and cleaned out his bank accounts!"

Sheriff Beck was grinning at Lieutenant Reynolds and said, "I knew it. Now we've got that son of a bitch for sure!"

49

After Sheriff Beck left, Jeff sat in his office trying to absorb all that he had heard from Red Waters. He couldn't begin to imagine the turmoil that the young man had gone through since his experiences with Decker. He told how he had been coerced into working for Decker without pay to cover the so-called expenses of his father's funeral.

He told of riding with Decker out into the forest on one occasion with a corpse enclosed in a body bag in the rear of the hearse. He said he had no idea what was going on until Decker asked him to help carry the body bag deep into the woods. They had parked almost exactly where Jeff had parked his Blazer that day.

He said that he didn't know what was happening until they had walked some considerable distance. He told how Decker had unzipped the body bag and unceremoniously pulled the body out and laid it in a weedy area. With that, he folded up the body bag and started back to the hearse.

Red said he had stood staring at the naked body of an old lady until Decker yelled at him to 'come on'.

Returning to the funeral home, Decker threatened Red not to say a word to anybody about what they had just done. He told Red that he was now an accomplice and he'd go to jail for a long time if anybody ever found out.

He told how they had made two additional trips after that to pretty much the same area. Then Decker ordered him to take a body by himself to the wooded area.

Beck thought, "That must be when Beasley saw him."

Finally Decker let him go. But, he warned Red to keep his mouth shut and just forget about the whole thing, or, he'd find himself lying out there in the woods with those bodies.

Decker claimed it had only been a temporary thing and maybe someday he'd go back and pick up those remains and bury them proper. Red said that Decker had laughed like a mad man when he had said that.

Red told them that Decker had him go to a local veterinarian clinic and offer to carry away their trash for a time. He was given a five-dollar bill or sometimes a ten for taking trash bags to the local landfill. Decker was waiting for him a couple of times and opened the bags looking for ashes from animals that had been cremated.

So there it was. The whole story. The Sheriff had taken out the handheld tape recorder and recorded the entire conversation. When Red was finished he said "Red, if I can get you immunity from prosecution, will you testify in court, under oath, to what you just told us?"

Red replied, "Yes sir, I will. That guy had us both scared out of our wits. I can't live with this any longer. It's driving Birdie and I both crazy." Then repeating, "I'll testify. Even without immunity! Just telling you today has helped a lot."

Red had gone back to the factory and as the Sheriff was about to leave, Jeff had said, "Sheriff, if for some reason you can't get immunity for that young man, I will supply him with all the legal defense he might need. He's just a kid really, and he and his young wife have been carrying a pretty heavy burden for quite a while."

The Sheriff had assured him that he would be able to get immunity from prosecution. He didn't want to see the young man's life destroyed over this either.

Jeff tried to call George again. This time he answered on the second ring. "Hi George. I wanted to know if I could stop out and visit with you for a little while."

George sounded pretty much like his old self-saying, "Sure, sure, I'm just starting to get some stuff together for my trip to Florida. Come on out."

George was waiting on the front porch again for him to drive up. He came down the steps and met Jeff holding out his hand. Shaking hands he said, "I'm glad you stopped out. I wanted to talk with you. How are you feeling? That's a pretty hat you're wearing," pointing at the orange stocking cap. "I came down to see you in the hospital but they had you pretty well sedated. Did you know I was there?"

"They told me the next morning," Jeff said as they climbed the steps into the house.

"Come in, come in, this cold weather seems to bother me more every year. How about a cup of coffee?"

"Birdie," he called toward the kitchen. "Would you bring us some coffee please? Two mugs."

Jeff was pulling off the stocking cap as Birdie walked in with two mugs of coffee. Seeing Jeff she stopped and stared at the shaved areas and bandage pads covering them on his head.

Jeff laughed at her expression and said, "It's okay Birdie. I keep a hat on when there's little children around."

Birdie said, "Oh my, does it hurt much. Oh Mr. Lawson, you look so ..." tears were streaming down her face.

"Easy, there, easy," Jeff said and stepping forward took the coffee mugs from her. "I'm doing fine. I'm going to be okay. Don't get so upset please."

She was wiping her eyes and returned to the kitchen area and Jeff looked at George in wonder. "Wow, I must really look bad. She really got upset."

George smiled and said, "She's a tender hearted young woman. She treats me like an old grand dad." With a wry smile, he said, "Which I would like to be one of these days!"

Jeff grinned and said, "That's only one of the reasons I'm here." George was looking at him in surprise. "I came out here to ask you if you'd have any objections to my marrying your daughter."

George jumped up, almost spilling his coffee and exclaimed, "What? Objections? Why in the world would you think I'd have any objections? I'm just sorry it's taken you two this long to get together. When? When are you going to do it?"

Jeff was taken aback at George's enthusiasm saying, "Gee George, I really don't know. I just asked her last night! I was so happy she said 'yes' that I didn't take it any further than that."

"Well, you've got to do it before I go to Florida! No, you don't either! Don't wait until spring either. I know,"

George was bubbling enthusiastically. "You can get married in Florida. I'm going to Naples and they tell me that's a real nice place. How about that? You can come down there in the nice warm weather, sandy beaches ...."

Jeff was laughing at George's excitement. He had never seen him get this worked up in all the years he'd known him. Holding up his hands he exclaimed, "Whoa, whoa, slow down George, I just asked Brenda last night. I don't know what she might have in mind. How about if we have dinner together tonight and discuss it."

"Sure, sure, that's right. That's a good idea." George was grinning happily, and then he said "No, no come to think about it, that's not a good idea. You two decide what you're plans are then tell me. The last thing I want to do is interfere with your plans."

Jeff laughed and said, "Well, I think it might be a good idea for me to grow some hair back first. I might scare the preacher if Birdie's reaction is any measure."

Then serious, Jeff asked, "George, I'm sorry you had to learn about Lydia from the Sheriff. I had hoped that I was mistaken. When Sheriff Beck told me for sure, I could have cried I felt so bad. Are you okay? Is there anything I can do for you?"

"Jeff, my boy, you've just given me the best gift I've ever had. As soon as they no longer need to keep her remains, I've made arrangements for her to be buried here in the little cemetery by the church."

"It was a terrible shock to learn what that man did, but I had done my grieving when Lydia died. I was appalled at the thought of her lying out there all those months. But I feel she has been vindicated now. The man who did this awful thing is in jail and I hope he rots there!"

"Well, from what Sheriff Beck tells me, he probably will!"

Jeff gave George as many details as he could, including what they had just learned this morning. He told George that he had told the Sheriff that he was going to hire an attorney if it became necessary to defend Red.

"He's had enough problems in his young life, without letting that Bastard ruin the rest of it."

Birdie had been listening in the kitchen and she gasped when she heard what Red had told the Sheriff and Mr. Lawson. She couldn't believe what she was hearing. Red had told them everything! But it sounded like he was not going to be arrested. She heard Jeff say that he had gone back out to work after the Sheriff left.

Upset, she undid the apron she had been wearing and quietly slipped out of the back door. She had driven her father's old S-10 pickup today and she started it up and slowly drove away.

Meanwhile, George was asking Jeff about the wounds to his head. "I'm going back down to the hospital in the morning and the doctor is going to remove the stitches. Hopefully, all I'll have then will be a couple of extra large band aids on my head."

With a laugh, "And as soon as he's done with me, I'm going to see a barber and get the rest of this mop cut off. It won't be pretty, but maybe it won't be as bad as this either."

George got up and walked to a window and said, "There goes Birdie. I haven't even paid her yet." Suddenly, with a look of understanding he said "Oh, oh. I'll bet she heard what you were telling me about Red and that asshole Decker."

Jeff said, "Well, she doesn't have to worry anymore. The Sheriff said he was positive he could get him immunity for testifying. Red sure was relieved to get that off his chest."

"George, I'm glad you're handling this thing as well as you are. I was really worried." Jeff said. "I was going to tell Brenda Monday night, but then somebody put my lights out before I could tell her."

"What about that?" George asked. "Any ideas who did that to you? The sheriff didn't seem to know much of anything when I talked to him on Tuesday. That's when he told me about this business with Decker. That was quite a shock! I felt bad for Brenda, she was there too and she was very close to her mother."

They sat and talked for the next hour or so and finally Jeff said, "I guess I'd better go home and have a sandwich and get some sleep. I'm beginning to feel pretty tired."

"Good," George said, "Do that, but let me call down to the 'Jam' and have them fix you something to go. How's a burger sound?"

50

J eff had stopped at the Log Jam and picked up the sack with the hamburger in it and drove on out to his cabin.

As he opened the door, he suddenly realized that he hadn't locked it again! He stuck his head in and looked around, but there was nobody there. But before sitting at his counter and eating the sandwich he carefully walked through the rest of the rooms just to make sure.

"I'm getting paranoid," he said to himself and returned to the kitchen. After eating the hamburger he stretched out on the couch, turned on the TV and promptly fell asleep.

When he woke up, the phone was ringing and as he struggled to come awake, he heard Brenda say, "Hello, yes it is. Oh Hi Sheriff, yes he is. He's just waking up. Looks like he's been taking a nap. Hold on."

She handed him the phone and he heard the Sheriff say, "Must be nice to be able to take naps in the middle of the day. Are you feeling okay?"

"I'm feeling fine," he said smiling at Brenda. "What's up?"

"I just wanted you to know that the D.A. is going to give Red Waters total immunity for his testimony. I just talked with him and told him about it. He's going to come in tomorrow morning and give an affidavit."

Jeff said, "Oh man, that's good news Sheriff. I'm sure glad you were able to work this out."

"Well, it didn't take a lot of convincing. When I gave the D.A. some of Red's background, he agreed without taking any exceptions." Beck continued, "Aren't you going to be down here in the morning, to get your stitches out or something?"

When Jeff said he was Beck said, "Why don't you stop by here when you're free and I'll take you to lunch. Bring your lady friend too."

"Oh, you mean my fiancé," Jeff asked? And Brenda smiled at him.

The Sheriff said, "Is that right, well congratulations. Sure thing, bring her along. She'll brighten up Duffy's for sure."

As he hung up, Brenda walked over and kissed him saying, "Hello. I understand that you went out to see dad today. He must have left five messages on my answering machine when I got home. He had me scared to death until he started in by saying how happy he was for us!"

"Yeah, I've been worried about him. He seems to be taking the news about your mom pretty well though," Jeff said. "And, I thought I should at least ask for his permission to marry his only daughter. He approved by the way!"

"Don't I know it? He's already talking about the wedding. I told him we hadn't discussed anything about the wedding yet." Then looking at Jeff she asked, "Have you thought about it at all?"

"No, not really," Jeff said. "There's only one thing I want, other than you, that is. But if at all possible, I want Dwight to be my best man. What do you think?"

"I think that's a wonderful idea," Brenda said. Then "Do you like spaghetti?"

"What? Spaghetti? Sure, doesn't everybody?" Jeff answered.

"Good, because I've been slaving over a hot stove this afternoon making spaghetti. I'll put some garlic bread in the oven and we can eat in about ten minutes."

They spent the evening talking about all the things that had happened to them during the past few weeks. They spent some time making minimal wedding plans and at some point.

Jeff suddenly said, "Hey, I forgot all about it until just now, but I still want to have a mortgage burning celebration! We could make it an engagement announcement thing too. How about next Saturday night? What do you think?" he asked her?

They were working on a guest list when Jeff suddenly moved next to her and said "I know you told me that last night was a one night stand, but we've got the whole weekend ahead of us now."

As he looked at her he moved his eyebrows up and down in a questioning manner. "Maybe we should try it one more time, just to make sure we're compatible. Don't you think so?"

51

"Ow, that one hurt" Jeff squirmed as Doctor Sing removed a stitch from his head. "How many more have you got anyway? Seems like you've been pulling away on those things forever!"

"Oh there's just a few more. We're almost done."

Brenda was sitting on a chair in the small examining room while Jeff was stretched out on an examining table. The nurse had raised the head of the table somewhat, so Jeff could at least sit up and was not flat on his back.

A few minutes later, the Doctor said, "There, that's the last of them. These have healed very nicely Mr. Lawson. I don't think there'll be much of a scar from any of these. We'll put some light bandages on for the next day or so, just to keep them from getting infected. Try and keep them dry when you take a shower for a couple of days. If you have any problems, give me a call."

As they were leaving, Jeff recognized a nurse that apparently was just coming on duty. "Hello there Mrs. McDuff, or should I say Mrs. McNaughton."

She smiled at Jeff and said, "Well, well. Look at

you. And walking on your own. You don't even need a wheelchair today."

"Yes maam, I'm very happy to say. Thank you for your tender loving care while I was in your charge. I'm grateful."

"Just doing my job sir," she replied. "But you were a very good patient. A lot of them aren't. I'm glad you're doing okay." She continued into the hospital lobby.

Brenda said, "She seemed very nice. Was she the one that helped you pee regularly?" she asked innocently

Jeff laughed and said, "Come on, let's get over to the Sheriff's office. I'm getting hungry for some of Duffy's soup."

It was snowing again as Brenda parked in the courthouse parking lot. Jeff said, "Maybe George has got a good idea about our getting married in Florida. I'm sick of snow already."

"Florida," Brenda asked? "What about Florida?"

"George said we should go to Naples, Florida to get married. With this kind of weather, Florida sounds pretty good."

"Nope," Brenda said as Jeff held the courthouse door for her, "I want a simple wedding right here in my home town."

Grinning at Jeff she said, "We could always go to Florida on our honeymoon couldn't we?"

When they came in the Sheriff's office, they stepped up to the counter and Jeff saw Sheriff Beck through his open doorway. He had a can of Coca Cola in one hand and was leafing through some papers on his desk with his other hand.

A woman stepped up to the counter and asked if

she could help them and Jeff pointed to the Sheriff and said "That gentleman in there promised to buy us a very expensive lunch today."

She smiled and before she could get to the Sheriff, he had met her at the door motioning for the two of them to come in.

"Hello Jeff, and it's very nice to see you again Mrs. Dexter. I understand that's going to change to Mrs. Lawson one of these days. Congratulations to you both."

"Thank you. Please call me Brenda, Sheriff," she said "And yes, we were just talking about that when we drove up."

"Mrs. Dex... excuse me Brenda, would you mind taking a seat for a few minutes. I have something to show Jeff. It'll only be a few minutes and we'll be right back. Would you like a cup of coffee while you wait."

"No thank you Sheriff. You're not going to lock him up are you? I wouldn't want to lose him now."

The Sheriff laughed and hustled Jeff out of the office and down a hallway. They stopped at a door on the side of the hall. And the Sheriff said, "We've got the person that attacked you in here. They came in and turned themselves in this morning."

"They?" Jeff said. "There was more than one?"

"Well, there was only one that attacked you, but there's actually three people in there now." The Sheriff was shaking his head sadly and said, "Would you like to meet them?"

Curious, Jeff said, "Yes I would. Why did they turn themselves in anyway?"

The Sheriff replied, "I think maybe you should ask them yourself. Go ahead on in."

Jeff opened the door and walked in. The two women looked up in surprise at the entrance and a small baby lay kicking and cooing on a blanket spread on the table. Jeff didn't recognize the older woman, but he didn't have any trouble recognizing Little Bird Waters!

Turning to the Sheriff he said, "Oh no, Sheriff this has to be a mistake. What have you done? This is Red's wife and baby. I don't know the other lady, but this must be a mistake."

"She's my mother, Mr. Lawson," Birdie said quietly. "It's no mistake. I waited for you and bashed you with a bait bat!"

"What?" Jeff stumbled. "What's a bait bat?" Then before Birdie could answer he said, "What are you talking about? Why would you do that?"

Birdie had tears streaming down her face. Her mother sat stoic as any picture he had ever seen of a sober faced Indian. She never looked at Jeff, but stared straight ahead. Her eyes only strayed occasionally to the baby in front of her.

Birdie was trying to get herself under control but she was racked with sobs coming from deep within the recesses of her soul! Jeff pulled out a chair and sat down across the table from Birdie and her mother. The baby lay cooing happily in between. The Sheriff remained standing in the doorway.

Jeff was nearly in a state of shock. All he could say was "Why? Birdie, Why did you do this?"

Suddenly, Jeff thought he knew why. He asked softly "Was it because I had asked you about Red working for Decker that morning?"

Birdie sat, unable to speak, tears still streaming down

her face. She nodded and tried to speak but the emotion of the moment was too great. She simply sat and sobbed.

"You must have been mighty afraid I was going to talk to somebody about it weren't you?" Jeff sat back and looked up at the Sheriff and shook his head. "What's going to happen to her Sheriff? What can I do to help her? I don't want her in trouble for this. Can you help us here?"

The Sheriff grinned and said, "You know I should be a gambler instead of a lawman. I'd have bet everything I own that you'd react just this way. Okay, you want to help her out of this mess? She's admitted she attacked you and could go to prison for something like that, but," and the Sheriff paused, "If you were to tell me, that you wouldn't prefer charges and any admissions made here were off the record, I think I could just tell these ladies, that they're free to go!"

"That's right," Jeff said, "I do not wish to prefer charges. No sir. No charges! Is that all there is to it?"

"That's it," the Sheriff said, and then to Birdie and her mother, "You ladies are free to go. I appreciate your coming in. Red will be done with the D.A. in a few minutes, if you'd like to wait for him in the lobby." With that he turned and walked back down the hallway.

Birdie was staring in disbelief at what had just happened. She had stopped sobbing, but the tears were still streaming down her face. "Oh Mr. Lawson. After what I did! How can you not want ..."

Jeff interrupted her saying, "Birdie, I'm sorry that you were so frightened as to do something like that. I have some experience with that kind of fear and it's a terrible thing. I remember being so terrified when I was in Iraq that I thought I was losing my mind!"

"You and Red have got a good life ahead of you and I want to see this young fella, playing football for Lakeview High someday."

He was grinning down at the baby. "Come on, I'll walk you up to the lobby."

Birdie's mother wrapped the baby in the blanket and gently picked him up. Birdie came around the table and hugged Jeff and with tears still streaming down her cheeks, she said, "Thank you Mr. Lawson. You're a wonderful man. We'll never forget what you've done for us. God Bless You."

They walked to the lobby just off the main entrance and they sat down to wait for Red. Jeff reached down and smoothed the coal black hair on the baby's head and said, "Bye there W.W. I'm sure we'll be seeing you again."

As he was walking back to the Sheriff's office, he was thinking about what had just taken place and suddenly realized that Birdie's mother had never uttered a word.

When he walked into his office, the Sheriff was talking on the phone. Brenda jumped up and came to him and wrapped her arms around him saying "You big dodo, the only reason you let her off the hook was so you wouldn't lose a house keeper."

Glancing at the Sheriff, he said, "Okay, okay. It's no big deal. I don't want anybody, and I mean anybody, to know about this, okay? I don't want those kids having to live with a lot of gossipy old women talking about them all over town. As far as this is concerned," he said pointing at his head, "It's an unsolved case of attempted robbery!"

The Sheriff hung up his phone and said, "Come on. Let's go eat. Maybe we can beat the rush at Duffy's if we hurry."

As they were walking out of Beck's office, Jeff said, "What's a bait bat?"

52

There was a bitter cold wind blowing and snow was swirling across the back yard behind Jeff's cabin. The twenty or so people that were standing around a charcoal grill on Jeff's patio deck didn't seem to mind the cold at all. It was probably because for the past hour and a half they had been drinking a variety of alcoholic beverages and consuming shrimp, cheese and crackers, peanuts and an assorted variety of additional snacks.

Jeff was about to burn his mortgage. But someone in the group started chanting 'Speech, Speech! So Jeff stopped and looked blearily around the group standing there and said, "I can't tell you all, how happy I am to light this little fire in front of so many people. When this paper starts to burn, it won't warm me nearly as much as the friendship you are sharing with me tonight."

The group responded, "Hear, Hear!"

Jeff relit the small propane 'match' and held it to a corner of the papers folded up on the grill. They began burning immediately, and the wind suddenly lifted a burning page and drifted it toward the cabin. A voice in the crowd said

"Somebody grab that. He doesn't want to burn the place down now that he owns it."

The group responded with loud guffaws and as the last of the papers burned to ashes, Jeff said, "That's it. It's burned to a crisp. Let's get back inside and finish off whatever is left of .... Whatever is left!" More laughter as the group moved inside.

Brenda walked with him into the cabin and asked, "Should we tell them now, what do you think? Some of them already know and are probably whispering behind our backs about it. Let's tell them," she urged.

"Okay, hey Dwight," he called. Then, "And Short Round. Come on over here please."

When Myra and Dwight had joined them Jeff raised his voice and called "Could we have your attention please." Several people continued with conversations but were quickly shushed by the others.

Jeff said, "As you know, everyone was invited here tonight to witness the mortgage burning thing, but, Brenda and I also have another reason to party tonight. I guess it's probably no shock to anybody here that I've fallen madly in love with this beautiful specimen of womanhood," referring to Brenda.

She was beaming. "And a most wonderful thing has happened that still has me befuddled," he continued. "But, I found out a week or so ago that, unbelievable as it may seem, she has told me that she's fallen in love with me!"

The group was laughing and applauding this news. Jeff continued "So, when two people find that they feel like that for each other, they usually decide to do something about it! And that is why my friend Dwight Sutherland and Brenda's friend Myra Noonan are standing here. They have agreed to stand as witnesses to our marriage, which will take place as soon as my hair grows out!"

The group was applauding enthusiastically now and one by one came forward and shook hands with Jeff and kissed Brenda on the cheek. Even Sheriff Tommy Beck and his wife were there. Jeff had asked him at lunch a week earlier.

Last in line was George Gunderson. He stepped in front of Jeff and said, "I still think you should come to Florida to get married. Naples is very nice this time of year."

Then he embraced Jeff and Brenda together and kissing his daughter said, "I know you'll both be very happy."

Dwight and Donna were the last to leave. Dwight gave Brenda a hug and kiss on the cheek and turned to Jeff and said, "Well old friend, looks like your days of living fast and loose are over. You are about to cross over into a new life and I hope you two will always be as happy as you are tonight."

Jeff was genuinely moved by his friend's good wishes and said with feeling, "Thank you Dwight. I hope we will too."

Donna gave Jeff a good night kiss and said, "Are you sure you don't want us to stay and help clean up this mess?"

"Nope, don't worry about it. Birdie told me she'd come out sometime after church tomorrow and clean up for us."

"You should give that girl a big tip for coming out here on a Sunday. She wouldn't do that for just anybody you know," Dwight said.

As he was about to go out the door he turned and said,

"Did you read in the paper today where that undertaker guy has been charged with murder. Said he admitted to killing five guys a number of years ago and then, just a month or so ago, he murdered the county coroner! Can you beat that? An undertaker of all things! He must have been killing people when business was slow!"

Dwight stood weaving in the door and said, "Why would a guy like that, do something as terrible as that? And your bones too! He's going to jail for that too, Why would he do something like that?"

Jeff replied, "I think there are some people that are just plain evil and Dexter is one of those kind of people. Somewhere along the line, he found himself on the path of evil and chose to follow it to the end!"